Black Conley

By

Shari Dare

Published by
Melange Books, LLC
White Bear Lake, MN 55110
www.melange-books.com

ISBN: 978-1-61235-727-0 Print

Cover Artist: Caroline Andrus

Black Conley
Shari Dare

Raised on a ranch run by whores Black Conley has come full circle. As a US Marshall he's been sent to find out who is rustling steers from Belle Barton otherwise known as Ball Buster Belle. As soon as he meets the beautiful blonde boss, he knows he doesn't want any of the other girls in his bed.

Belle has returned to Montana to run her father's ranch only to find out no man will work for her. Instead she's turned to the local whores and although they ply their trade at night, during the day they work hard for the Double Bar B. Not wanting a man in her bed, she offers Black the choice of her 'girls' but forbids him access to her bed.

To Sherry Derr-Wille for allowing me, Shari Dare to come out of the closet and write this story.

Chapter One

Laramie, Wyoming 1886

Black pumped against the whore he'd bought for the night. The act represented nothing but self-pleasure and release. He'd put his emotions aside years ago. There was no place in his life for such things.

This woman was no more to him than any of the others he'd had over the past fifteen years, but he didn't care. She was warm, she was somewhat pretty, and she allowed him to vent his anger and satisfy his longings.

"Deeper, Baby, deeper," she crooned.

Unlike things he'd heard about whores only pretending, he rarely left a woman wanting in that department. "Are you certain?" he said, as he withdrew his cock from her cunt.

"Positive," came the whispered reply.

He repositioned himself and turned her onto her belly, then instructed her to get on her knees.

"You ain't gonna fuck me in the ass are you?" the girl said.

"Hardly. You said you wanted it deeper. Well, this is as deep as I can get." He shoved his cock in from the backside of her cunt and buried it all the way to his balls.

The girl screamed in delight. To add to the enjoyment, he grabbed one of her tits and played with it while he pistoned against her.

"More, more," she demanded.

Black was more than willing to accommodate her and slowed his actions to prolong the hard-on he wanted to satisfy. When at last they both came, he was careful not to collapse on top of her. Instead, he rolled off, and turned her over to face him. While he lay there, spent and exhausted, he played with her clit until she again moaned with pleasure. A long time ago, he'd learned women could go all night, while men had to recuperate before they could again take a woman.

It didn't take long for her to come again and mix her velvety juice with that which he had deposited only minutes earlier. Convinced he had, indeed, satisfied her, he pulled himself into a sitting position and lit a cigarette. Beside him, the girl continued to kiss his chest while she played with his balls. He knew it wouldn't take much of this type of attention to make him ready to take her again by the time he finished his smoke. He liked to get the most for his money, and this girl was more than ready to give it to him.

He crushed out his cigarette and started sucking one of her tits in preparation to shove his cock into her cunt when a knock at the door interrupted him.

Cursing a blue streak, Black disentangled himself, grabbed his gun, and went to the door. It was evident the young boy who stood there with an envelope in his hand was embarrassed.

"I … I have a telegram for you, Mr. Conley," he stammered, looking alternately between Black's gun and his cock that stood out as stiff as a poker.

"Well, give it to me," Black ordered, before going to get his pants so he could give the boy some money. By the time he returned, the boy had focused his attention on the whore in Black's bed.

"Cover yourself," he growled, as he pulled a coin from the pocket of his pants.

Once the boy left, Black slammed the door.

"Come back to bed, Sweetie," the girl crooned. "Whatever is in that wire can wait until we finish our business."

"Like hell it can," Black retorted, ripping open the envelope.

What the hell was the big rush in getting this to him? He silently scanned the contents of the wire. Why wreck a perfectly good fuck just to give him his next assignment?

The only answer he could think of was that the telegraph office hadn't gotten it to him when it first arrived. He'd have a talk with the telegraph operator when he went across the street to send the return wire.

Rather than going back to the whore, Black threw some money on the bed before he got dressed. Although the girl pretended to pout, he knew she was counting his money while anticipating getting another man

6

to pay her tonight. If she was smarter than she looked, she would give the bartender only his usual pay while keeping the rest for herself.

"I guess this means you're done with me," she said, as she pulled on the dress she'd discarded earlier.

The deeply cut neckline made him wish he didn't have to leave her. Of course, he knew he couldn't stay after reading the contents of the wire. Work always came before pleasure in his book. With this wire coming from Denver, he had no choice other than to read it and find out where he went next.

Once she left, he read the wire from his boss, Ed Heath, more thoroughly. His assignment would take him to Larson's Gap in Montana and a ranch called the Double Bar B. According to Ed's wire, the woman who ran it, Belle Barton, was in trouble. She'd been losing cattle and couldn't get the sheriff to help her find the rustlers. It would be Black's job to find those responsible and put them under arrest. Ed doubted the local sheriff would be any help, but he said it was worth a try.

After sending a return wire to Denver, Black packed his gear in his saddlebags, tied his bedroll to the back of his horse, and prepared to leave Laramie behind. A glance inside the saloon revealed the girl he'd bedded earlier was already attaching herself to a cowpoke with more money than brains. At least he was the first one to have her tonight. If she was like most of the women in these places, he doubted she cleaned herself up between customers. There was nothing worse than fucking a woman who was full of some other man's cum.

As he rode Buck, his Appaloosa gelding, out of Laramie, he thought about his life. In the past, he'd done everything he could to make a living. He'd started as a gunslinger and somehow ended up as a lawman. Since he'd become a U.S. Marshal he'd found a job that was to his liking. The life of a gunslinger was iffy, and he really didn't enjoy killing people, but it was what he did best. With the title of U.S. Marshal, he did the job that he'd done when he'd killed his first man.

His mind turned to the memory of Mike Slade. If ever a man needed to die, it was Slade. He'd killed Black's mother by beating her to death with her own bullwhip, and for what? He'd done it to gain title to the Circle C, the ranch his father built for his family in East Texas.

Black had only been three when someone killed his father. It wasn't until after Slade lay dead in the street that he found out the man had killed his father as well as his mother to get the ranch adjoining his. At the time, Black called it revenge, but now he knew he'd only saved the county the cost of a hanging.

He remembered how hard it had been for his mother. She'd ended up running the place with the help of several whores who were ranch hands by day and whores by night. With the proof he carried in his saddlebags, he regained title to the Circle C. From there he went to the bank telling them sell it to the first man with enough money to satisfy them. He knew Slade was well respected in town and getting anyone to work for him would be difficult. He didn't want the ranch, but didn't want Slade to have it. He'd been only fourteen at the time and the life of a gunslinger seemed more to his liking than herding a bunch of dumb cows. He trusted the banker and knew the man would keep the money safe for him.

Even though he hadn't done any ranching in over fifteen years, a job on one of the ranches would give him the perfect cover to investigate the rustling. Ranching was hard work, but it wouldn't hurt him to ride herd on a bunch of cattle in Montana for a while. At least he'd get to eat three square meals a day and be able to sleep somewhere other than outside. That was better than where most of his assignments took him. With winter coming, it sounded damn good.

He didn't need to work, but the situation demanded he blend in with the locals, and what better way to do that than to work as a cowhand. Besides, spending the winter in a hotel room with nothing to do was as far from his liking as was sleeping outdoors. It would do little but draw attention to his presence. Working with the locals usually raised a whole lot less suspicion about why he was in this small town rather than where his gun could make him a hell of a lot more money.

When he arrived at Larson's Gap, the town looked about as lively as a Sunday school picnic. Outside the saloon, two horses waited for their owners to return. At least he didn't have to guess where the saloon was. He could get a drink without having to make any explanations about who he was.

Inside, he stepped up to the bar. "Whiskey."

The bartender looked up. "Don't serve Injuns. It's best if you get your ass out of here."

Black pulled his gun and pointed it at the man. "Look, you son-of-a-bitch, I'm no Injun."

"You got black hair and your dark skinned. You're an Injun all right."

"My ma was Mexican, and my pa was white. That makes me pure Texican. Push me too far and you'll find out why they say there ain't nothin' meaner than a Texican when you rile him. Trust me, mister, anyone who takes me for an Injun riles me no end."

"Yes sir, Mr...."

"The name's Conley."

The man began to shake as he poured the whiskey. "I shoulda known from the way you drew that gun of yours. Is it true you killed thirty men?"

"Probably. I don't keep count, especially since every one of them lost their lives in a fair fight."

"How can it be a fair fight when that gun of yours comes out of the holster like a rattler when he's ready to strike?" the man at the far end of the bar said.

"When a man is drawn on he has to defend himself. That's all I intend to say on the subject. I don't lead that life anymore. I was hoping to find out if there are any ranches in the area hiring for the winter."

The man laughed. "Just the Double Bar B, but no one wants to work up there."

Black hid his pleasure at hearing the name of the ranch where he was supposed to look for work as part of his assignment. "Why not?"

"Because word is that the Double B in the name of that ranch stands for the way that bitch can bust a man's balls."

"Bitch?"

"Her name is Isabelle Barton. She took over the ranch after her old man died and left it to her. She spent most of her life in the East, and what she doesn't know about ranching could fill a book. She calls herself Belle, but that hardly fits her. I just call her ball buster. I worked for her for about a week. As much as I wanted to get in her pants, one of her tongue-lashings was enough for me. I lit out the next day."

"I hear tell she's got a bunch of women up there trying to run the ranch. Have you ever heard of anything so ridiculous? What in the hell do women know about ranching? The only thing they're good for is fucking, if you get my drift."

"Thanks for the warning," Black said and downed his whiskey. "Which way is it to the Double Bar B?"

"You ain't serious. Why would you want to work for that bitch?"

"Why not? I've always liked a challenge. This sounds like one I want to tackle."

"You'll be sorry. I'll be here waiting for you when you decide you've had enough of her high and mighty ways."

"Thanks again. I hope you don't hold your breath waiting for me."

Black left the Purple Moon Saloon and mounted Buck. The Double Bar B was the ranch he sought and would be the perfect place for him to spend the winter. If Belle Barton was anything like his ma, it could be an interesting relationship.

As he rode, his thoughts turned to the way his mother ran the Circle C once his father died. Slade hired away most of the hands that worked for his pa. In their place, she brought in whores and allowed them to ply their trade at night, as long as they worked the ranch during the day. It had been a good relationship, and his mother made a good living, not only from the cattle she was able to sell to the trail herds but also from the money the women brought in at night. With the split being fifty-fifty, they all prospered. If it hadn't been for Slade, Black would have grown up to run the ranch. Instead, he'd been driven off the land.

It took a year for him to return to get vengeance. So much had happened that day, he didn't even like to think about it. Not only had he killed his first man, but he proved the Circle C had been taken from him unlawfully. It probably would have been for the best if he'd stayed on to run the place. Unfortunately, he'd tasted blood and wanted to use his guns more than his hands. After selling the ranch to the highest bidder, he left East Texas forever.

Now he'd come full circle. If he could persuade Belle to allow him to work on the Double Bar B, he'd once again be working with women who were ranch hands by day and whores by night.

* * * *

Belle Barton looked out her front window. This was her empire. She'd come here ten years ago to be with her father only to have him die months after her arrival. Everything she knew about ranching she'd learned from her father's journals, her own trial and error, and her father's former foreman, Roy Heath. Within six months of her father's passing, she'd lost most of her hands. Those that came to work for her later usually tried to see how far they could push her and soon learned Belle wasn't about to be pushed. She'd grown tough. Over the years she'd earned the name of Ball Buster Belle and wore it proudly.

The idea of bringing other young women to the ranch had been pure genius. The way the people in town treated the whores who found their way to her door was deplorable. As far as anyone knew, the women worked for Belle and that was it. Of course, there was more to it than that. With the stage line agreeing to allow her to run a way station from her home, she was able to provide the drivers and male passengers enjoyable companionship for the evening as well as a good meal and a soft bed. Her women were told they couldn't bed down with the neighboring ranch hands, but the stage line didn't disapprove of them plying their trade to the passengers as long as they didn't offend any females who were traveling.

To accommodate the passengers, the stage line agreed to help finance an addition to the house. She'd insisted the passengers should be able to spend the night in a place that resembled a hotel. Most of the places where she'd stayed on her journey from Ohio to be with her father were shacks.

Just last fall she'd lost Amy, one of her best women both in the saddle and in the bedroom, to a guest who returned and asked her to marry him. It had been a beautiful wedding. He'd even brought a preacher all the way from Denver because he knew that pompous ass who presided over the church in town wouldn't want any part of the ceremony.

Her mind turned from the women to Clayte Adamson from the Diamond A. He'd been begging her to let him buy her out since the day her father died, leaving her with clear title to the Double Bar B. In the past few year, he'd become more adamant, especially when she landed the contract for the way station.

A month ago she'd gone to the funeral for his wife, Nettie. Clayte told everyone Nettie had taken a bad fall down the stairs and hit her head. By the time he got to her she was dead.

Even though Belle knew that was the official cause of death she also knew the underlying reason they were putting Nettie in the ground. Clayte worked his wife to death. In the nine years they were married, she'd given birth to seven children and was pregnant with the eighth when she died. That much childbearing coupled with the work Clayte expected her to do was enough to make any woman throw herself down the stairs to get away from it all.

Two weeks after the funeral, Clayte was at her door. "I've come up with a solution to our problem," he began when she set a piece of pie and a cup of coffee in front of him.

"I didn't know we had a problem," Belle said, as she poured herself a cup of coffee.

"Of course we do. You're running this spread alone, and I have a passel of younguns that need a ma. If we were to combine forces so to say, I could take over the running of your ranch, and you could take care of my kids and me."

The memory of Clayte's words still grated on Belle's nerves. As soon as he'd spoken them she'd grabbed the coffee pot and dumped its contents over his head. He'd yowled in pain and vowed she'd regret her actions.

Since then several steers from her herd went missing. One or two here and there until the total was over thirty. She knew Clayte was behind it, but couldn't prove it. What she needed was a man and not in the way everyone would think. She needed someone who was good with a gun and just sneaky enough to catch Clayte in the act. Her problem was where she would find such a man. Looking through the paper, that came ever week from Denver, she got an idea. She'd advertise for a hired gun. It wasn't like she couldn't afford it. She had enough money to pay for several such men, but for now, one would be enough to satisfy her.

From the parlor she heard the stage driver as well as his two passengers sweet talking Janna, Lacy, and Cara. The women would make good money tonight meaning that in the morning Belle's share would be added to the money she used for running the ranch. If business for the women remained this brisk, Janna would have enough money to move on to California soon. Belle hated to lose her, but that was part of the business. Janna wanted to open her own house in San Francisco, and Belle couldn't blame her. With winter coming, things here would slow down, and, by spring, there would be a new girl knocking on the door wanting a job.

"There's a lone rider comin' in," Kate said, as she returned to the kitchen after checking the stock.

Belle nodded. "Don't know who it could be, but be ready just in case you don't get the night off after all."

"It's not like I couldn't use the money, Belle, you know that, but I sure do hope he ain't wantin' a roll. I'm dog-tired."

"You go on up to bed then. If he's from town, I'll try to steer him away. I just heard Janna go up as well as Lacy. With luck Cara will join them, and I won't have to do any explaining about why the women are entertaining men in the parlor."

The words no more than passed her lips than she heard Cara's light step on the stairs followed closely by those of a man's heavy boots.

Outside, the sound of a horse's hooves signaled the arrival of the stranger. Rather than wait for him to come to the door, Belle grabbed her shawl and shotgun before going out to the porch to greet her visitor, giving Kate time enough to get upstairs.

"Something I can help you with, Mister?" she said, once the door closed behind her and she pointed her gun directly at his chest.

"Heard you were lookin' for ranch hands for the winter," the man replied, as he carefully dismounted, holding his hands in the air.

She assessed him as he walked the short distance that separated them. He was dressed in black and wore a pair of six-shooters on his hips. They were hung low, as though he needed them at just the right height for a fast draw. Once he mounted the steps of the porch, he put his hand on the barrel of the shotgun, pushing it harmlessly down toward the board floor.

"Seein' that gun pointed at my heart makes me a mite uneasy. What do you say we talk about that job I heard about?"

His manner and the fact he disarmed her so easily made her want to raise the gun and fire, but his strong hand holding it down stopped her. "If you heard that, you also heard that they call me Ball Buster Belle. I didn't get that name without working for it."

"So I heard. Now if you'll just put down that shotgun maybe we can talk about the fact you need a hand more than I need a hole in my chest."

"You seem to have me at a bit of a disadvantage, but don't think for one minute that I won't shoot you if you give me any cause or I just feel like it. I expect a hard day's work and pay top wages, but I don't take none to being pushed by any man."

She watched as he took off his hat to reveal a mane of black hair that fell to just below his shoulders. "Heard all about you in town. I doubt you'd be able to scare me off quite as easily as you could some of the others. The name's Black, Black Conley, and I'm lookin' for a job for the winter. Won't fool you none, I plan to move on come spring, but I still need a place to bed down, three meals a day, and a job to do. I think I know all about your operation. You see my ma ran a ranch like this in Texas. She made damn good money from the cattle and as much from the women who worked for her, if you get my drift."

"I get your drift. Are you any good with that gun?"

He laughed heartily. "I would have thought that once I told you my name you would have figured out who I was. It worked for them fellers in town. Had the bartender shaking so hard he could hardly pour me a glass of whiskey."

She nodded. Black Conley wasn't exactly what she'd expected him to be, but she knew about him all right. From the stories she'd heard, he'd killed over thirty men and all of them in fair fights. She'd thought he would be older and more hardened, yet his brown eyes told her it was possible a little boy still rested behind them. He didn't use the offensive language most men used when they came here looking for a job. To be truthful, he sounded like an educated man. So why was he here, on her doorstep offering to work as a ranch hand? For that matter, why was he here in the middle of nowhere when his guns could make him more money in one of the bigger frontier towns? In thinking about it, she knew if he was as good with his guns as the papers said, he was exactly what she was looking for.

"I do know who you are, Mr. Conley. Come on in, I can't offer you whiskey, since I don't allow it in the house, but I can get you a cup of coffee, while I heat you up some of the stew we had for supper. It looks like you could use a good meal."

He agreed and followed her into the house. Once inside, she would get a better look at him. The long black hair framed a dark skinned face, with brown eyes that any woman could easily drown in. His background could be anything from Mexican to Comanche, considering he said he came from Texas.

"If you take this job, my rules are simple. Like I said, I allow no whiskey at this ranch. If you want to drink, do it on your own time and do it at the Purple Moon in town. If you come home so drunk you cause a disturbance, you're fired. Do your work during the day, and, at night if the women aren't otherwise occupied, you can take a poke at them, but not for free. They're working women and what they do at night brings money into the coffers of this ranch. Another thing, I pay a good wage, and I expect loyalty in return. What goes on here stays here."

"Fair enough. My ma's rules were pretty much the same. 'Course she didn't have too many men who would come to the ranch for anything other than the women. How much do your women get for a night? I came here to work, but nighttime entertainment might not be such a bad thing."

"Depends on the customer. The stage driver gets his for two bucks a roll while the passengers pay four. As for you, I would imagine we could work out an arrangement where you could get yours for let's say a buck and a half."

"It sounds fair to me. A good roll never done anyone any harm, just so long as it doesn't get in the way of what a man has to do during the day. I saw you eyeing my guns before. Any reason why you're so interested in them?"

She ladled the stew into a bowl for him before replying. "Guess there is. I was thinking of putting out an ad for a hired gun. I've been having a lot of trouble with rustlers. Of course, I'm certain I know who's behind it, but I need proof. I need someone who is willing to find out just what's going on and use his guns if necessary. I'm losing the cattle on the range that borders the Diamond A. Clayte Adamson wants this ranch, and he wants me. If he's the one stealing the cattle, it would certainly answer a bunch of questions."

"I take it you don't want him."

"That's right, I don't. Him and my pa had some harebrained idea about the two of us getting married and putting the ranches together. I set my pa straight the first week I was here. Clayte was harder to convince.

"About a month ago he lost his wife, and he was sniffin' around two weeks later. He had the nerve to suggest we get married to combine the ranches and give his seven brats a mother. That's about the same time I started losing cattle. It wasn't hard to put two and two together, and I came up with four and not some other number."

Black's smile was unnerving. "I take it you told him what he could do with his offer and did so in no uncertain terms."

"You bet I did. He's probably still nursing the burns from the coffee I dumped over his head."

"Like I said, I need a job for the winter, and I came here to work. You can depend on me doing good work for you. Just don't get in my way while I'm doing it. If I ain't mistaken, you need my guns more than you do my skills at ranchin'. I'll make certain you get both. I can live by your rules, Ma'am, and I can take care of that little problem. I won't kill the bastard, but I can make him wish he'd never messed with you or the Double Bar B. Just point me to the bunkhouse, and I'll stow my gear as soon as I take care of my horse."

"We haven't used the bunkhouse in years. This place has six bedrooms and I usually only have four to five women working for me at any given time. Right now there's only four, so I have an empty bedroom. As soon as you get your horse stabled, come back up to the house and I'll get you settled."

He nodded and left the warmth of the kitchen. As she watched him go, she couldn't miss his tight ass and the broadness of his shoulders. The two of those things made her wonder what he would be like in bed. Where did that thought come from? She must be losing her mind. The last thing she needed was a man in her bed. Ten years ago she promised herself never to be taken in by a sweet talking man. She refused to go back on her promise.

Belle's mind drifted to the years she spent in the East with her Aunt Mable. She'd been only five years old when her mother died. Her father knew he couldn't run a ranch and take care of child at the same time, so he wired his wife's sister to come out and get Belle. In Aunt Mable's home, she'd received the love and attention she deserved as well as a good education.

She'd been sixteen when Preacher Martinson's son, Ronald, came sniffin' around her aunt's door. Ronald had been handsome and, when their meetings turned sexual, he assured her there was nothing wrong because they were in love and as soon as her aunt agreed they'd be married. He'd known the right way to make love to a woman, and she'd been ripe for the picking. In the months they experimented with sex, she'd been transformed from girl to woman. When she told him she was carrying his child, he denied it could be his.

As soon as news of her condition became public knowledge, Preacher Martinson and the good women of the town branded her a whore. It was then that her aunt sent her to a convent not far from their home. There, she'd abided by the strict rules of the nuns and gave birth to a beautiful baby girl who was taken from her within hours of the birth. She prayed her child had been given to a loving home.

Once she left Ohio, she came back to the Double Bar B and her father, vowing never to let another man touch her in that way again. She'd kept her vow and wasn't even tempted by the sweet talking men from the East who wanted her more than they did the other women. So why did Black make her drawers wet when he took her hand to shake it?

Just the thought of him sleeping down the hall from her was enough to make her change her mind and reopen the bunkhouse. Of course, she knew she wouldn't do that to him. The bedroom wasn't being used, so why heat another building all winter. She'd just have to make certain the man kept his distance from her and occupied himself with the other women.

Once she told Black where his room would be and watched him walk toward the barn, she went upstairs to tell Kate about the new man. "That stranger who just rode in is here for a job. He's a gunslinger. Can't say I'm upset about him coming here. I gave him the room across from yours. You being forewoman here, I thought you should know."

"A gunslinger, you say? What's his name?"

"He calls himself Black Conley. I've heard of him. Seems he's killed over thirty men and all in fair fights, if you can believe what they write in the papers."

"Black Conley," Kate replied, the name rolling off her tongue as though she was contemplating it. "I've heard of him. His ma ran an operation like this in East Texas. I should know. One of the women I worked with in Nevada worked there for a while. He might be interesting company for tonight."

"Thought you were dog tired."

"Things change, especially when Black Conley comes calling. I'm sure you gave him a deal on being with each of us. I think tonight will be on the house though. You know sort of a welcome to the Double Bar B."

Belle nodded. "All I ask is you keep him busy. I don't want him getting any crazy ideas about me, if you get your drift."

"I get it, Belle, but somehow I think this one has you interested. You really should try it. If you don't, you won't ever know what you're missing," Kate teased. "I'm certain you'd like it a lot better when you're getting paid for it."

"I like it a lot better when I'm the one taking the money and handling it for you. I don't want any part of the other, thank you."

* * * *

After learning where he would be bunking, Black left the ranch house with a smile a mile wide on his face. He didn't care about the other women. The one he wanted was the boss. She was just about the prettiest thing he'd seen in a long time. Her long white-blond hair was styled into the latest fashion, and her green eyes were ones any man could die and not mind once he'd seen them. It was no wonder her neighbor wanted her in his bed. Any man would have to be a fool not to want to call Belle Barton his own.

He'd just have to bide his time. The stories he heard in town could prove wrong. Just looking at her, he could tell she wasn't some tight virgin who didn't know the pleasure of being with a man. Somewhere along the line someone had done her wrong, and she wasn't about to fall into any man's arms. That was all right by him. She said there were four whores working for her and trying each of them could probe to be an interesting pastime for the long winter nights ahead of him. Sooner or later he'd melt the ice that Belle had around her heart and, when he did, he was certain she's prove to be a more interesting companion than any of her whores. If he'd stayed in her kitchen any longer the bulge in the front of his pants would have given her a clue as to his intentions toward her.

Once his horse was stabled he realized his hard-on wasn't about to go away any time soon without getting some relief. A quick hand job behind the barn would take care of it until the lovely Miss Belle could be persuaded to let him into her bed. He prayed it wouldn't take him long to get into her pants, since he didn't relish jacking off any more than he did sticking his cock into the other women. They'd give him relief, but it wouldn't be the one he wanted and therefore not the same. He didn't give himself to a woman unless she was special and Belle was damned special in his book. Paid companions were all right for a night or two, but a woman like Belle was what he wanted for a lifetime and at twenty-nine, he decided that lifetime should be a hell of a lot longer than it would be if he continued working as a U.S. Marshal.

He shook his head in disbelief at his thoughts. He had no right to think about happily ever after with a woman. In his line of work he was much better off sticking with whores. They expected no more than what he paid them to give him. He knew he still wanted Belle, but on his terms, not hers. She would grace his bed and it would be because she wanted to not because she was paid. Once he satisfied his curiosity about her, he'd be free to go on to the next assignment when this one was finished.

Maybe it would have been different if she hadn't been wearing those tight fitting pants and the shirt that was open far enough for him to get a good look at her breasts. She was a fine woman, a fine woman indeed, and by the end of the winter she would be his woman.

After getting the relief he craved, Black made his way back up to the house. He'd grabbed his gear and was more than ready to spend the night in a real bed. It would be a novel experience, since he'd been sleeping under the stars for the most of the summer as well as the trip from Laramie to Larson's Gap. Why should he waste money on a hotel room or even one at a boarding house when he had the open range as his bedroom? Of course, such sleeping conditions didn't allow him the pleasure of a woman. When the need arose, which was often, he'd hightail it to the nearest town and visit the whores who plied their trade above the saloon.

Belle sat in the kitchen sipping her coffee when he returned.

"I waited up for you. I wanted to make certain you got your horse stabled. Morning starts early around here, and I wanted to let you know you'd be riding with the forewoman, Kate."

"Much obliged, Ma'am," he replied, aware of her staring at the front of his pants. Had she noticed the bulge that he'd gotten rid of behind the barn? If so, was she sorry to see it gone? Was she thinking about slipping into bed with him tonight? If that were her plan, he'd be more than willing to accommodate her.

She didn't say anything that would give answers to his questions. Instead, she led him to the staircase in the parlor and up to the second floor. "I'm going to bed for the night as well, so we might as well go up together. Once I do, I'll be turning out the lights. Wouldn't want you to get lost."

As they walked down the door-lined hallway, he expected to hear couples enjoying an evening of sexual delights. To his surprise, the silence was almost deafening.

He thought about what it would be like listening to the love sounds coming from behind the closed doors and transporting him back to when he'd been a young boy. Then, he'd been on the outside listening without being able do more than wonder what such delights would be like. Even though he knew what the women did behind those doors, he still wished he could watch. Hell, he'd wanted to participate, especially with Salina.

She was a feisty little Mexican gal who got kicked out of her Pa's house for fucking one of his vaqueros. She'd made her way to Texas and his mother's place. There, she'd plied her trade and made damn good money while doing it. Just thinking about her, made him swell for the second time tonight. She was to have been his present on his thirteenth birthday. Instead he'd found his mother beaten to death and instantly become a man without ever having a woman.

Instead of a night of pleasure in Salina's bed, he had taken the women to Mexico and his grandfather's ranchero. His mother's death had made him well aware of the danger that surrounded the Circle C where the women were concerned. Like his mother, he knew that these women, and their safety were his responsibility.

Once in Mexico, he had not been allowed to be with Salina. She'd left to go back north to the life she enjoyed shortly after their arrival. Instead, he had lost his virginity to a beautiful girl on the same night she lost hers. Neither of them had the experience to show the other the pleasure of sex. For that he was sorry. For the experience, he could never feel sorrow.

"Looks like you could use a little relief," Belle said, as she glanced down at the crotch of his pants.

His thoughts of the past dissolved as he looked toward her. "Guess I could at that." He reached out to grab her hand, but she backed away.

"Kate is waiting for you in your room. Earlier she said she was dog-tired, but when she heard Black Conley was here, she perked right up. This one's on the house, sort of a welcome-to-the-family present, you might say."

Black concealed his disappointment the best he could. "Thanks, Belle, I'll see you bright and early in the morning."

"You bet you will. We start here with breakfast at six, and we hit the saddle by seven. Hope you're up to it. It doesn't matter what goes on at night, during the day I expect my hands to be up and ready to ride as soon as I am."

Black turned from the woman who was to be his boss afraid he wouldn't be able to hide his disappointment. As soon as he entered the room, he saw a scantily clad woman lying on the bed.

"You must be Kate."

"Don't sound so disappointed, Mr. Conley, I'll give you a good roll."

Her voice carried the hint of a Spanish accent and on closer inspection he saw she was a dark complexioned as he. For a moment, it was as though Salina was in his bed waiting to give him his thirteenth birthday present.

"Is there a problem with me being here? I'd hate to think you didn't want me after all I've heard about you."

"Where would you have heard about me?" he said, as he took off his gun belt and made his way to the bed.

"About ten years back I worked with an old whore in Nevada. It was my first job, and I was green as grass. Salina took me under her wing and said she was repaying a favor to the first woman she ever worked for. When I asked her about it, she told me that she worked for your ma and even though you were a kid, she wished she'd been able to give you a good roll for your thirteenth birthday. Of course, we both know why she couldn't. I'm pleased to see you've turned into a man. I'm anxious to see if you're half as good as they say you are."

"What else did your Salina say about me?"

"Ah, so I've piqued your curiosity. She said that you were a good kid, but every now and then you needed to be spanked. Do you still like to be spanked?"

Her question caught him off guard. Without waiting for him to answer, she got up from the bed and came over to start undressing him.

Expertly, she took off his shirt and unbuttoned his long johns. As she ran her hand over the matt of black hair on his chest, his thoughts of home and Salina disappeared. This woman was well trained, but of course she'd had the best teacher available. He hardly realized when she slipped the top of his long johns down around his waist.

Once his chest was exposed, she began kissing his nipples and then sucking on them with occasional love bites. Even though he knew what was coming next it surprised him when she unbuttoned his pants and reached inside the flap of his long johns to grab his cock.

"Ah, this is one of the best cocks I've had in a long time. I think I'd like to play with it for a while before I allow it to enter me."

As though she had a calf by a rope, she led him to the bed by holding him firmly in her grip. Once there, she pushed him down to a sitting position.

"Take off your pants," she ordered. "How do you expect me to give you a good fuck when you're fully clothed?"

"I … I didn't…"

"Of course you did. You just thought it would be Belle in your bed. Well, you can get that damn fool notion out of your head here and now. You can enjoy the rest of us, but Belle is off limits. Now, let me help you with your boots so we can get down to business."

Black thought about the kind of business Kate was referring to and decided it was better than going to bed alone with a hard-on.

She pulled off his boots while he took off his gun belt and slid his pants and long johns down around his ankles. She did the rest of the work for him. Once he was completely naked, she pushed him down on the bed and told him to spread his legs for her.

He felt like a damn fool lying spread eagle on the bed with his cock sticking up like the lodge poles he'd seen in the Indian villages he'd visited over the years. There he'd found that a little kindness got him many young women who were more than willing to share his bed for the night.

To his amazement, Kate crawled up onto the bed with him and took his cock in her mouth so she could suckle it like she was a baby taking nourishment from her mother. In all of his life, he'd never had a woman do something like this to him. While she sucked him, she played with his balls until he could contain himself no longer. With a force unlike any he'd experienced in a long time, he came into her mouth. To his surprise, she swallowed his cum and teased him until he was again erect.

"Did you like that?" She licked her lips as though she was afraid she'd lose even one drop of his cum.

"Like it? Hell yes I liked it. It's a shame you can't bottle that sensation and sell it in one of those medicine shows. I bet you could make a million dollars in less than a year. Where did you learn to do something like that?"

"Salina said that when she moved on from your ma's ranch, the next place she worked told her it was mandatory. At first she didn't like it, but once she learned how to do it correctly, she found it to be very stimulating, both for her and her partner. She taught me how to do it when I first arrived at her place. If you enjoyed this, wait until the next time we're together and I suck your balls. Of course, for that you will have to pay. Now that you're satisfied, I need you to do the same for me."

She lay down beside him and pulled him on top of her. After what he'd just been through he wondered if he would be able to perform, but once he slipped his cock into her cunt, he knew there would be no problems in that department. While he pumped against her, he grabbed her breasts and manipulated her nipples into hard pebbles. She moaned in pleasure, and he knew he was the one responsible for it. Whores had a way of moaning even if they weren't feeling anything, but it wasn't anything like this.

He'd just leaned over to take one of her nipples into his mouth when she slapped him squarely on the ass. He jerked his head up and looked at her. To his surprise, that slap had made him even harder inside her.

"What did you just do to me?"

"I gave you a spanking, you naughty boy. As a little kid it hurts like hell, but as a man it only heightens the pleasure. All of this is only a prelude of what's to come if you want me in your bed again."

"What happens if I spank you?"

"Maybe someday we'll find out. For now, this works for me."

The more she spanked him the harder he pumped against her until they finally both came at almost the same time. He rolled off of her and pulled her into an embrace. He'd learned, a long time ago, that women, even whores, liked to be cuddled after being fucked.

"You were good, Black, really good," Kate said. "You'll be even better once you get that damn fool notion out of your head that it's Belle you want in this bed. There are four of us here, and we all like our men in different ways.

"Little Cara takes it any way a man wants to give it to her, but if she had her choice, she'd be tied up to the bedposts and fucked until dawn. Lacy has a cute little whip. She uses it on the men and lets them use it on her. She says it's more fun than regular sex. That brings us to Janna. She's into feathers and the like. What that girl can do with a feather is downright indecent. Of course, they all do it the way the customer requests, but every once in a while, the guy says they can do what they want.

"It's then that we make the big money. I heard tell one man paid Lacy twenty dollars just because she used that little whip of hers. As for me, my specialty is sucking a man's cock and balls 'till he cries for mercy. I never make less than ten dollars a night since the men appreciate what I can do for them."

"I can see why. I certainly did."

"You'll get to enjoy each of us and believe me, you'll get your buck-fifty worth, especially if you let the women do what they do best."

"I don't know about the whipping part. Is it anything like that spanking you gave me?"

"They say it's more intense. Someday I might try it for myself, but never on a permanent basis. I don't like pain that well. A good spanking is one thing, but a whipping is something else."

Black kissed her long and hard and fell asleep with her in his arms.

Chapter Two

Black rolled over and reached for Kate. To his dismay, she'd left his bed. He wondered if it would have been different if he'd been a paying customer. The answer to his question echoed in his mind. Of course, it would be different. He'd be in her bed and not his.

He felt around until he found a box of matches. Once he struck one of them, he lit the lamp on the table beside the bed. He reached first for his shirt and then the cigarettes that he knew were in the pocket. He needed a smoke. Usually after he bedded a whore, he liked to smoke a cigarette, but last night had been different. Holding her in his arms and enjoying the softness of her body next to his had overruled the need for a smoke.

After taking a long drag on the cigarette, he reached for his pants so he could find the pocket watch he always carried. It was the only thing he had left that had belonged to his father. From his mother, he had his memories, but he'd been too young when his father died for any of those.

He opened the face of the watch and, once his eyes focused, saw it was five in the morning. Since breakfast was served at six, he'd have plenty of time to wash the sex from his cock and put on fresh clothes. His others were covered in trail dust and smelled to high heaven. When he finished work tonight, he'd take them down to the creek and get them clean.

With his sponge bath and shave finished, he pulled on his clothes and boots before heading downstairs. The smell of bacon and eggs made him realize last night's activities had given him a good appetite.

He was surprised to see an older woman in the kitchen cooking and all of the women wearing dresses and looking fresh as daisies. "Morning ladies," he said, as he entered the room.

"Good morning, Black," Belle greeted him. "Girls, this is Black

Conley. I hired him last night. If everything I've heard about him is true, he can use those guns he's wearing, and he knows how to work a ranch. He'll be riding with you this morning, Kate. You can show him around especially up where we've been losing all the cattle."

He watched as a petite brunette stepped forward. "I'm Janna," she said, extending her hand. "I can hardly wait to get to know you better. Kate told us about last night. It should make quiet nights around here more enjoyable."

She stepped aside as a saucy red head stepped forward. "I'm Cara and this is Lacy," she said, introducing a pretty blonde. "We're all looking forward to getting to know you better."

From what Kate told him last night, things could get really interesting. He could see Janna with her feathers, Lacy with her whip, and Cara tied to the bedposts and all of them ready and willing to do whatever he wanted. After last night with Kate, he was getting hard just thinking about it.

Outside he saw the stagecoach he'd glimpsed earlier. It was evident that this was a regular stop for the stage line. If that were so, the reason he hadn't heard anything from the upstairs rooms could be that the women were occupied elsewhere with the gentlemen from the stage. "So where are your overnight guests?" he said to Belle, after exchanging pleasantries with each of the women.

"They'll be down soon," Belle assured him. "They each have their own rooms in another section of the house. After the women are finished with them for the night, they enjoy a good night's sleep without having to worry about waking up their companion. They all know that the women have to be up and ready to ride at the crack of dawn. Now, if you'll tell Annie how you like your eggs, she'll fix them for you."

Black had just finished telling the cook about his eggs when the passengers from the stage came down for breakfast. Most of them were fancy Dans from the East heading for God only knew where. He certainly hope they paid well.

He laughed at his silent thoughts. Those were the words he'd heard his mother say whenever her women had gentleman callers. If the men paid well, there would be more money in the ranch accounts. By splitting fifty-fifty with the women, she made damn good money and so did the women, especially with their pay, three good meals a day, and a roof over their heads.

He decided that all the passengers must have been men since there wasn't a woman in the bunch of them.

"It was a right fine night, Miss Belle," the driver said. "I hope these gents enjoyed themselves as much as I did. Next time, I'd like to try Miss Kate. I haven't had her in quite a spell. Nothing against the other women, but I do enjoy variety."

Janna sashayed up to the driver and allowed him to slide his hand down the front of her dress. "I understand, Jeb. I like variety as well. You just keep bringing all these handsome men here, and we'll all do our best to keep you happy."

"I trust you've been with all the women," a man with a British accent said. "My evening with Miss Cara was far beyond my expectations. It's a shame that I won't be coming this way on my return to London, but my business will take me in the opposite direction."

As soon as the men arrived, Black saw Kate leave the room. Within minutes, she reappeared, the fancy dress gone, replaced by work britches and shirt.

While the passengers ate their breakfast, Black and Kate went out to hitch the team to the stage. "Does the stage come through here often?" he said.

"About once a week eastbound and the same westbound. Later today, Belle will take the mail into town and stop at the bank to deposit the money the women made last night."

"You let her take care of your finances?"

"Why not? She's fair about everything. Don't know if I'd trust a man as much as I do her. I just wish she didn't have the problems this ranch gives her."

"Problems? You mean by not having men to run it."

Kate laughed at his statement. "Good heavens no. Her problems come from Clayte Adamson. That son of a bitch wants this place. He has ever since her pa died ten years ago. Now that he's single again, he's been bird-dogging her with his empty proposals and offers to buy her out. Since she's not interested in either, he's been taking our cattle. I'd like to catch him in the act and unload a shotgun full of buckshot in his fat ass. Maybe that would keep him on his side of the property line."

Black shook his head. "Can't picture you on the business end of a shotgun. Do you even know how to shoot one?"

Kate looked indignant. "Of course I do. In my line of work a gal needs to know how to protect herself from the scum that think they can beat her or even worse. Salina said she never had to learn how to use a gun until she left your ma. She said the first man who bought her for the night beat her senseless and left her for dead. She decided that would be the last time a man, any man would do something like that to her. Once she made her point by threatening one of her gentlemen, she never had to do it again."

Black laughed heartily. He'd heard about men who liked to beat the whores they bought. Usually, they were upstanding citizens and didn't want it known that they beat women. When that was they case, they didn't dare do anything like that to their wives. He'd run into his share of them and always wanted to do to them as they did to the women they took to the rooms upstairs at the saloons.

Of course, he never acted on his impulses. It wouldn't do for him to step on the wrong side of the law. No matter how many men he'd killed, there wasn't a one of them who hadn't drawn on him first. Every lawman from here to Texas knew that about him. Black Conley was a gunslinger, but he'd never done anything outside the law, and he intended to keep it that way. The story of Black Conley was good enough to give him the perfect cover when he was investigating things like the rustling that was going on at the Double Bar B.

"Are you just going to stand there watching the dust from the stage?" Kate said.

"Guess not. I'd like to get up to the boundary line between the two properties. Maybe I can catch a glimpse of this Adamson."

"You don't know him. He'll have his men up there, but he keeps his fat ass at the ranch. He doesn't like to get his hands dirty."

"What about moving the cattle from that area?"

"We were planning to round them up and bring them closer to the house last week, but Clayte kept us busy in other areas. Now that you're here, I was hoping to start the roundup today. I have to talk to Belle about it first, though."

"What do you have to talk to me about?" Belle said, causing both Kate and Black to turn toward the house.

Black was pleased to see her in the tight fitting britches and shirt. They certainly accented her womanly curves. Behind her, the three other women were similarly clad. He'd seen them at breakfast but they looked much different without their low cut dresses that accented only one of their assets.

"I'd like to start the roundup today," Kate replied. "We can't afford to lose any more cattle to Clayte, and, if we leave them on that east range any longer, we could lose every steer we have up there."

"You're right," Belle agreed. "I was going into town, but if we're going to do the roundup I think it's best if I stay here. I can put the money in the safe in my office and be ready to join you in just a few minutes."

"Good," Kate continued. "I'll get your horse saddled, and we'll be ready to ride as soon as you get out here."

Earlier, Black hadn't noticed that the three other women each wore a gun belt with a single revolver positioned over her right hip. Under the circumstances, he was surprised to see that neither Belle nor Kate wore one.

"The others have gun belts. Why not you and Belle?" he observed once Belle returned to the house.

"I'm more comfortable with a rifle, but I do wear a gun. I don't like keeping it in the house, so I have it in the barn. As for Belle, she'll have her guns on by the time she joins us. If you recall, she was planning to go into town. That said she wasn't wearing them, since the people in town don't quite understand what it is we do out here. For her to wear a gun to town would be like raising a red flag in front of a mad bull. They'd have her locked up quicker than scat."

"Locked up? Why?"

"Because, according to the town fathers, good women don't carry guns, so they passed a law against it, back about eight years ago. Up until then Belle, didn't go into town without them. I think it was Clayte's doing. If Belle were locked up, he'd find a way to get this spread away from her. That is his plan, you know."

Black thought about what Kate said while he saddled his horse. It made sense, especially if this Adamson feller wanted this ranch so damn bad. He'd heard of men, especially Mike Slade, killing for less. It was a wonder that Belle was still alive.

By the time Belle arrived, they were all mounted, and Kate had put her rifle in the boot of her saddle. Each girl rode a horse that seemed to fit her personality. Kate rode a chestnut mare, Janna a brown and white paint gelding, Lacy a palomino mare, Cara a sorrel gelding, and Belle a white stallion who matched her silver blonde hair. He wondered if she ever used him for stud, then noticed the horses in the corral. They looked as though the stallion had sired most of them using the palomino as well as the chestnut for breeders.

"I'm ready to ride," Belle said, shoving her rifle in the boot of her saddle.

The ride to the east range took about half an hour, leaving Black awed by the expanse of the ranch he now called home. Once there, it was evident someone had been trespassing on the Double Bar B. The barbed wire fence had been cut and tracks of several animals led away from the property.

"That son of a bitch, he's hit us again," Belle spat. "You five can handle this, I'm going into town. This time that bastard of a sheriff is going to have to listen to me."

She wheeled her horse and took off at a fast gallop in the direction of the town Black had left the night before.

"Let's get to work," Kate ordered. "We've lost enough cattle to Clayte and his bunch. We can count them and check our losses when we get them to the pasture closer to the house."

Black made a mental note that he would come back up here tonight and see just who was stealing the cattle. He promised himself he wouldn't do anything he might regret tonight, but he knew he had to get evidence before he went off half cocked and did something that would push the law to come gunning for him.

* * * *

Belle thought about going back to the house to get rid of her guns, but by the time the idea entered her mind she was halfway to town. She was too mad to turn around now. Besides, this time she had proof. She had five witnesses, including one man, to back her up about the fence being cut.

Just outside of town, she stopped long enough to take off her guns and stash them in a clump of bushes where she could pick them up later. There was no need to give Joe Calhoun any reason to arrest her today. She purposely left her rifle in the boot of her saddle. As long as she wasn't wearing her guns she would be safe from the law. If anything was said about her rifle, she would point out that Lightning was a stallion and therefore wearing a gun wouldn't be against the law, since males could all wear them in town. It was just females that the law pertained to and one look at Lightning told anyone who was interested he was all male.

Town was as quiet as she would have expected it to be so early in the morning. The banker was just opening up for the day and the general store had its door open so that customers could come inside and the owner could enjoy the last of the fall breezes that would soon turn to winter winds.

When she entered the sheriff's office, she found Joe in his usual position, sitting behind his desk with his feet propped up on the top of it while he read the wanted posters that seemed always to be in front of him. He was so engrossed in the posters; he didn't even look up when she entered the office. Unceremoniously, she shoved his boots off the desk, almost toppling him over in the chair that was precariously balanced on two legs.

"What the hell do you think you're doing, Belle?" Joe sputtered.

"I wanted to get your attention. This time you're going to listen to me and do some investigating, or I'll have to bring in my own detectives from Denver."

"What the hell do you need detectives for, Belle? I heard that fancy pants gunslinger headed out to your place last night. Why not use him?"

"If you're referring to Mr. Conley, I hired him on as a hand not a gunman."

Joe shook his head. "From what I hear you may want him as a hand, but he's more used to using his guns than herding cattle. So what imaginary problem are you here to complain about this time?"

"It's not imaginary. I lost more cattle last night."

"Now that's a real shame. I hear tell there's a pack of wolves up around your place. Maybe what you need is a wolfer to track them down and eliminate them for you."

"Wolves don't cut fences, and they don't take off with the cattle. They kill them and eat their fill at the kill site. This time, my crew, along with Mr. Conley all saw the cut in the fence and the trampled grass. If I'm not wrong, they probably got off with about a dozen head. That makes almost forty head of cattle in the last two weeks. It's as plain as the nose on your face that it's Clayte's men who are taking them, so what are you planning to do about it?"

"Do?" Joe questioned. "I don't do for whores. Everyone knows what goes on out at your place. If you were half as worried about your cattle as you are about bedding down the passengers on the stage, you wouldn't be in this predicament. From what I hear, your gals are right good in bed. I was thinkin' of comin' out there and havin' a poke at one of them myself. Just how much would you charge me for a good roll?"

"More than you could ever afford. Since I can't get any satisfaction from you, I'll be sending a wire to the U.S. Marshal in Denver. I'm certain he'd be more than willing to come up here and see why you aren't doing your duty. We'll see how far you get with someone in authority."

"Now wait just a minute. The U. S. Marshal don't have no jurisdiction here. This is a civil matter."

Belle smiled at how flustered she could make Joe. "Maybe it is, but I know enough about the law to know that if you aren't doing your duty, I have every right to bring in a marshal."

"Do you think anyone here would send that wire for you?"

"Hell no. I plan to send it from my place. The stage line put in a telegraph so that their passengers could use it if necessary. I can send my own wire. I learned how to run it when they put it in. Now, if you'll excuse me, I have a wire to write and send. Have a good day, Joe, and don't overexert yourself reading all those flyers. Do say hello to your wife for me. I haven't seen her in church lately. I do hope she's not feeling poorly."

Belle turned on her heel only to be stopped when Joe called her name. "Let me put my deputy in charge here. Then I can ride out to your place with you and see for myself what you're talking about."

Belle smiled. She knew if she threatened Joe with a U.S. Marshal he'd change his tune. From everything she'd heard, Clayte ran not only the Diamond A, but also the town council. Since Joe and Clayte had grown up together, it was only logical that the sheriff would be on Clayte's side when it came to any dispute between him and her. This time she held the trump card. She decided that she'd wire Denver anyway. Ed Heath was the son of her father's former foreman and knew more about Larson's Gap than anyone he could send. If she was lucky, he'd come himself. If not, she knew he'd send the best man he had.

"You know where my ranch is, Joe. I'll ride on ahead and meet you at the house."

Joe sputtered, but finally agreed. For Belle, not having to have him ride with her was a relief. He'd certainly question her about why she was stopping along the way and the look on his face when she strapped on her guns would be one of pure disgust. It was better if he didn't see her armed until he got to the ranch. There she could do as she pleased, since she would be on her own property.

"I could arrest you, you know," Joe said from behind her, causing her to turn to face him.

"Arrest me? For what?"

"For carrying a gun in town."

Belle laughed in his face. "I think you're reading the law all wrong, Joe. As I recall it says that no woman can wear a gun in town. I'm not wearing any guns."

"What about that rifle in the boot of your saddle?"

"To be technical, the saddle is being worn by my horse, and, in case you haven't noticed, he's all male. So you see, I'm breaking no laws. Of course, if you want to search me, maybe it's best if you get your wife to do the honors. I wouldn't want to have to press charges that you took advantage of a woman."

"Have it your way. I'll meet you out at your place in about an hour."

Belle turned back to her horse and mounted effortlessly. As she rode out of town, she thought about Joe's wife, Nora. From the gossip she'd heard at church, she decided it was common knowledge Joe beat the living shit out of the woman whenever he was drinking and that was every Saturday night. It was no wonder she didn't come to church on Sunday morning. The bruises alone would be enough to give credence to the rumors that were running wild about the goings on in the Calhoun household. The beatings were only part of the gossip. If she could believe everything she heard, Calhoun was allowing Clayte to take a poke at Nora whenever he needed a woman and at half the price he'd have to pay at the Purple Moon.

* * * *

As soon as they started driving the cattle to the winter pasture, Black remembered why he hated ranching so badly. The dust that choked him also made his eyes water. At least they weren't driving them to market. Hopefully someone would be putting together a herd, and Belle could get her cattle to the railhead that he knew was about two hundred miles away, without having to do the work herself.

"How far are we taking them?" he said, when he rode up next to Kate.

"There's good range land up by the house. We've got a large box canyon up there that makes a good corral. That way we can keep an eye on them and get food to them if necessary. Belle's pa built shelters on three sides of it so that the cattle can get in out of the wind and snow when winter hits. It works really well for our purposes."

32

Black nodded and returned to his position at the back of the herd. At the pace the steers set, they'd be lucky to be back to the house by noon. Once he got something to eat, he'd take his bedroll and go up to fix the fence that had been cut. He'd seen an area that would be perfect to watch the comings and goings around that part of the ranch for the night.

Belle was waiting for them when they returned to the ranch. "Did you get a head count?" she demanded as soon as they put their horses in the barn.

"From what I could see," Janna said, "we lost about twenty head this time. At least down here, one of us can ride night hawk."

Before Belle could answer, a man rode into the dooryard. Black wondered if this was the infamous Clayte Adamson, but as soon as he saw the badge on the man's shirt, he decided it had to be the sheriff that Belle had gone off to see earlier.

"Just when did you put on them guns of yours, Belle?" Joe said when he dismounted.

"As soon as I was outside of town. I'm breaking no laws by wearing them."

"What kind of laws would that be?" Black said, pretending ignorance about the laws in Larson's Gap.

"I don't see where it's any of your business, Mr. Conley, but it has to do with wearing guns in town."

"I'm impressed you know my name, but I was wearing my guns last night and no one arrested me."

"That's because you ain't a woman, Mr. Conley. Women ain't allowed to wear guns. As for how I know who you are, bad news travels fast."

"Black, this is Joe Calhoun, our not so honorable sheriff. The fool tried to arrest me for having my rifle in the boot of my saddle until I reminded him that I wasn't wearing the rifle, Lightning was, and he's pure male."

Black and the women all enjoyed a good laugh at the sheriff's expense. "Just how did such a law come to be?" he said. "I ain't never been in a town where women had such a law passed against them."

"That's because you've never been in a town with Ball Buster Belle. Once you get to know your new boss, you'll find out she's trouble with a capital T. Now are you going to take me up to where you say this fence was, cut or are we going to stand around here all day jawjackin'?"

"I certainly would hate to keep you from your more pressing duties,

Joe. The crew can handle things here. Would you ride along with us, Black? I certainly wouldn't want Joe telling people I took advantage of him out on the range."

Black chuckled as he watched the sheriff's face go from pink to crimson in the blink of an eye.

"You know I wouldn't do no such thing, Belle."

"One never knows. Before we leave, you might as well join us for dinner. I'm certain Black is as hungry as I am."

Before going into the house, Black stopped at the well and drew a bucket of water so he could wash the trail dust from his hands and face. It didn't surprise him to see the sheriff bound up the steps onto the porch and enter the house ahead of Belle. He decided Joe Calhoun was one man who didn't miss many meals.

When Black finished cleaning up, he headed for the house. He was pleased to see Belle waiting for him on the porch. He didn't dwell on why she was there as much as he did on the swell of her breasts straining against the buttons on the man's shirt. He could remember his mother telling him that a man's shirt was never made to accommodate a woman's breasts. Now he understood why. If he got lucky, those buttons would pop off giving him an eye full of what he wanted to see. Somehow, he decided, he going to have to get her naked and in his bed. When he did, he'd guarantee she wouldn't bust his balls, but she would make them feel a hell of a lot better.

Chapter Three

Black eyed the sheriff from across the table. The man had the manners of a three-year-old child. He piled food on his plate like he hadn't eaten in weeks and ate like a hog at a trough.

"I'll say this for you, Belle," he said, with his mouth so full of food it ran down his chin with every word, "you do set a good table. It's a good thing you got someone here who can cook for you. I doubt any of the females at this table know their way around the kitchen."

"We all know how to cook, Sheriff Calhoun," Kate replied before Belle could open her mouth. "We work our asses off on the ranch so having someone here to fix our meals when we're working is a Godsend."

"I doubt you know much about God, Missy. What you do know is about working on your back. I offered to come out a take a poke at any one of you, but your boss doesn't seem to like my money."

"I can understand why," Cara said, her voice so sweet it was as though it was laced with honey. "We're all very particular about what cocks we let into the henhouse. If they aren't clean enough, we don't want anything to do with them."

Joe immediately looked down at his plate as though he wanted to say something, but after on look from Black he remained silent throughout the remainder of the meal.

"You ready to ride, Black?" Belle said when he finished his pie.

Black nodded as he got up from his chair. The sheriff made no move to join them.

"If you're coming with us, you'd better get a move on," Black said as he left the table. "I'd hate to have you get lost trying to find the range where the rustling took place."

The look on Joe's face was one of pure disgust as he pushed back his chair and followed Black and Belle out of the door.

"You know, I know the reason why you took up with Ball Buster Belle," Joe said, as they mounted their horses.

"And just what would that reason be?"

"Bein' an Injun there's not a rancher around here that would want you within a hundred yards of their place."

"Look, you son of a bitch, I had this talk with the bartender last night, and, if I don't miss my guess, you heard it all word for word. If you think I'm going to draw on you and give you cause to arrest me, you're dead wrong. I don't like repeating myself, but I'll make an exception in your case. My ma was Mexican and my pa was white. That makes me a Texican, and, like I said last night, it don't do anyone any good to get a Texican riled."

"Didn't mean any offence. It's only a logical conclusion. I mean with your coloring, I assumed you were an Injun just like they did at the saloon. It does make a body wonder what you're doin' around these parts."

"Do you know what happens to people who assume too much?" Black said. He watched as a dark cloud of incomprehension crossed Joe's face. "When you assume something you make an ass out of you and an ass out of me."

"I don't get it," Joe replied with a shake of his head.

"Well, I do," Belle said. "Of course, both Mr. Conley and I are educated. When you spell the word assume it is a-s-s-u-m-e. In other words ass comes before you, just like it does me. Now do you get it?"

"Can't say that I do, but then I didn't go to one of those high class schools in the East like you did. I'm just a good old country boy doin' my best to keep the law."

They stopped at the place where the fence has been cut, and Joe got down to examine the ground. "It looks like someone drove your cattle through here, but I doubt it was anyone from the Diamond A. Even if it was, I don't know how you would even go about trying to find twenty steers among his cattle. He runs five thousand head. Can't see you checking the brands on every single one of them. I'll take a ride over to his place and see if he lost any cattle last night. Probably the same bunch raided his place on the way to God only knows where." Joe remounted his horse and rode in the direction of the Diamond A.

"That bastard," Belle muttered once he was out of earshot. "I'll bet he and Clayte have a good laugh over all of this when he gets to the Diamond A. I'm even more determined to wire the U.S. Marshal in Denver and get him up here."

"There's no need for that, Belle. It's no coincidence that I'm here and Joe has good reason to wonder about me. Someone already contacted the marshal's office, and they sent me up here to see what's going on. You probably aren't the only one losing cattle to the Diamond A."

"You? Why would they send you?"

"I'm a U. S. Marshal, but that's not for public knowledge. I was sworn in several years ago, and when they need someone to go in without being noticed, they send me. I was just lucky that the men in town directed me out to your ranch last night. I've been told to investigate both Adamson and the sheriff while I'm here."

"It's hard to believe you're a marshal. I mean you do have a reputation. From what I've heard, you're more comfortable on the wrong side of the law than on the right one."

Black tilted back his hat and looked her squarely in the eye. "Let's get one thing straight. I ain't never been on the wrong side of the law. I ain't wanted for anything, other than my speed with a gun. Every time I've had to use it I was drawn on first. I don't want to have to use it against anyone around here, but if I'm challenged, I won't hesitate. My orders are to find out who's behind the rustling and put an end to it. If I find out that Joe Calhoun is in this with Adamson, I have the authority to arrest him too."

He looked into her eyes and saw her confusion mirrored there. "So why work for me?"

"Why not? It gives me the perfect cover for what I have to do. It also gives me three meals a day, a place to lay my head at night, and the prettiest boss I've ever seen."

On impulse, he pulled her into his arms. Her breasts against his chest made him wish he could take her here and now, but during the day he was on duty. He'd have to settle to a feel and a kiss. She struggled against him until he covered her mouth with his. As she relaxed enough to enjoy what he was doing to her, he cupped her ass with one of his big hands and pulled her so close she couldn't miss the feel of his cock as it pressed against her.

"We ...I ... you can't do this," she protested once he freed her mouth.

"Why not?"

"Because I'm not one of the women who works for me. I told you last night you could have your pick of them at a reduced rate, but you couldn't have me."

"That doesn't answer the question. Why not? You're ten times more desirable than any of them. I can see why they would call you Ball Buster Belle, if you'd earned the title, but to me you're just an ice princess."

"You don't know anything about me, Mr. Conley and I'll thank you to keep your hands off me. I'm not for sale, and I'm no man's plaything. I expect you to respect my wishes. Tonight, I'll make certain one of the women comes to your room to relieve that bulge you have in your pants. Just remember, it won't be me."

He watched as she turned and hurried toward her horse. The sight of her ass swaying in defiance, as she mounted made him want her even more. It would be a long winter and, sooner or later, she'd give into him. He had nothing but time. He was willing to wait until she was ready for him.

* * * *

Belle had never been so flustered in all her life. It was true the boy in Ohio had gotten into her pants when she was young and dumb, but since then she had distanced herself from any man who crossed her path. Those who had been bold enough to kiss her soon learned it was the wrong thing to do. One tongue lashing from her had doused their ardor and given her the reputation that earned her the hated nickname of Ball Buster Belle. So why was it when Black kissed her she imagined herself in bed with him? It didn't matter. Whatever the reason, it had to stop here and now. She couldn't afford to become a weak woman like the rest of the ranchers' wives in the area. She certainly didn't want some man dominating her and that was just what would happen if she allowed Mr. Black Conley to get too close. When she first took over this ranch, it would have been easy to succumb to Clayte's charm, but what would that have gotten her other than an early grave like Nettie?

As she swung into the saddle, her pussy ached for the release she knew she could find if she put aside her principals and went to Black's bed. As soon as she was out of sight, she squirmed in the saddle in an attempt to relieve the ache, but doing so only intensified the sensation, reminding her of the feel of her nipples pressed against his chest. Control of her life could easily get out of hand with Black around. She should fire him, but she needed him to find out what was going on with the rustlers more than she needed to put temptation safely out of her reach.

As she neared the ranch house, she saw the women coming in form the canyon where the cattle would spend the winter. Just seeing them made her wonder if one of her own hands had sent the wire to Denver. It was entirely possible, since they all knew how to run the telegraph. Of course, it could have been someone altogether different. Maybe she wasn't the only rancher in the area who was losing cattle on a regular basis. It wouldn't hurt none to ask around at church on Sunday.

She knew which men were loyal to Clayte and which ones hated his guts. A few questions posed to the right people could do her a world of good. Until now she hadn't thought much about anyone else having problems. She'd thought it was just Clayte's way of getting her to sell out and become a wife to him and mother to those wild Indians he called his children.

"Did Joe do anything about the rustling?" Kate said when Belle rode up.

"Are you kidding? That bastard probably still thinks it was wolves that raided us. If it was, they were about the most intelligent animals around. Maybe we should round them up and sell them to the circus."

Her comment brought hearty laughter from Kate. "What did he really say?"

"He went over to the Diamond A to see if they'd lost any cattle. When I pointed out that I thought Clayte was behind this he said there was no way he could search for our cattle among all the ones in Clayte's herd."

"Sounds like a lame excuse to me."

"Me too. I didn't get a chance to talk to you this morning. I was wondering how Black was last night."

"Why, Belle Barton, I never thought I'd see the day when you were interested in how a man performed in bed."

"I'm not interested in that. I was just wondering if the other women would be pleased with him on slow nights."

"Like hell you were. That man has gotten to you, and I can understand why. He's about the most handsome drifter I've ever seen, in bed, well, that cock of his was so big, I thought he was going to tickle my tonsils with it. One roll with him and you'd forget all about that piss ant in Ohio. From the way you tell it he couldn't have been much more than a boy. I think it's high time you took on a man. It could be an interesting experience for both of you."

Belle sensed her cheeks suffused with a blush. "I'm certain it's what Mr. Conley wants, but what any man wants is in direct contrast to my desires. I'll keep him so busy with you and the other women he won't have time to worry about me."

"Suit yourself, but I think you're making a mistake you could regret for the rest of your life. That man has tricks up his sleeve that could curl your toenails if you let them."

Belle made no comment. There were a lot of things Belle would like to have Black curl, but her toenails weren't on the list. She'd learned a long time ago if she wanted sexual satisfaction she could give it to herself. The last time she'd visited Denver, she'd found a unique little shop that catered to the pleasures of women. There, she'd bought a contraption that looked like a man's cock. It wasn't soft and pliable, but at least it did the job when she needed to rid herself of the frustrations of her self-imposed celibacy. If it were bedtime, she'd be upstairs using it right now to take away the frustrations Black had ignited with his kiss.

* * * *

As soon as Belle was out of sight, Black set to mending the fence. It didn't take long to pull the wire tight and splice the cut ends together with another piece of wire. It was a procedure he'd become quite familiar with in all the years he'd investigated rustling cases. He wondered what it would take to get these men to realize that sooner or later they'd all get caught.

"Just what in the hell do you think you're doing on the Double Bar B?"

Black looked up at the sound of the man's voice. "What's it to you?"

The man looked down on him from the saddle of his black stallion. "I'm Belle's neighbor and fiancé. I don't like people trespassing on her land. Sheriff Calhoun was just at my place telling me how she's been losing cattle. I was just on my way over to see if there was anything I can do. Guess I didn't get here any too soon. How many more of her cattle were you planning to take?"

"I wasn't planning to take any. I work for Miss Barton. I'm here mending the fence rustlers cut last night."

The man laughed heartily. Black decided it wouldn't be long before Clayte Adamson laughed out of the other side of his face. He'd taken an instant dislike to the man. It was no wonder Belle was so anti-man if this was the only choice she had for a husband.

"Guess it makes sense. Belle always did have a soft spot in her heart for drifters and strays. Leave it to her to take on an Injun for her pet project."

Black's anger flared. "Look mister, I'm gettin' right sick of being taken for an Injun. The proper term is Texican and I'll thank you not to forget it. Now if you'll excuse me I have more work to do. I figure if this fence is cut in one spot, it could be cut in more places. I plan to ride the length of this fence before nightfall. So if you'll excuse me, I'll be on my way."

"Suit yourself, but if you're planning to get on Belle's good side so you can slide into her bed, you'd better think again. She's mine, and, once we're married, she won't be spreading her legs for anyone but me. I can hardly wait to give her a good fuck and show her what a woman's place is in life. It certainly isn't running a ranch. That bitch needs to be tamed and I'm the man to tame her. Once she's taking care of my younguns, she'll learn what it's like to be a real woman. After that, I'm certain she'll give me some fine healthy sons rather than those whiney brats I got from my first wife."

Black mounted up and rode on without responding to Clayte's boast. If he stayed any longer, he'd have to take the man down a notch and he couldn't risk losing his cover over an ignorant bastard like Clayte Adamson. His time would come and, when it did, Black was certain, the man would be wearing the shackles Black carried in his saddlebag and not the black eye a fight would give him.

Even though Black was certain he'd find no more breaks in the fence, he rode along the line of barbed wire for about half an hour. That was just enough time for Clayte to get to the ranch house and confront Belle.

Spurring his horse to a gallop, he rode back to see exactly what was happening. Rather than make his presence known, he left his horse in a grove of trees and snuck up to the house.

From his vantage point, he saw Belle on the porch talking to Adamson. Their words reached him loud and clear.

"I don't recall asking you to come calling, Clayte," Belle said.

"Come on, Belle, I know you've had some problems with rustlers. Joe was just over at the house and told me of your troubles. I sent my men out right away to see if we lost any cattle last night. Once they were gone, I realized you were over here all alone and decided that you could use my help. I met up with that half-breed drifter you got working for you. I wouldn't put it past him to be the one takin' your cattle. You know you can't trust an Injun when there's stock ripe for the taking."

"I'll trust who I want. Even if Black were a breed as you say, I'd trust him a hell of a lot further than I would you. Now why don't you slither back to that hole you came from? I don't need or want your protection."

"What you need is a good man to fuck you until you understand what a woman's place in life is and I'm the man to do it. I think I'll start right now."

Black cringed as he watched Adamson take a step closer to Belle. He was about to grab her when she pulled her gun.

"I wouldn't come any closer if I were you. If you value those balls between your legs, I suggest you get off my property. In case you don't know it, I'm a crack shot, and I'd take great pleasure in castrating you like I do the steers."

It was all Black could do to keep from laughing out loud. The look on Adamson's face was one of pure terror.

"You'll regret this, Belle Barton. Mark my words, you'll regret turning me down. One of these days you'll come crawling to me on your hands and knees and then I'll take you like a dog takes a bitch in heat."

"It sounds like you're the one in heat, Clayte. Maybe it would be best if you went into town tonight and took on one of the new whores at the saloon. I hear tell that Lester brought in some new women all the way from Denver. Makes the Purple Moon Saloon sound like just the place for you. Just remember you hadn't better get caught slapping any of them around the same way you did Nettie. Lacy told me Lester has a knife that he uses on anyone who beats on his women. I'd hate to see someone other than me getting the pleasure of castrating you."

Adamson turned on his heel and mounted his horse. He took off fast from the dooryard. It wasn't until he was gone that Black came out from behind the woodshed.

"You handled yourself quite well," he said as he approached Belle.

"You … you watched? Why didn't you make yourself known and

help me out?"

"I aimed to, but you were doing such a good job I didn't want to stop your fun. Besides, I don't want to tip my hand too soon. I'd rather give Adamson enough rope to hang himself. From the look on his face, he was disappointed to see your cattle moved. Did he ask where they'd been taken?"

"He asked and I told him it was none of his business. Do you think you can get enough evidence to arrest him?"

"Don't see where it will be much of a problem, although it could take all winter. With your cattle out of his reach, he just might wait until spring to make his next move. That should give me plenty of time to find out just who sent that wire to Denver. If he were raiding the other ranches, I'd just as soon know who's siding with us and who's siding with him. From what I saw of the sheriff, I doubt we can count on him to help us. We're on our own until I learn differently."

The tension he'd seen in her face earlier returned, but she regained her composure fast. "Why don't you come in and have a cup of coffee? We don't have to worry about Annie overhearing us. She's over at her place until it's time to fix supper."

"Her place?"

"She and her husband have a house on the ranch. They worked for my pa for years. She's always done the cooking here and her husband, Roy, was my pa's foreman until he got his ribs stove in by a bull. That was right after Pa died. Since then, he and Annie have stayed on. I see him every night when he comes with Annie for supper when he gives me lots of tips on how to handle the ranch. Kate enjoys visiting with him as well. He was the one who suggested she should be the foreman out here."

"What did you say Annie's last name was?"

"I didn't say, but it's Heath. Why do you ask?"

"No reason, just wondering. I like to know the folks I'm dealing with. I think I'll ride out to see them. Which way is their place from here?"

After getting the directions from Belle, he left the house and went back to where he'd tied his horse. Just hearing the name of Heath solved the mystery of who had requested a U.S. Marshal to be sent to this area. His best friend, Ed Heath, was also one of his superiors. It was Ed who had sent him the wire that brought him here from Laramie

The close proximity of the Heath home came as a surprise to Black.

It was no wonder the woman was able to go home in the afternoons. She could easily make the walk between the two places in a few minutes.

A man who could be Ed, only older, answered his knock.

"Wondered when you'd get here, son," Roy greeted him. "Come on in and Annie will get you some fresh apple pie. Never saw a boy who would turn down a piece of Mama's apple pie."

Black didn't want to offend Roy so he accepted the invitation. It was a smaller replica of the ranch house and just as well kept.

"Mama does a good job not only here but up at Belle's place, too," Roy said, once they were seated at the kitchen table enjoying pie and coffee.

"The pie is good," Black admitted, "but that's not the reason I came. It was you who sent for me, wasn't it?"

Roy nodded. "I sent for someone. Didn't know it would be you. Mama knew the minute she laid eyes on you this morning. I would have, too. Since Ed's described you enough in his letters."

"So what's your stake in this? You certainly haven't lost any cattle."

"No, but our girl has. You see her pa and me was best friends for longer than I care to admit. When his wife died, Annie and me tried to talk him out of sending her back east, but he was set on it. He kept saying that his wife's kin could take better care of her than he could. Maybe he was right, but it almost broke our hearts when he sent her away. I always thought that her and Ed would get married, but young folks have different ideas than the older generation."

"What Roy is trying to say," Annie said when she joined them at the table, "is that this is our home. Both Belle and her pa have been very good to us. What affects the Double Bar B affects us as well. Belle doesn't think I know about the rustling that's been going on, but I'd have to be blind and deaf not to have caught wind of it."

"Mama and me figured that if we asked Ed to send us one of his men we'd be able to at least have a hand in getting the rustling stopped. As much as we'd wanted our boy to come home, we knew it would be best if he sent someone else. We asked for the best and that's what he sent us. He tells us no one is better than Black Conley. Maybe you can get our little girl out of this trouble she's in and remind her she's a woman with a woman's needs. I can't believe she hasn't let at least one man in her bed, what with all the goings on over there."

"What a terrible thing to say, Roy," Annie scolded.

"Don't see why you'd think it's so terrible. We both know what them women do at night with the passengers from the stage. A good roll with a good man might be just the thing Belle needs. Even at our age it's good to warm up the sheets now and then."

Black laughed at the banter between husband and wife. Even if he agreed that Belle needed to be fucked, preferably by him, he didn't come right out and say it.

"From what I can see, Belle needs to have someone catch that no good neighbor of hers in the act. What can you tell me about Clayte Adamson and Joe Calhoun? I have a gut feeling the two of them are in this together."

Once Annie went back to the ranch house to fix supper, Roy filled Black in on the thefts that had prompted his letter to Ed.

"Is anyone else getting hit?" Black said, once Roy stopped for a bite of pie and a sip of coffee."

Roy nodded. "There are four ranches that have lost cattle. Pete Morison's spread is to the north of Clayte's place, Jeb Taylor to the south, and Zeek Willows to the east. If you ask me, which you didn't, I think they've lost steers to take the suspicion off Clayte. If it were only Belle getting hit, everyone would suspect Clayte. The others are all friends. You know, the kind who drink together every Saturday night, take a poke at the whores who work upstairs at the Purple Moon, and act pious as hell on Sunday morning in church."

"What about Joe Calhoun?"

Roy's brow knotted and a dark look filled his eyes. "That son of a bitch runs after Clayte like a puppy dog. Clayte says shit and Joe asks what color and how much? He's as bad as Clayte when it comes to the way he treats his wife. She ain't been to church in weeks. It's probably because she's too ashamed to show her face. Word is that Clayte pays Joe to let him fuck her. It's a real shame. She was a sweet gal before Joe got her in a family way. He's kept her like that ever since. Him and Clayte are certainly cut from the same pattern. For a while, I thought the two of them were having a race to see who could have the most kids the fastest."

"Then you think the two of them are in this together?"

"I don't have to think, I know."

Black finished his coffee. "Saturday night I should take a ride into town. I haven't had a night of drinking in a long time. It always fascinates me just how much you can learn when you're buying drinks for the house."

Chapter Four

Belle sat at the table long after Black left the house. She was still sipping her now cold coffee when Annie arrived.

"Was there are reason you sent Black over to our place?" Annie said.

Belle wondered if she should tell Annie what Black told her when they were alone on the east range. "Ah..."

"You don't have to say anything, honey. We know who Black is and why he's here. Roy wrote to Ed and asked him to send us the best man for the job. We had hoped it would be Ed who came, but we certainly weren't disappointed to find out it was Black. Ed speaks highly of him."

"Why didn't you tell me?" Belle replied. "Shouldn't I have known a U.S. Marshal was coming here? If I had, I wouldn't have kept going into town to be humiliated by Joe Calhoun."

"What if we would have gotten a letter from Ed saying he couldn't spare anyone? What good would knowing have done you? It was better this way. You hired him thinking he was nothing more than another drifter. Now you know he's here to help you out of this predicament. When I left the house, Roy was filling him in on all the other ranchers who are losing cattle. Of course, I doubt they'll side with us. You know Clayte and that bunch are as thick as thieves. They watch out for each other. I'm afraid it's us against them in this fight. Have you told the girls yet?"

Belle shook her head. "I really haven't had a chance to talk to any of them. I thought Kate should know, but I'm undecided about the others."

"Roy and I think all of them should know. They have a stake in this the same as you do. It would be like not telling family. That's what we all are here, you know."

Belle agreed. They were a family. For the past ten years it had been her against the rest of the ranchers around Larson's Gap. At first Roy and

47

Annie had been her only allies, but slowly the women started coming. Kate was the first and then the rest followed. It wasn't right that they should be kept in the dark about what was happening.

After washing the grime of the days work from her body, Belle went back to the kitchen to help Annie. When she was at the house at this time of the day, she helped with the preparation of meals, but those were few and far between. She enjoyed it when she could.

* * * *

Black was surprised when the clock struck five. He hadn't expected to stay at Roy's place for over two hours.

"I guess we should be getting back up to Belle's place for supper," Roy said. "Mama don't like folks being late for meals."

"You take your evening meals at Belle's place?"

The old man nodded. "Belle's pa and I came here together from Texas since we didn't like the way things was looking with the Mexican government. That was back in thirty-five. We didn't want to get mixed up in that mess with Santa Ana. We were only sixteen and thought running away from home and striking out on our own would be a wonderful adventure. We worked a lot of ranches in the year before we made it to Montana. That was when we decided to let our folks know where we were. Matt's folks were so glad to hear from us they sent him the money to buy this spread.

"We weren't without our troubles, but at least we were together. That was when the wagon train arrived with Annie on it. She was the prettiest little thing I ever laid eyes on. As soon as I saw her, I was as gone as a lovesick calf in the springtime. I knew I wanted her. I was real surprised when Matt hired her on as the cook and the rest as they say is history."

"What about Belle's ma?" Black said.

"Now that's a real sad story. She was the daughter of the man who ran the trading post. Right after she was born, her ma ran off with a trapper and no one ever heard from her again. Old Andy raised that girl in the right way. When we arrived here she was the prize of Larson's Gap.

"Her and Matt hit it off and, before you know it, he was sayin' 'I do' and acting like a real husband. They tried having kids right off the way me and Annie did, but Janie just wasn't meant to be a mother. She lost

48

about three babies before they finally had Belle. After that she lost two more and, when Belle was three, she carried one until it was ready to be born. The birth went wrong and both Janie and the boy died.

"It damn near killed Matt. That's when he sent Belle East to be with Janie's aunt. He said it was because he couldn't raise her right, but I knew better. It was because she looked too damn much like her ma. He never looked at another woman after Janie died. He did visit the whores once the Purple Moon opened up, but that was just to relieve the longings that come on a man."

Black was grateful to Roy for answering the questions that crowded his mind concerning the reason Belle wasn't better accepted in the community. He didn't have to be a genius to figure out she was an outsider where Adamson and the other ranchers in the valley were concerned. Now he knew the reasoning behind it.

"Mama will have my scalp if we're late for supper. You'd better be prepared those gals get all gussied up just to eat supper. Mama says it's because they don't like wearin' those britches. If you ask me, I'd say it was because they want to look special for them men on the stage. On nights like tonight they just want to feel like ladies. You can say what you want about them gals working that ranch, but they're all damn good at it. If I weren't so old and crippled up, I'd give them a roll, but Mama would have a fit about it. Besides, Mama is damn good in bed herself. Anyone would think that she used to work above the Purple Moon rather than those youngsters."

Roy laughed heartily, bringing on Black's own deep chuckle. Somehow he couldn't picture Annie as anything but a sweet little ole granny lady. She was gray haired, plump, and the deep dimples in her cheeks gave her an almost angelic appearance. He doubted she would make her way in a place like the Purple Moon Saloon.

"Somehow I just can't picture Annie plying her trade for strangers, like..." he left the rest of the sentence unspoken. Even sixteen years after the death of his mother, he had problems talking about what she did with the men who came to the house after the lights were out at night.

"Like your ma," Roy said finishing Black's statement. "Don't look so shocked, son, I know all about you. I should, I've read enough of the letters Ed sends home to say nothing about the accounts about you in the newspaper. I just have one question. Why did you become a U.S. Marshal?"

Black ran his tongue over his lips as he considered his answer. He rarely had to account to anyone about why he'd decided to work for the law because he usually worked undercover with his badge out of sight. People knew him as a gunslinger and, as such, he was able to gain the confidence of the folks who were close enough to the ones he was investigating to build his case.

"At the time your son made it sound damn appealing. It sounded like it was something I could do with my guns and not have to worry about some piss ass sheriff arresting me. It's turned out to be more work then I thought it would, but it's good work. At least when I go to bed at night, I'm satisfied with what I'm doing. That's more than I can say for when I was hiring out my gun to whoever paid the most money."

"So, do folks think you're here as a hired gun?"

"Doubt it. The first night I made it quite clear, I was looking for work and that I didn't do anything with my guns anymore except maybe scare people. As far as I'm concerned, it's best if you folks and Belle are the only ones who know the real reason I ended up in this town."

"You'd better rethink that son. Annie is over at the house right now persuading Belle to tell the women about you. We both talked it over, and it's only right. Those women work their asses off in more ways than one for the Double Bar B. They deserve to know. Trust me, no one else will have any idea what the real reason in that you're working for Belle this winter."

Even though the idea hadn't appealed to Black at first, it was starting to grow on him. He couldn't work with these women or play with them if the need arose, without them knowing his real assignment in Larson's Gap.

"Guess you got a point, Roy. If breakfast was any indication of the kind of cooking Annie does, we'd better get over there before those gals eat it all up."

* * * *

Belle went up to her room to wash and change. It surprised her to see the dress Annie laid out for her to wear. It wasn't unusual for Annie to do such a thing, but the dress her friend chose for tonight was certainly not something Belle would have chosen. The neckline was dangerously low. She was certain to give Mr. Black Conley a good look at her breasts if she wore it.

Rather than put on the dress Annie selected for her, she went to her closet for something more suitable only to find the remainder of her wardrobe had suddenly disappeared. Belle knew what Annie was up to. She should. Annie had tried to set her up with enough men in the ten years since she'd come home. She wondered what Annie had against seeing a woman without a man in her life.

Out of defeat, Belle put on the dress and fussed with the neckline in the hopes of making it less revealing. Unable to pull it any higher, she brushed out her hair and secured it away from her face with a ribbon the same shade of blue as the dress.

It surprised her to see Black leaving his room when she stepped into the hall. When had he come upstairs? She hadn't heard him. Maybe what everyone was saying was true and he was part Indian.

"Good evening, Miss Barton," he said as soon as he saw her. "Roy told me you all dress up for dinner. I was surprised to see this suit laid out on my bed. I trust it was from one of the gentlemen on the stage. I will have to thank Annie for her kindness when I get downstairs."

Belle assessed the suit. It hadn't been left by anyone other than her father. The last time she'd seen it was when she'd packed away the clothes that were hanging in his closet and had Roy take them to the attic. It was evident Black filled out the suit and shirt much better than her father did. His broad shoulders ran in a line down to a narrow waist and hips. Without his guns and with his hair slicked back, he looked so handsome.

"The suit belonged to my father. I must thank Annie for bringing down the trunk containing his things. It will be much easier for you to have more than one change of clothes."

Black nodded. "May I have the honor of escorting you to supper, Miss Barton?"

The tone of his voice coupled with the formality of his speech took her completely by surprise. "Ah … yes, you may."

He took her hand in his and tucked it into the crook of his arm as though he was a fancy gentleman escorting a lady to one of the dances she'd attended when she lived in Ohio. In all the years she'd been on the Double Bar B, no one had treated her in such a way.

His close proximity brought a shiver of delight to her nether regions, and she willed the sensation to subside. It certainly didn't help that he was looking at the mounds of her breasts like a hungry man eyeing a steak.

"I'm not the main course, Mr. Conley," she said, her voice only loud enough for him to hear.

"The more the shame. You are a beautiful woman, Belle Barton. Someday I hope you realize just how lovely you are. It's a shame you hide your best assets with the sham that you're tough as nails. Something tells me with the right man you could be downright dangerous in bed."

Belle fought the urge to slap his face for making such a suggestion. As her employee, he had no right to say such a thing to her. Rather than act on her intensions, she held her tongue. Being her employee was only a ruse so no one could figure out what he was doing on the Double Bar B before he had the evidence he needed to convict Clayte Adamson of rustling.

* * * *

Black enjoyed watching Belle squirm. Of course, the view of her breasts was an added bonus. They were large enough they would fit perfectly in his hands. From what he could tell from the britches she wore earlier, her woman's mound was just as large. It, too, would fill his hands, and give him pleasure beyond his wildest dreams.

He'd bedded many whores in his day and that was exactly what they were, whores, receptacles for the pent up need that filled his cock as well as his mind. They were not the women of which dreams were made. Belle Barton was such a woman.

He could almost imagine slipping his cock into her velvety folds and riding her like he would a wild mustang. It would be an adventure to teach her the joys of being with a man. His only regret was that she was a virgin. As such he'd have to go slowly so as not to hurt her. He'd only ever taken the virginity of one woman and, although it had been satisfying to be the first man to lie with her, he had regretted his actions. It wasn't right to take a woman for the first time unless you planned to spend the rest of your life with her.

Trying to get his mind off Belle, he concentrated on the lovely girl on his grandfather's ranchero. Her name had been Teresa, and she'd been the daughter of his grandfather's foreman. She'd dogged him until he finally gave in and took her in the back of the barn. When her virginity had given way to him, she'd cried, but urged him to go further until at last they were both lost in the troughs of passion. She had lost her virginity on the same afternoon as he lost his. It had been pleasant, but at the same time he was ashamed. She deserved better than him. The next day he left the ranchero to take care of the unfinished business he'd left in Texas.

When they reached the bottom of the stairs, Roy and Annie greeted them. "I told you Black would look good in Matt's old suit," Annie declared. "Tomorrow I'll wash up the rest of the clothes in the truck and get them put in the drawers and closet."

"I can take care of my own clothes," Black protested.

"You'll learn that you can't argue with Annie," Belle teased. "I should know. I've lost enough arguments with her. Speaking of which, where are the rest of my clothes?"

Black smiled at the exchange between Belle and Annie. He wondered why Belle had chosen this particular dress to wear. He'd hoped it would be to impress him, but he was mistaken. The provocative dress was Annie's idea of a way to push Black and Belle together.

"Oh, dear," Annie said, wringing her hands in mock distress. "Did I forget to bring your clothes in off the line? It was such a perfect day I thought I should air them out before winter."

"Sure you forgot," Belle replied. "When you were cleaning, wasn't it just convenient that this was the only dress you didn't take out to air? As a matter of fact, it isn't even my dress. Unless I'm wrong, it belongs to Kate."

Black laughed at her statement. "I think it was an appropriate choice," he said, as he tightened his grip on her hand. "As much as I like the way you look in those britches and shirt, this dress is ten times better." With his free hand, he reached up to trace a line from her jaw down her neck. Before he reached her breasts, he felt her tense and pulled back.

The look on her face, said she enjoyed his touch, but her eyes said she was terrified that he would move his hand enough to enjoy the feel of her breasts and bring her nipples to hardened nubs.

"I'll thank you to keep your hands to yourself, Mr. Conley," she said. The sound of her voice told him she meant business.

"I've never seen the boss so flustered before," Cara commented. "Just what kind of magical spell do you have cast over her, Black?"

"There's nothing magical about it," Belle replied, a bit too quickly. "If Annie hadn't been playing matchmaker again, none of this would have happened."

Black was glad he wasn't taking the brunt of the blame Belle was laying on Annie.

"Well, someone has to play matchmaker," Annie retorted. Her smile said that she wasn't one bit upset about Belle's accusations. "You certainly aren't a sweet young thing anymore. You're getting close to thirty and that's the time that a woman should be thinking about settling down with a husband and a passel of younguns."

"I suppose you think I should be considering Clayte's proposal to become his wife and mother to his brats. Well, if that's what you have on your mind, Annie Heath, you can jolly well forget it. I'd sooner bed down with rattler than to get myself in that situation."

"That's not what I was planning and you know it, young lady. Now, if you don't hurry, supper will get cold and no one will enjoy it."

"Whatever you say, Annie, but please make up your mind. Am I a young lady or an old maid? You can't have it both ways."

From the tone of Belle's voice, Black could tell, Belle's earlier annoyance had been replaced by a more playful mood. He decided the two women participated in this matchmaking battle on a regular basis. Had the older woman hoped to have Belle as her daughter-in-law? If she did, she'd have a long wait. Ed Heath was a bachelor, but far from an eligible one. He was married to his job and women were the farthest things from his mind.

Black thought about Ed as he escorted Belle to the table. The man never ceased to amaze him. While Black visited the whores in whatever town he stopped, Ed never seemed to have those urges. He often wondered about that, but decided his friend was more dedicated to his job than most men.

The conversation at the table was the kind you'd expect to hear. Each of the women talked about the work they'd done during the day, while Belle listened. Black could tell she was making mental note of every word in order to plan for the next day's work.

Black wondered when the subject of why he was at the Double Bar B would come up. When no one broached it, he cleared his throat.

"There's something I need to get off my chest," he said, once he had everyone's attention. "It's no accident I came to the Double Bar B to work. I was sent here by Roy's son to investigate the rustling." He paused to allow his words to penetrate. While he did, he reached into the inside pocket of his suit and pulled out his badge.

"I'm a U. S. Marshal. Ed wanted me to come here because he didn't trust the sheriff to do right by Belle. I tend to agree. I've met the man and trusting him would be like sending the fox into the hen house to guard the chickens. I think he's up to his eyeballs in this rustling thing. That said I trust the truth of my identity will remain just between those of us at this table."

It took a moment for the women to absorb what he'd said. When they did, he was amazed at how four females could all talk at the same time.

"One at a time," he said, "I'll answer all your questions, but not when you're all talking at once. I can hardly hear myself think."

"Chickens in the hen house," Roy said with a grin.

"Just what do you mean by that, Old Man?" Annie said.

"That's what it sounded like in here when all the women were talking at once. It sounded like it does when the chickens are all clucking at the same time when you walk into the hen house."

Everyone laughed at Roy's observation before they began asking questions. They were the usual ones Black expected, the questions that were asked again and again when people found out what it was he did for a living. Still, they were ones that deserved answers if he intended to work with these women in putting the people responsible for the loss of the Double Bar B cattle in jail.

One by one Black answered the question the women posed for almost an hour. He was certain their comments and concerns would go on far into the night if someone hadn't knocked at the door.

The prospect of a late night visitor silenced the women as Belle rose to answer the insistent knocking. With the silence in the room, Black couldn't help but overhear the conversation between Belle and her visitor.

"Why did you have to go and hire a gunslinger, Belle?" he heard the man at the door ask.

"I didn't hire a gunslinger," Belle replied.

"Like hell you didn't. If you don't know the reputation of your new hand, the rest of us do. Black Conley has killed over thirty men. What are you planning to do, have us all shot in our sleep so you can increase the size of the Double Bar B?"

Black listened to Belle's answer, but refused to allow her to face the man at the door alone. He pushed back his chair and ignored the warning glance he received from Roy.

"Do you have a problem with me, mister?" Black said, as he pushed past Belle. "If you do, I suggest you accuse me to my face and leave

Miss Barton out of it. Now, who the hell are you anyway?"

"Black, this is Jeb Taylor, one of my neighbors," Belle said as she introduced the man.

"So, Conley," Jeb began before Black could speak, "how do you plan to help Ball Buster Belle runs us all out? Can I expect a bullet in the back, or are you helping Belle steal my cattle?"

"Taylor, I did get the name right, didn't I?" He paused to allow the man to nod his head. "Good, then that means your place runs across the south side of the Diamond A. Why is it that you're accusing Belle of stealing your cattle?"

The man ran his tongue over his lips as though contemplating his answer. "Let's see, she runs this place with a passel of whores. I doubt old Matt was sure she was even his daughter. Then, you show up right in the midst of her rustling spree. I lost another ten head last night, and now I see her herd is moved. What more proof do I need?"

"To begin with, Belle wouldn't have to use whores, as you call them, to run her place if the men in this area weren't so lily livered they couldn't get past the notion of working for a woman. I doubt you've ever worked with these women when they're ranching, but I have, and I've never worked with a better bunch of ranch hands. What they do at night is their business, but I guess you don't fuck your wife at night. Come to think of it, I've even heard that you seem to like visiting the whores above the Purple Moon Saloon. What does your wife think of that? I'll tell you what I think. I'm not above taking a poke at a whore, but I don't have a wife at home waiting for me. If I did, you can stake your life on it, the Purple Moon would be the last place you'd find me."

"You can't compare a man havin' a little fun to women who get paid to fuck a man to women trying to run a ranch can you?"

"Of course I can. I really can't see why a man would spend his hard-earned money on a whore when he has a wife waiting for him at home, but then maybe I'm different than you. That brings us to Belle and who she is or isn't. From what I hear, Belle is the spitting image of her ma.

"Besides, if she were out to get something for nothing, why would she come to a godforsaken place like this? I can't imagine anyone wanting a ranch in Montana where the winter comes straight from the gates of hell and summers are far too short. If her intentions were getting something for nothing, I can think of a lot better places to do it than Larson's Gap."

"That brings us to you. Why are you here?"

"Like I said at the saloon the other night, I found myself in this part of the country and didn't like the thought of spending the winter outdoors. I can't afford to rent a room for the whole time. When I asked about a job, I was told to try the Double Bar B. No one told me you or any of the others around the area were hiring. If a man wants to eat, he has to work and, if that means working for Belle Barton, then that's what I intend to do. The bed is nice and soft and the meals are good. As for the work, it's nothing I've never done before. You mentioned the fact I was a gunslinger, and you're right, but the men I've killed have always drawn on me first. The first one was in East Texas when I was fourteen. After a while, I realized it wasn't a really stable profession. I don't hire my guns out anymore, and I don't shoot people in the back."

"But what about my cattle?" Jeb protested.

"What about them? I reckon they're in the same place as the fifty head Belle's lost over the past few weeks."

"I want to check Belle's herd to see what brands are on them."

Black nodded. "I think that's a right fine idea. We eat breakfast here at six. I'll be ready to ride with you and any of the other neighbors by seven. We'll start with the cattle that have been moved up by the house, then we'll check out the other ranges. There's nothing here that needs to be hidden and the sooner you and your friends realize it, the better."

Jeb turned on his heel and started down the steps of the porch. "We'll be here at six," he called over his shoulder. "I don't want you to move any of them cattle without us."

"If that's the case, I'll tell Annie to fix extra for breakfast," Belle replied. "My hands don't ride on an empty stomach and neither should you."

Black listened as the man muttered to himself all the while he mounted his horse. When Black at last turned back to Belle, she was slumped against the door jam.

He stepped toward her and took her arm as though to steady her. Once she leaned on him, he escorted her to the porch swing and helped her to seat herself. Even the cool of the evening breeze seemed comforting in comparison to the heat of the argument they'd just had with Jeb.

"That man has a powerful hate for you," Black said. "Of course, that whiskey on his breath probably had a lot to do with what he said. Tomorrow ought to be an interesting day."

"I guess I ruffled a lot of feathers when I didn't sell out after Pa died. Jeb and the others were certain I'd turn tail and run. I just couldn't do that. Pa and Roy worked hard to build up this place. I couldn't let it be split up between Clayte, Pete, and Jeb."

"I can understand. It's good you stood up for yourself. When my ma died, I was too young to fight for our place. It wasn't until I was sure of myself with a gun that I went back and righted the wrong that had been done to me."

"You own a ranch?"

"I did when I was fourteen, but I didn't want anything to do with the East Texas of the Circle C. I sold it to a friend I'd made when I was growing up. He needed a ranch, and I needed the cash. It all worked out for the best."

"Don't you miss the land?'

"I miss my ma and the women who worked for her more. If I'd run it, things would have never been the same. I got a good education growing up there."

She relaxed against Black's shoulder and allowed him to put his arm around her. "Do I have to guess what kind of an education you got?"

"It's not what you think. I was a kid, too young to be taught those things. On the day my ma died, I turned thirteen. That night I was supposed to get my first lesson in such things, but that never happened. What Ma and the women taught me were manners, to speak and read Spanish, and to read and respect the teachings in the Bible."

"Do you still respect those teachings?" she said, looking up at him.

"I do, but the Lord probably doesn't like the way I twist them to fit my needs. After the first man I killed, I didn't have a hunger for it, but word got out about how fast I was and trouble just seemed to follow me. It wasn't until I met up with Ed that I realized my guns could be used for good. Things have turned around since then."

She snuggled closer to him, and his hand wandered to the soft mound of her breast. As much as he wanted to cup it in his hand, he refrained. He had all winter to win her over and take her to his bed. For now, the swell of her breast against the fabric of her dress was enough to assure him that sooner or later she would be his in every way, especially the ones that counted the most for a man.

Chapter Five

Belle lay awake long after the house was quiet for the night. The events of the last few hours replayed in her head, keeping sleep at bay. She was thankful Black had come to find out who was responsible for the rustling of her cattle, but why did he have to be so damned desirable.

She let her mind wander back to when they sat on the porch swing after Jeb left. It had been a long time since she'd sat like that with a man. The last time, she could remember, Ronald shared the swing and told her how beautiful she was. As a girl of sixteen, she fell for his line and allowed him to take liberties he had no business taking. When she'd told him she was pregnant, he no longer called her beautiful or even came to call. She wouldn't fall into that trap again.

Getting up, she lit the lamp beside the bed and went to the dresser to search for the toy the woman at the shop had called a dildo. It had been a long time since she'd last used it, but tonight she needed some sort of relief.

She'd been embarrassed when she realized the way Black's hand caressed her breast had made her drawers wet. She'd prided herself on control, but tonight her body had betrayed her.

As her hand touched the wooden object hidden under the clothes in her dresser drawer, she thought about the man sleeping just down the hall from her. It was be so easy to slip out of her room and into his bed. Instead of the hard wooden cock, she could have the real thing. From what Kate told her, Black's cock would be hard, but it wouldn't be unyielding.

Rather than dwell on things that went against her grain, she took the dildo from the drawer and returned to bed. Self-gratification would be much less complex than going to Black's bed and becoming involved in a loveless relationship just to satisfy her wonton needs. It was all right for the women because it was their trade, but not for her. When she gave herself to a man, it would be because she truly loved him. She could hear her aunt screaming at her. 'Sex should be for love and not lust, Isabel. Men lust after whores and unfortunately, even though I tried to raise you right, you have become as bad as the girls who ply their trade down at Dirty Gertie's place. I can only pray the nuns can teach you what I couldn't.'

That memory prompted another one. She had been sent to the convent within days of learning of her pregnancy to avoid embarrassing her aunt or Ronald any further. She was the outcast, the fallen angel. While she went to the convent and spent the better part of every day on her knees on the stone floor praying for her salvation, he was free to deflower another young girl and then deny the child.

She shook her head to rid herself of the horrible memory accompanied with thoughts of Ronald. He was probably living in sin somewhere, but she wasn't about to fall into that trap again. When her body called for relief, the little wooden toy would take the place of a man who used her only as a receptacle and then threw her away at the first opportunity.

She made her way back to the now cold sheets. After pulling up her nightdress and turning down the lamp to a soft glow, she concentrated on her favorite fantasy. As usual she started by cupping her breasts in her hands and manipulating her nipples in the same way Ronald had done so many years ago. Instead of the dream lover who appeared behind her closed eyelids, the man was Black and his large calloused hands were doing wonderful things to her breasts.

The sensation traveled down her body until it reached her woman's soul causing her to move her hands lower to stroke her clit and become wet in the process. Once her juices began to flow, she put her fingers into her cunt until she ached for the relief that only the dildo could provide.

As soon as she slid the hard object inside her, she imagined Black hovering over her ready to send her to the heights of passion with his cock. She knew the dildo wasn't the same as having him inside her, but at least it perpetuated the dream she'd formed in her mind.

* * * *

Black lay in bed, the memory of Belle's breast against his hand fresh in his mind. Even thinking of her made his cock swell until it was downright painful. He had two options when it came to taking care of that hurt. The first was to go down the hall to Belle's room and take her here and now, but he didn't approve of rape. The woman had to be willing, and he had yet to find a paid companion who wasn't ready to take his cock inside her. The second was to jack off into the piss pot that sat beside the bed.

The first option seemed like the best, but he refused to take Belle against her will. She was a beautiful woman and deserved much better than him. He could easily go to Kate's room and offer to pay for satisfaction, but that option just didn't seem right tonight. The woman he wanted was Belle and no other.

Rather than lay on the bed and be miserable, he pulled on his pants, boots and shirt and made his way to the door. He didn't light the lamp because the light of the full moon was enough to illuminate the room.

Once in the hallway, he made his way toward the stairs. He would go out behind the barn for the release he craved and then come back to bed.

As he passed Belle's door, he heard her moaning softly. He couldn't help but wonder if she was dreaming and whether he was in that dream. If so, was he fucking her and bringing on the moans of pleasure coming from behind the closed door.

"Black," she called, causing him to stop dead in his tracks. "Oh, Black."

Her voice sounded as though she was in distress. Unwilling to allow her to continue in the nightmare, he opened her door and stepped into the room.

To his surprise, a soft light showed him her naked body lying on the bed with her hands between her legs manipulating an object that looked like a man's cock. She was so lost in her sexual passion she didn't even hear him enter the room.

He smiled at the scene he'd just witnessed and backed out the door, closing it softly. At least he wasn't the only one who was going to be jacking off tonight. He'd heard about women who got sexual pleasure from such objects as the one he saw Belle using. He'd just never seen one before.

It pleased him to think that when she was in the midst of pleasuring herself, it was his name she called. In the past, he'd had women who fell in love with him and wanted him in their beds, but not as quickly as

Belle seemed to have done.

As he went down the stairs, he started to think about the woman herself. She wasn't a virgin, because if she were, she wouldn't know about such things as dildos and how to give herself pleasure. There had to have been a man in her past who had taken her to the heights of pleasure.

From what he'd heard since arriving at the Double Bar B, it hadn't happened in Montana. Roy said that she'd been raised in Ohio. Had someone there taken the one thing a woman cherished and, if so, why had she come back to Montana instead of enjoying the life of a married woman with a loving husband?

Once out at the barn he did his business then pulled a smoke from his pocket. Leaning against the building, he enjoyed the cigarette, all the while watching the window he knew belonged to Belle. The light burned until at last he saw her get out of bed. The nightdress that had been bunched up around her breasts now covered her completely as she made her way to the washstand across the room from the bed. He smiled at the vision he could see from this vantage point. If she knew just how visible she was from the barn, she'd invest in shades. Of course, she certainly didn't expect anyone to be outside watching her every move.

From just beyond the barn, he heard horses approaching and quickly stubbed out his cigarette. He stepped back into the shadows and watched as Jeb and two other men dismounted.

"It looks quiet to me," one of the men said.

"Well I ain't taking any chances," Jeb replied. "Check the corral to make certain their horses are still there. I wouldn't put it past that bitch to move our cattle before we have a chance to check things out."

Black heard the men go to the corral and count the number of horses that were there.

"It looks like they're all there," the third man observed. "I don't know why you dragged us out of bed on this wild goose chase. You don't really believe Belle is behind the rustling, do you?"

"Clayte says she is and that's good enough for me. I don't know about the rest of you, but I don't want her to make off with our cattle just because she knows we suspect her."

Black's anger began to boil. He wished he had his guns with him, but that would only perpetuate the rumor that he was here as a hire gun.

"Something I can do for you boys?" he said as he stepped from the shadows.

All three men turned to face Black.

"Just making certain you and Belle aren't making off with those cattle of ours that you stole," Jeb replied.

"Makes sense," Black commented. "I tell you what, why don't I go up to the house and get a coat. Once I do, I'll get my horse saddled and ride up to the canyon where we took the cattle with you. That way you can see for yourself those women aren't trying to cheat you."

"It suits me, but what were you doing out here anyway?'

"I needed to take a piss and have a cigarette. Never did like smoking in the house when everyone else was asleep. I was taught better than that."

Without further comment, Black went up to the house to retrieve his coat.

"What's going on?" Belle said when he entered the kitchen. "I thought I heard voices."

"You did. Those neighbors you invited for breakfast didn't want to be late. They showed up to make certain we didn't take their cattle out under the cover of darkness. I told them I would ride up to the canyon with them and keep watch on the herd tonight. There's nothing for you to worry about. Just go back to sleep."

Before he could turn toward the stairs, she put her arms around his neck and hugged him tightly. She had no idea what her hardened nipples pressing against his chest were doing to him. If she weren't careful, he'd take her right here on the kitchen floor and explain his actions to anyone who came in and found them together in such a position.

"Be careful," she whispered.

"I will, but for now I have to go out and keep an eye on those yahoos who think you're up to something."

He disentangled her arms from his neck and hurried upstairs to get both his coat and his guns. When he returned to the kitchen, she was still standing there, looking like an angel in her white nightdress with her hair hanging loose around her shoulders.

"Tell Annie I'll have a powerful hunger by the time I get back in the morning. I'm looking forward to a good breakfast." The tears in her eyes surprised him.

"Why are you crying?" he said as he took her in his arms to kiss their salty wetness from her cheeks.

"I told you I'm scared and with good reason. It's hard telling what lies Clayte has been putting into the heads of Jeb and the others. They're likely to shoot first and ask questions later."

"I'm not worried about getting shot. None of them are good enough with a gun to get the draw on me and besides they're all so drunk they couldn't shoot straight anyway."

She tipped her head slightly so that her mouth was perfectly aligned with his. Without restraint, he leaned over and kissed her. Instead of the indignation he would have expected, she accepted his kiss and returned it with a passion he didn't think possible from someone who had known him for such a short period of time. Maybe he wouldn't have to wait for an entire winter to get into her bed.

"I'll see you in the morning. Don't worry. I can take care of myself, especially when the men I'm up against are dead drunk and already arguing among themselves."

"They're all drunk?"

"Yup. I figure Jeb started making the rounds and had a few drinks with each of the others. I take it they're Pete and Zeek. They're bound and determined you and the women are going to cut out their cows from our herd and run them off by morning. It won't hurt me none to ride nighthawk."

"Maybe I should get dressed and go with you."

He cupped her chin in his hand and raised her head so he could look into her eyes. The urge to kiss her was one he couldn't deny. After pulling her into his arms he covered her mouth with his. Feeling her supple lips beneath his made him want to forget the men who were waiting for him. The way Belle responded to his kiss told him she was hot and she was his for the taking.

"Are you comin' or are we leavin' without you?" Jeb called from beyond the kitchen door.

Reluctantly, Black tore himself away from Belle and headed toward the door. He certainly didn't want to add any more fuel to the anger these men had building within them.

* * * *

Belle stood at the kitchen window and watched as Black mounted his horse and rode toward the canyon where her cattle had been taken earlier in the day. As she did, she could feel the wetness between her legs increase. She knew it wasn't left over from when she'd pleasured herself.

That sensation didn't last this long. This was new.

"He can't have his effect on me. He just can't," she whispered to the darkness. "He's a stranger and…"

"And he's enough to make any woman wet just by looking at her," Kate said, finishing Belle's statement in an entirely different way than Belle had intended.

"I didn't know you were up."

"I heard the commotion outside and decided to investigate. What's going on?"

"Jeb came back with Pete and Zeek. He said they wanted to make certain we didn't move the cattle under the cover of darkness. Of course, it was the whiskey talking. It had to be."

Kate fussed around at the stove starting a pot of coffee before she returned to the table to join Belle. "I didn't mean about the men in the dooryard. I could hear them shouting clear up to my room. I don't understand why men think everyone goes deaf when they get drunk."

"Then what did you mean?"

"I heard Black come back upstairs. I figured he was getting his guns. I peeked out my door when he went downstairs and saw he had his coat as well. I figured he was riding out with the others, but then he stopped in the kitchen. I was coming down to see what was going on and saw him kiss you. Are you falling in love with him?"

"How can you ask such a question? I don't even know him. He's a stranger, and he took too great a liberty by kissing me like that."

"I didn't see you pushing him away. He was sincere. I could tell. He's had it bad for you since he first arrived. You don't have to deny it. I could tell when I went to his bed last night. He allowed me to take care of his needs, but it wasn't me he wanted."

"That's ridiculous. All men want women. It's the nature of the beast. He only thinks he wants me because I told him he could take any of you to his bed but not me. You know what they say about forbidden fruit."

"I don't think he's the only one lusting after that fruit. I heard you in your room tonight. When you were lost in the pleasuring you were giving yourself, you called out his name."

"I … I what?"

"You called his name a couple of times. It was clear you wanted Black in your bed and not that wooden cock you seem so fond of."

"You're right, I do want him in my bed, but it won't happen. I won't have another fiasco like the one with Ronald. I refuse to be branded a whore for a second time."

Kate laughed loud and hard. "Honey, you already are branded a whore just for having us all here, so why not reap the benefits? I fall in love with every man who beds me, but it's gone as soon as he is. It's time you got Ronald out of your system and found out what it's like to be with a real man."

"Is Black a real man as you call it?"

"Yes, he is. I thoroughly enjoyed last night. I wouldn't mind another poke at him, but he seems to think he wants you. It's as plain as the nose on your face."

"Well, I'm not sure I want him in my bed. When things quiet down, I'll send Cara to him. She'll be able to take any notion of bedding me out of his head."

"Think what you want, but you're wrong. He's not the kind of man who gives his heart easily. He'll enjoy Cara, but it won't change his feeling for you. Trust me on this one, Belle. I know what I'm talking about."

"He can't be that taken with me, Kate. He just arrived last night and…"

"And nothing. It's something I've only seen once and when it happened it was sheer magic. I was working in a whorehouse up around Reno with a gal by the name of Salina. She had been at that ranch Black's ma ran in Texas. One night this man came in. We were all sitting in the parlor and he walked right up to Salina. I saw the expression on his face and so did everyone else. For a solid week, he came back and paid the high price Salina got for being with the men. At the end of that week, he told her he was going to marry her and by the end of the month they were on the stage heading for California together. I still hear from her, and she's happier than ever. They have three kids and a little ranch. That's what is called love at first sight. I saw the same expression on Black's face last night, and it certainly wasn't for me."

"Well, he can get that damn fool notion out of his head. I'm going to bed and so should you. Those men will be back bright and early tomorrow morning wanting their breakfast, and it wouldn't do for us to be still in our nightclothes."

Belle went up to bed and listened as Kate cleaned up in the kitchen before following her. Behind the closed door, Belle fingered the wooden dildo. What would it be like to be with Black?

As soon as the thought crossed her mind, she thought of the times she'd been with Ronald. The first time, she'd been in so much pain, she hadn't wanted to do it again, but Ronald promised it wouldn't hurt if they did it again. He'd been right. There was no pain, but the act happened so quickly she hardly had the time to enjoy it. He'd gotten his pleasure and left her wanting. If that was what it was like bedding a man, then she wanted no part of it. The satisfaction she'd learned to give herself over the years was enough. What bothered her was that she'd called out Black's name without even thinking. When she'd pleasured herself she'd imagined Black making love to her. She would definitely have to be more careful in the future. She hoped Black hadn't heard her outcry.

She considered taking the dildo to bed with her, but decided against it. The unyielding piece of wood usually worked, but tonight it wouldn't be able to take away the ache Black's kiss had planted in her cunt.

* * * *

Black left the house and headed toward the barn where the three men waited for him. They were impatient and ready to get started.

"What took you so long?" Zeek growled. "Did you have to take a poke at one of them there whores? Don't know how you do it. I'd sure like to live in a house with five whores all ready to let me get in a good fuck whenever I want it."

"Ain't been here long enough to have had that pleasure," Black replied as he swung into his saddle. "You know I wasn't considering riding nighthawk tonight, but since that's you're intention, then so be it. At least there's a full moon. I'm sure you'll soon see there are no brands on those beeves other than the Double Bar B. I should know I rounded them up this morning. Now, gentlemen, I don't think you left your warm beds and hot wives to sit here and discuss my love life."

He spurred his horse to a gallop and led the way to the box canyon where they cattle were settled for the night. It surprised him to see Roy ride out to greet them.

"What are you doing here?" Black said, once he rode up next to the older man.

"After Annie and me had our lovin' for the night we both decided someone should be ridin' nighthawk on these steers. I know Belle talked about sendin' one of the women out here, but it ain't work for a woman. Besides, I need to do something to keep my hand in the runnin' of this place. Matt would expect me not to make his little girl do things all by herself. I've been slackin' far too long."

"Good grief, Roy, what's gotten into you?" Zeek said. "At your age you should be sittin' by the fire and enjoying yourself. It's just too bad you can't give Annie the good fuck she deserves. 'Course we all know a woman's juices dry up at about the same time a man's do."

"Speak for yourself, Zeek. Annie and I have no problems in those areas. From what I hear, you don't have a problem when you're at the Purple Moon. How does Mattie feel about you going there when you should be takin' care of business at home?"

"This ain't the time for such a discussion," Black interrupted. "These boys want to see if they can find their brands on any of the steers Belle has pastured here. I told them I'd come along and help them look."

"I would have sent them packing. I know, as well as you do none of these animals are stolen. Hell, I helped the women with the branding last spring, and there wasn't a cow or steer on the property that shouldn't have been there."

"Just the same, these boys have it in their heads these cattle don't all belong to Belle. It's high time we set them straight."

Roy grumbled as the three men rode around the herd. Black knew what they were finding and that the proof of Belle's innocence was coming as a bit of a shock to them.

He was enjoying a smoke, when he heard more riders approaching and with them were cattle.

The neighbors immediately joined Black and Roy to confront the strangers. Shots were fired and the cattle following the newcomers scattered. When the smoke cleared, three men were down and a fourth had gotten away.

"This one's dead," Jeb declared. "What about the other two?"

"This one's dead as well," Pete said.

Black knelt beside the third man. "Who sent you here?"

The man looked up at him. Whatever he said Black knew would be the truth. Men who were dying didn't want to do so with a lie on their lips.

"Don't know. Just got to town and this man paid us to bring these beeves to this pasture. He … he…"

The man choked on the blood that was beginning to run from his mouth, closed his eyes, and died.

"Who would've done such a thing?" Zeek said.

"Probably the same son of a bitch who has been stealing our cattle," Jeb replied. "It only seems right he would want to put the blame on Belle. She ain't well liked in these parts."

"Whoever it was, doesn't matter now," Black observed. "Let's get those cattle rounded up and find out just whose they are."

It was almost dawn before the last of the cattle were gazing peacefully just outside the box canyon. The brands were from Zeek, Jeb, and Pete's ranches as well as some from Clayte's herd.

"Whoever is behind this was probably going to hit Belle's herd again before taking these cattle to God only knows where," Roy said. "We'll divide up the cattle so you can take back your stock. Black and I will return these cattle to Clayte after we have breakfast. We can leave them here for now, and go down to get something to eat. You boys all know Annie doesn't abide by folks bein' late for meals."

Chapter Six

Belle had been up since four. The thought of Black riding nighthawk after working all day bothered her. She would insist he do nothing today other than rest. The fact she'd been without sleep for most of the night didn't matter. It was Black she worried about. By the time Annie arrived, Belle had already started preparations for breakfast.

"Land sakes, child, what are you doing up an about this early?" Annie greeted her.

"I … I couldn't sleep." She went on to explain about her late night visitors. "What if the three of them did something to Black? I'd never forgive myself."

"Never is a word that shouldn't be thrown around too lightly. I seem to remember my ma saying she'd never go west and yet that's exactly what we did. Before we left Virginia, I said I'd never marry a dirt-poor farmer. The man I was destined to marry would be able to give me fancy dresses and I'd ride in a fine carriage. When I got here one of the first people I met was Roy. He wasn't dirt-poor, but he couldn't give me fancy dresses. As a matter of fact, the only carriage I've ever had was the buckboard and at times it needed repair. Learn from my mistakes, honey. Love or anything else you vow will never happen. It comes at you when you least expect it."

"I wasn't talking about love, Annie. Black is out there alone with Zeek, Jeb, and Pete. What if they do something foolish and shoot him. The way they were liquored up it's entirely possible."

"He's not exactly alone. After Roy and I went to bed last night we did a lot of lovin', but that's nothing unusual. What I'm getting at is he decided to go out to the canyon and ride nighthawk. Like he said, this ranch is our home and, even if he can't work every day, he can do something to help out."

"You let Roy ride out there alone?"

"Wouldn't be the first time. It bothers him when he can't do the things he used to do. Many nights he's been out there. I'm just glad those weren't the nights when the rustlers hit. I couldn't stand to lose that old man. We sort of fit together. Without him, I'd never be complete."

The sound of horses in the dooryard alerted Belle the men had returned. Rushing to the door, she gasped when she saw three horses with men draped across their backs along with Black, Roy, Zeek, Jeb, and Pete.

She rushed out onto the porch. "What happened?"

"We ran into the rustlers," Jeb announced as though he was proud of the fact they'd killed the men who were responsible for the disappearance of so many cattle from the area.

"We'll explain everything over breakfast," Roy said. "I'm so hungry I could eat the ass end out of an old dead skunk."

"I wouldn't go that far," Black said, "but I could use some coffee. It was a long night. These other fellers are just as tired and hungry as we are."

Belle held open the door to allow the men to enter the kitchen. Once everyone was seated around the table, Kate asked about the rustlers.

"It was like you and me talked about last night, honey," Roy replied. "Someone was dead set on making it look like we were the ones takin' the cattle. They were running steers from every ranch in the area straight toward the canyon."

"I think they were getting ready to add Belle's steers to their take for the night," Zeek said. "I can't believe anyone would purposely plant evidence on this ranch that didn't belong here."

* * * *

Black held his tongue. It wouldn't do him any good to tip his hand this soon. These rustlers had gone from taking five or ten head here and there to taking twenty to thirty head a night. Why would there be exactly ten head from each ranch? He knew the answer all too well. From what the men who had joined them said, ten was the number of cows they had each lost over the past few weeks. It was only Belle who was losing more. By cutting out the cattle that had been taken from the other ranches, along with ten head from the Diamond A, it would look like a usual raid to these men. Black knew differently. They were being planted on the ranch for the men to find in the morning when they were due to arrive and look for their missing steers.

Annie and Belle served up platters of flapjacks along with bacon and eggs. The more the men ate, the more they bragged about how they'd killed those rustlers. Each man took credit for one of the rustlers, when Black knew his bullet had struck home twice and Roy had downed the other man. It was just as well the men thought they were the ones who had killed the rustlers. Black's expertise with a gun was well known, but he didn't want to take credit for any of the killings last night.

With breakfast finished, the three neighbors mounted up to take their steers back to their own ranches. Once they were gone, Black pushed back from the table.

"I'm taking those steers back to the Diamond A," he announced.

"You need your rest," Belle protested. "You've been up all night. The women and I can take them back."

"Black's right, honey," Roy said. "It's best if he take back those steers. It's not hard thinkin' what Clayte would do to you if you went alone. Nettie's not there anymore to ride reign on him. Besides, the women have work to do here. Kate and I will take those hombres into town and alert the sheriff as to what happened last night."

"But you need your rest, too. I can't let you do something that should be my responsibility."

"Let him go, Belle," Annie said. "I know better than to cross him when he's got his mind set on something. Roy and Joe go back a long way. There won't be any arguing about who killed who or what those men were doing on the Double Bar B."

Black saw the light of understanding in Belle's eyes. She needed to learn to trust men and what better ones to start with than Roy and himself.

After finishing the last of his coffee, Black went to the outhouse to take care of business before going out to where he'd left his horse. In the corral, the cattle he was about to drive back to the Diamond A milled around as though confused by being taken from their home pasture, driven across Double Bar B land, and now being penned up.

To his surprise, Belle led her white stallion from the barn. "Just what do you think you're doing?' Black demanded.

"I'm going with you. I'm your boss, you know. It's my place to return Clayte's steers to him."

Black didn't argue. It would give him some time alone with Belle.

He wanted to get to know her better and try to figure out why she distrusted men so much.

"Suit yourself, but I hope you plan to keep up. I don't have time to be playing nursemaid to anyone who can't keep pace."

The look of indignation on her face brought a smile to his lips. Together they herded the cattle from the corral and started across Double Bar B land to get to the Diamond A. It came as no surprise to see that the fence had been cut in the same place Black mended it the day before.

"On our way back we'll stop and mend that fence," he said as he rode up next to her.

"It will be a good place to have lunch. Annie packed some sandwiches for us. She knew we wouldn't get back in time to eat with the others."

Black dropped back to round up a stray that had stopped to graze. As he did, he thought about eating lunch with Belle. He liked being along with her. It made even the thought of mending the fence sound less like work and more like something enjoyable.

They met Clayte just beyond his ranch house. "What the hell are you doing on my property?" he demanded as he rode up to him. "Did you come to steal more of my cattle?"

"Hardly," Belle retorted. "These steers were being driven across my land last night along with those from the other ranches. It's hard telling how many head I would have lost if Black, Roy, Zeek, Jeb, and Pete hadn't been there."

Black watched the expression on Clayte's face change. "What happened to the rustlers?"

"Three of them are dead. Roy and Kate are taking them to town so the sheriff can get a good look at who's responsible for the rustling. The last one got away, but I think I winged him. Hopefully, this will stop the rustling, and you can all start to relax around here."

"This is your doing, Belle," Clayte accused.

"My doing? How can you even think such a thing? Why would I put Roy and Black in danger to say nothing of my own neighbors?"

"To throw suspicion off yourself."

"Well, if that ain't the most asinine thing I've ever heard," Black responded. "I think those men were trying to throw suspicion from themselves by planting those steers on Belle's place. When Jeb left the house last night he said he and the others would be back in the morning to check brands. Instead, they came back later and were there when the cattle were driven right to the box canyon. Now ain't it strange that those hombres knew exactly where Belle had taken the cattle?"

"Rustlers are a strange lot," Clayte said when he regained his composure. "They probably were watching when your whores drove the cattle to the winter pasture."

"It don't matter none how they knew," Black said, defusing the tension growing between Clayte and Belle. "For now you have your steers back, and we have a fence to mend again."

"Well, since one of them jaspers got away, don't be surprised if you get hit again. Once a rustler finds easy pickings, he usually strikes twice. They've found your ranch is a good one to hit. I wouldn't be surprised if you lost half your herd by spring."

"Thanks for the warning, Clayte," Belle said. "Like Black says, we have fences to mend, and you have cattle to get back to your herd."

"You know if you took me up on my marriage proposal, you wouldn't have to worry about rustlers. You could leave that to me."

"I'd rather ride herd on my own beeves than to do the same on that passel of younguns of yours. Find yourself another wife somewhere else. I'm not interested."

"You'll be sorry you said that, Belle Barton. I'll be the one to laugh at your funeral when you die a dried-up, old maid when you could have been doing what a woman is meant to do, raising children."

Black saw the anger flashing from Belle's eyes as they rode back toward the Double Bar B.

"How dare he?" she demanded of no one in particular as soon as they were out of earshot. "I don't care if I do end up an old maid. I would never lower myself so much as to say 'I do' to that piece of scum."

"I doubt you'll have to. I'm certain he's behind the rustling. He's the only one who knew where you took the cattle yesterday. How else would the rustlers been able to find them if they weren't in the East pasture?"

"You've got a point there. He was at the house quick as scat when he found out the cattle had been moved."

"If I'm not mistaken, he got the others all riled up so that they would be wanting to check the brands on the cattle you have in that canyon. He thought they'd wait until morning and he could get the men responsible for it to drive the stolen cattle up to your place last night. The last thing he expected was to have us waiting for them. Didn't you see how white his face went when I told him we'd met up with the rustlers?"

"I certainly did, and, when you told him that three of them were dead and the fourth got away, the relief was evident. He's scared and with good reason. How long do you think it will be before you can arrest him?"

"He's had a scare. I doubt he'll do anything more before spring. Things have gotten too hot for him now. Besides the outsiders he hired for this job are either dead or long gone. He'll have to come up with a new bunch, and no one is going to venture this far north during the winter. I think things will be quiet. If that's the case, then I'll be able to get more evidence on both Clayte and the sheriff."

"But how? You know no one is going to cross either one of them."

"That's why I'm the U.S. Marshal and you're the ranch owner. I have my ways, and, believe me when this does come to a head, it will do so very quickly."

* * * *

By the time they reached the cut in the fence, the sun was directly overhead. It was Belle who suggested they eat before mending the fence. She knew Black was tired and thought if they ate first, he might fall asleep so she could take care of the fence while he got the rest he so needed.

She unpacked the sandwiches Annie put in her saddlebags earlier in the day. Thick slices of fresh bread complimented the thin slices of cold roast beef topped with tangy horseradish. Just the meal for a hungry man. She had planned they would eat in this pasture so she'd packed nothing to drink. The spring fed stream that ran through her property would be enough to quench their thirst.

"After that breakfast Annie fixed, I didn't think I'd be hungry," Black said, "but those sandwiches look damn good to me."

She handed him a sandwich and watched as he took a big bite. From the look on his face, he had gotten a good helping of horseradish along with the meat.

He swallowed what he had in his mouth and followed it with a good healthy drink of water. "What's on this beef?"

"It's horseradish."

"It can't be. I've had horseradish, and it's never this strong."

"That's because it's fresh. Annie made Roy take her somewhere to get it last spring. He always puts up a fuss, but in the end they go there together, and she spends the next several days putting it up for use in the winter. When I first tasted it, I thought it was some sort of poison. After a while it sort of grows on you."

Black laughed. "Guess it does. It's not that bad, but it was a shock when I first tasted it. After a couple of these sandwiches, I'll be ready for something sweet."

"Annie packed some of her apple pie," Belle said.

"That's not exactly what I had in mind." He took her in his arms and kissed her.

Any control she had over her body the night before was completely gone. Here in the middle of the east pasture, there was on one to see them, no one to pass judgment. When his tongue darted between her parted lips she realized she wanted more than just his kisses. Kate was right. This man was different. She wanted him in the way a woman wants a man. Her dildo could never produce the spasms of excitement that ran through her body until they reached the sensitive area between her legs the way Black's kiss did.

She reached up to put her hands on the back of his head and pull him closer to her, but he was even quicker. His free hand was working the buttons on her shirt. Without breaking their kiss, he untied the ribbon that held her camisole shut to reveal her breasts. The cool September air against her sensitive nipples made her gasp.

When she didn't protest, he manipulated her nipple between his thumb and forefinger as he trailed kisses down her neck. She became wetter and wetter as his lips caressed first the top of her breast and then captured her nipple between them. As he sucked, she worked the buttons on his shirt and long johns until his chest was exposed to her view. She ran her hands over the matt of black hair the peppered his chest and rubbed his male nipples until they were as hard as her own.

She hardly realized he had unbuttoned her britches until his hand touched the mound covered by the vee of hair that guarded her womanhood. Even if she had wanted to turn back, it was too late. His fingers had found her clit. Until now, she had been the only one to touch that sensitive place. Ronald had shoved his cock into her leading her to believe that was the only way to have sex. His pleasure had been first and foremost in his mind and he had left her left wanting.

It wasn't until after the women arrived at the ranch and talked about the pleasures of sex that she found her little toy. Once she bought it, she began exploring her body and learning about the things they told her. It always amazed her that something so small as the nub the women called their clit could give her such erotic pleasure.

As Black rubbed her in a circular motion she realized she'd only skimmed the surface when it came to giving and receiving sexual favors. Colors exploded like the fireworks in her mind like those she remembered watching on the Fourth of July with her aunt back in Ohio. The sensation also did wonderful things to her body.

"Take me, Black, take me now."

With the expertise that could only have come with practice, he removed her boots. As each foot was exposed, he massaged her from her toes to her heels again bringing about unexpected shockwaves of delight. With her boots off, he removed her britches and bloomers, leaving her naked from the waist down. The only garments remaining on her body were her shirt and camisole, and they were open, exposing her breasts. Nothing about her was hidden from his view.

Before returning to the business of loving her, he took off his shirt, boots, pants and long johns. As he did, she gasped at the sheer size of him. In full erection, he made her dildo look like a small stick.

"Are you certain you're ready for this?" he said as he positioned himself over her.

She reached up to touch the part of his body she knew would give her great pleasure. "I'm more than ready."

Before he entered her, he again massaged her clit, while putting his fingers into her cunt. She had never been this wet before and wished he wouldn't prolong her agony any longer.

While he played with her, she explored the entire length of him with her hand. During her exploration, she accidentally touched his balls. He moaned with delight prompting her to glide her fingers over the velvety sack. Before, she had kept her eyes closed when Ronald fucked her and her dildo didn't have anything this delightful to play with.

"What are you doing to me, woman?" he said, as he removed his fingers and proceeded to slide his entire length into her body.

With him inside of her, she couldn't even begin to answer his question. He was riding her as though she was an unbroken mustang, and she loved every minute of it.

Their lovemaking lasted much longer than she remembered it lasting with Ronald. Time after time Black brought her to the brink of orgasm only to pull back to prolong the delightful agony. Finally, it seemed as though he could no longer deny himself release. They came at the same time and her internal juices mingled with his cum. She could feel it coursing into her body and warming her very being.

It was no wonder Kate said he tickled her tonsils. He had tickled far more than that in the time they had spent joined as God had meant for men and women to be joined.

* * * *

Black lay for several moments, his cock still within her cunt. As it shriveled to its normal size, he realized he had never had sex this good. Maybe it was because she wasn't a paid companion. Perhaps it had been so good because he knew she was relatively inexperienced. The way she touched his balls attested to the fact that the only good fuck she'd ever had had come from the wooden dildo.

Reluctantly he rolled off her. "Are you sorry?" he said, as he pulled a smoke from the pocket of his discarded shirt.

"Sorry?" she purred. "How could I ever be sorry about making love to you? That is what we did, isn't it? It wasn't just a good fuck like the women get paid for having, was it?"

He looked down at her. The look on her face was one of pure excitement. The innocence that had been there earlier had been stripped away over the past hour as they'd melded their bodies into one.

"It was far from just a good fuck as you call it. I thought maybe you were a virgin. One thing I won't do is take a woman's virginity. That's something best left for her husband to … Hell, I wouldn't have cared if you were a virgin. I've wanted you since I first laid eyes on you."

"Then you weren't disappointed about my lost virginity?"

Black laughed and pulled her into his arms. "I'm not at all disappointed. The truth be told, I rather enjoyed the way your body responded. Do you want to tell me about the first man to enjoy you?"

"Only if you tell me about the first woman you took to your bed. Was she one of your mother's whores?"

Black smiled at the memory of the promised fuck for his thirteenth birthday. "That was the plan, but my mother was killed and all of the plans were suddenly changed. I never got to enjoy Salina, but I'm certain she could have taught me more than one of her tricks. My first woman was a girl of fourteen. We lost our virginity together, and, after that, I realized I didn't want to do that to another woman. Teresa thought I would stay on my grandfather's ranchero and marry her, but I had other ideas. For all I know, she could have my child, but when I left Mexico, I cut all ties with my family. I knew my grandfather would never approve of the life I decided I wanted to live. However, he certainly would have approved of my killing the man to avenge my mother's death."

He was surprised to see tears running down her cheeks and brushed them away with his forefinger. "It's nothing to cry over. At thirteen, I wouldn't have been a good husband to Teresa. I had too much hate in my heart to even consider loving a woman."

"And now? Do you still have too much hate to love?"

"The hate burned out a long time ago, but I never found anyone worth loving, until now. I've never been with a woman I haven't paid. I always thought it was better that way. It was different with you. I can't explain it."

If his words bewildered her, it wasn't noticeable. Instead, she reached up and stroked his cheek, making him painfully aware of the fact he hadn't taken the time to shave before bringing the cattle back to the Diamond A. He had wanted everything to be perfect when he made love to her, and he had taken her as though he was a bull servicing a cow in heat.

"I think I know what you mean," she replied. "I never wanted anything to do with men, not after what happened in Ohio. Then you came along and, well, everything changed. I don't understand it, but I've wanted you so badly. I know it's only been a couple of days, but it seems like a lifetime."

Her words about Ohio piqued his interest. "Do you want to talk about Ohio?"

She bit her lip and nodded, but only slightly. "It was eleven years ago," she began. "I was just a kid really, but I thought I was a woman. The preacher's son, Ronald, came calling quite often. Aunt Mable thought he was a real catch and was already planning the wedding. Ronald said because we were going to be getting married, we should experiment with sex. He said no one would buy a pair of shoes without trying them on so why would we not try and see if we fit well together? I was so in love with the idea of being a wife, I agreed. The first time hurt, but he assured me it wouldn't hurt again."

"He used you?"

She nodded. "He most certainly did. It was all about his pleasure and to hell with mine. When I told him I was carrying his child, he denied it was his and accused me of being with every boy in the county. I was branded a whore, and my aunt took me to a convent. While I was there, I spent many hours on my knees on the stone floor praying for the redemption of my soul. When the baby was born, she was ripped from my arms. I only saw her briefly. They told me she would go to a good home and that I should forget I'd ever had her."

Sobs cut off her words, prompting Black to hold her while she cried. "Does anyone out here know about the baby?"

He could feel her shake her head no. "Everyone thinks I'm a virgin, everyone but Kate that is. She's the only one I ever told about what happened. She insisted I buy the dildo. She understood I didn't want anything to do with the men who came on the stage, but she said I needed some kind of release. It really helped, but it couldn't compare to what we just did."

"We have a long winter ahead of us," he whispered. "I promise I'll teach you everything I know about lovemaking.'

"And come spring you'll leave me."

He didn't like the sorrow he detected in her voice. "Yes, I'll leave, but it won't be because I don't want you. I'll leave because I have a job to do, and, when I've finished here, there will be another assignment waiting for me. Ed keeps me busy."

"I can understand that. I promise I won't make you stay when there's work to be done. I'll be thankful for whatever time we have together and there will be nothing to bind you to me when it's time to leave."

"I hope not, but I also want you to know what it's like to be with a man. The life you're living isn't right. There should be someone to make you complete. I don't want you ever to have to use that dildo again. It's downright unnatural."

They lay in each other's arms and surprisingly fell into a deep sleep. Black was the first to awaken, not so much because he had gotten enough sleep, but because a cold wind had started to blow, promising a storm in the making.

She stirred in his arms. "We must have fallen asleep." She stretched.

"We did, but there's a storm brewing. We'd best get dressed and get out of here."

He got up and pulled on his clothes. While she dressed, he mended the break in the fence. With the job completed, he turned to see her watching him intently.

"Did you mean what you said before we went to sleep?"

"Every word and more," he replied as he pulled her into his embrace. "I've never wanted a woman in the way I want you. I always thought it was best if I paid for the release I needed. Now I know I was only fooling myself. Paying for something that should come naturally isn't nearly as fulfilling as what we just shared. I know that's how the women at your place make their living, and I don't fault them for that, but I doubt I'll ever pay for it again."

She took two steps forward and wrapped her arms around his neck. "I was hoping you'd feel that way. I don't expect marriage, but I also want you in my bed for as long as you want to stay."

"What if you find yourself in the situation that you did in Ohio?"

"I won't. The women told me about a tea that prevents such things. I make it for them every night. Even though I wasn't having sex with anyone I've been drinking it as well. It's actually quite good and very relaxing."

Black pulled her into a tight embrace. He wondered if she was pleased that she wouldn't find herself in a family way, or if he was disappointed that she wouldn't be carrying his child. The thought was a sobering one. For the first time in the past fifteen years, he wanted to be part of a family. He wanted Belle to be his, not just for the winter but for always, but in his line of work, he couldn't ask her to wait while he went on his assignments. He would be content with what he had for the few months while at the Double Bar B. He might even write to his grandfather and let him know that no man's bullet had taken his life.

Chapter Seven

The storm hit as Black and Belle rode to the ranch. By the time they returned to the house, both were soaked to the skin.

"You go on in the house," Black shouted to be heard over the howl of the wind. "I'll take care of your horse."

Belle nodded. She was so chilled, it was all she could do to dismount and make her way to the porch. Once she stepped into the warmth of the kitchen, she began to shake with chills.

"Get her upstairs and out of those wet clothes," Annie ordered. "I've got water on heating so you can have a hot bath."

Kate came to Belle's side and guided her toward the stairs. It didn't matter that water dripped from her hair and clothes all over the clean floors Annie prided herself on. All Belle wanted was to be shed of the wet garments and to be warm again.

"What took you two so long?' Kate said, once she had helped Belle undress and get into a warm robe. "We were getting worried about you."

"We had to mend the fence again," Belle explained. "Before we did, we had the lunch Annie packed for us and then fell asleep."

Kate looked directly into Belle's eyes, then picked up the discarded bloomers. "You let him take you, didn't you?"

"I wouldn't say he actually took me. It was more like mutual consent."

"How could you consider such a thing? You hardly know him."

"You're a fine one to talk. Just last night you were saying I should try it. Well I tried it, and I liked it. I know him as well as I need to. Besides, you don't know the men who come to your bed."

"That's different."

Belle nodded. "It certainly is. Oh, Kate, I feel alive for the first time since I've come to the Double Bar B. I thought I could take care of my own needs, but there's nothing I can do for myself that can begin to match what Black did this afternoon."

"It was a foolish thing to do. What if he gets you in the same condition Ronald did? What will you do then, especially when he leaves for the next assignment, wherever that might take him?"

"I won't get with child. I drink the same tea you and the women do. What I need from you, from all of you, is to learn what to do to keep him interested."

"You want us to teach you the tricks of the trade? Do you think that's wise?"

"Yes, I do. This might be the only time I get to experience anything like this. I want to learn what to do with the feathers Janna uses, how to use the whip that Lacy has and what it's like to be tied to the bed and taken without being able to struggle. I also want to know how to do what you do."

"You want to learn how to suck a man's cock and his balls. Belle Barton, I didn't think you'd ever do anything like that."

"You do it, so why not me? I only have until Black gets enough evidence to arrest Clayte. Grant me this one thing. I doubt there will ever be a man who is as receptive as Black seems to be. He was actually concerned with my feelings, not just his own."

"Are you decent?" Roy called from beyond the closed door.

"Yes I'm decent," Belle replied.

"Good, 'cause I got two big buckets of hot water out here for your bath. If someone doesn't open the door soon, I think my arms will fall off."

Kate opened the door to give Roy entrance to the room. Behind him, Black stood looking like a drowned rat.

"I figured the two of you could share the same water. Just by looking at you, Annie figured out what took you so long. There's no use in filling the tub twice in one day."

He winked slyly and poured the buckets into the tub, then stepped aside so Black could pour in two more.

"The two of you have about an hour before the eastbound stage is due to pull in," Roy reminded them.

Belle and Kate stared at the two men in surprise until Roy took Kate's arm. "I don't think it would be proper for the two of us to stay and watch these two take their baths. Besides, you have to get all prettied up for the eastbound. There's bound to be some gents on there who will need your attentions, and you want to look your best. Annie already sent the other women up to change."

Once they closed the door, Belle began to laugh. "Can't put anything over on Annie, can we?"

"Seems not," Black said, as he took off his hat and started unbuttoning his shirt. "It was a bit unsettling when she first suggested I come up here and share your bath. She told me it was plain as the nose on your face what had happened and she couldn't be happier. That old woman is going to turn you into a whore if you don't watch out."

"I doubt it," she said, as she stepped forward in order to peel the wet shirt and long johns from his body. "There have been a lot of men come to this ranch, but never one that had the effect on me that you have. I've had more than my share of offers, but I've never taken anyone up on them. You're the first and will probably be the last. Ronald doesn't count. Even though he gave me a child I couldn't keep, he didn't awaken my womanhood the way you did this afternoon."

"I plan to awaken more than that, if you'll let me. Now, let's have that bath before the water gets cold. There's nothing worse than a cold bath."

He stepped out of his pants and underwear and for the first time she became aware of the fact he didn't wear boots. She smiled at his bare feet as he slipped the robe from her shoulders.

Unexpectedly, he lifted her into his arms and deposited her gently into the tub before climbing in behind her. The feel of his cock against her backside made her ready for him to make love to her again.

"Do you think…" she managed to say before he lifted her air and kissed the back of her neck causing her to become speechless.

"We can't make love now. There wouldn't be time, but later, I promise you later we'll learn more secrets about each other than we ever knew existed."

He reached in front of her for that cake of soap on the front edge of the tub and worked it into a rich lather. With his hands he rubbed it over her breasts, paying particular attention to her sensitive nipples. He worked his hands down across her stomach and then lathered up the hair at the juncture of her thighs. She rested against his chest as he slipped his finger into her pussy and messaged her clit.

"You are such a tease, Black Conley. You just said we couldn't make love because there wasn't enough time and now you bring me to the brink and leave me wanting."

"It's only a prelude of what's to come later tonight."

"Not when there's people from the stage in the house," she warned.

"Why not? They'll be so busy they won't know what we're doing. I promise I'll be back in my own bed by the time the sun comes up in the morning."

* * * *

Black stepped out of the tub and held out his hand to Belle. The way the lamplight shimmered off her wet skin sent shockwaves into his cock. She wasn't the only one who didn't want to wait until the house was quiet and the lights were out. Luckily, patience was one of his strong points.

He picked up the towel Kate left on the bed and dried the droplets of water from her shoulders and back as well as from the front of her body. When he finished she took the towel and dried him in the same manner.

"I'll leave you to get dressed," he said, as he started toward the door. "I wasn't thinking past the pleasure of bathing with you, or I would have brought in a change of clothes for tonight."

He took one last look at her magnificent body before he left the room. Never before had he wanted a woman the way he wanted her. It had been love at first sight and that was something he never believed. Ed had been a fool to send him here. It was evident Roy and Annie once wanted Ed and Belle to become man and wife. Of course, they had probably given up on that idea when Ed didn't hot foot it back to the Double Bar B when Belle arrived ten years ago. He couldn't help but wonder about the child she'd given away. Was it true the only one here who knew about it other than himself was Kate? Surely she had told her father as well as Roy and Annie. They were too close to think otherwise.

After shaving off the beard that had grown in the past day and a half, he dressed in the suit he'd worn last night. Wearing it made him feel like a real gentleman, one worthy of the company of Miss Belle Barton.

The atmosphere in Belle's dining room was more like a fancy dinner party, like the ones his grandmother delighted in planning, than supper at any stage stop he'd ever visited. The men from the stage were all dusty from their trip, but were thrilled to be enjoying the company of the ladies at the table. With the driver there were four men, enough so that each of the women would have a companion for the evening.

Belle sat at the head of the table, as though holding court. On either side of her were the women, each with a man by her side. Only the chair at the foot end of the table was empty.

"Mr. Conley," Belle said, as he entered the room. "I was beginning to wonder if I should send Roy to see if you would be joining us this evening."

"There was no need, Miss Barton," he replied, deciding he could play at her game of pretense. "As you can see, I'm more than ready for dinner."

Belle made a big production out of introducing Black to the driver of the stage, as well as the man from San Francisco who was traveling east on business, the salesman who was returning to St. Louis, and the card shark who had decided he wanted to get back to the Mississippi and the boats that traveled up and down the great river.

"I heard tell of a gunslinger out of Texas by the name of Conley. You wouldn't be him would you?" the gambler said.

"Yes I would, but that life is behind me. Now I'm just another ranch hand, and Miss Barton has been good enough to take me on for the winter."

"I've heard of you as well, Mr. Conley," the stage drive said. "Are you as good with those guns as they say?"

"I am, but it's nothing to brag about. When I was a kid, I thought I was special because my guns were faster than most. As I grew up, I realized I didn't like the thought of possibly losing my life every time some man decided he could out draw me. It was only a matter of time before one of them did, and I didn't relish being dead. I decided to come to Montana and try my hand at ranching to give the legend time to die down."

"That's a wise move, Mr. Conley," the man from San Francisco observed. "I would hate to live with such a sword hanging over my head."

Black knew the conversation was disturbing to the ladies. They knew of his reputation, but to hear it described in such a way had to be upsetting.

"I think we can think of better table talk than this. These lovely ladies don't need to hear such sordid details."

"I agree with Mr. Conley," the salesman said. "I am certainly looking forward to my evening with Miss Janna. The last time I was here I had the pleasure of Miss Kate's company. I'm afraid I've bragged about it so often my friend from San Francisco is eager to find out if I am exaggerating."

The comment brought laughter back to the table. Black was pleased the conversation no longer revolved around him. It was in everyone's best interests if his life remained private. Let these men think he had given up using his gun for his livelihood.

* * * *

Belle helped Annie and Roy in the kitchen while the women entertained the men in the parlor. After supper, Black had gone outside, and she wondered what he could be doing out there for so long.

Annie and Roy bid her goodnight, just as Belle heard the first of the women take her gentleman upstairs to enjoy the evening in the bedrooms added for the comfort of the passengers on the stagecoach. From the sound of the footsteps on the stairs, she knew Kate was the first to retire for the night. Soon each of the other women went up to bed, leaving Belle alone in the kitchen to ensure the house was secure for the night. She'd just turned down lights in the parlor when she heard Black enter through the kitchen door.

"I wondered where you were," she said, when she came in from the parlor to greet him.

"I was checking on the horses and rode out to the canyon where the cattle are bedded down. It all looked peaceful enough to me. Doubt anyone will try taking any cattle for a while. I'm sure Clayte will lay low until the hoopla about those rustlers we killed last night dies down. Once it does, he can blame it on the one who got away."

"At least we can get some rest tonight," she said, as she turned toward the stairs.

"Rest? Is that what you really have on your mind? I know it's not my thoughts on what tonight could bring."

He slipped his arm around her waist and guided her toward the stairs. Rest wasn't tops on her list either, but she didn't want to appear too anxious.

Once they entered her room and lit the lamp, Belle was surprised to see Black's belongings intermingled with her own. "Did you do this?" she said.

"Not me. I would never be so presumptuous. I thought you did it."

Belle began to laugh. "Hardly, I'm certain it was our friendly matchmaker, Annie, with her more than willing accomplice, Roy. They want to see me settled. I guess they think settled for even a short period of time is better than not settled at all."

"Well, if that's the case, then I won't argue. Tonight will be all about your pleasure. This afternoon was only a prelude. Since you're almost an innocent, I think it's time someone made you into an experienced woman."

Belle tried to protest, but he silenced her with a kiss that drove her to the heights of desire. His tongue snaked into the cavern of her mouth and sparred with her tongue until she thought she would die from the pleasure of it. When they drew apart, he undressed her, one piece of clothing at a time. She'd never been undressed like this before, and the feel of it intensified her erotic feelings.

When she stood naked, he looked at her as though for the first time. The heat of his gaze made her blush with wanting him.

He pulled down the bed covers for her. "Lay down," he commanded. "I'll be with you in a minute."

She watched as he undressed and wondered if he had become as aroused by undressing her as she was by watching him disrobe. Once he stood naked before her, she had her answer. He stood there for a moment, as though savoring the vision of her body before he joined her on the bed and spread her legs wide so he could lie between them. She reached out to him, but he stopped her by taking her slender wrists in one of his large hands and pulling them high above her head.

"Not tonight," he whispered. "What I have planned isn't about me. It isn't anything I would ever do with a paid companion. This is about your enjoyment, and I promise it will bring you pleasure. It's something I remember hearing the women who worked for my mother talk about, but it was nothing I ever wanted to do. I always figured the whores I bedded weren't clean enough. You, my dear, are perfect in every way and deserved to be worshiped and loved in a special way."

The thought of him thinking her worthy of such attention made Belle blush. In her lifetime, no man had ever thought her special. Ronald had used her and she knew it, but at the time, she thought she was in love. Now she knew better. His professed love was nothing more than lust. She had often wondered how many other women he had ruined in the name of love. All thoughts of the past left her mind as Black began to kiss her neck and work his way down to her breasts as he had done earlier in the day. All the while, he paid homage to her nipples. His fingers caressed her clit driving her to the heights of desire.

After what seemed like hours of delightful torture, he began kissing down her ribcage until he came to her maiden's mound. Once there, he shifted position and began to lick her pussy, as though he couldn't get enough of the taste of her. To her surprise, his tongue caressed her clit and pulled it into his mouth as though it were her nipple. With the sucking of her clit came teasing bites until she could no longer hold back. Her body betrayed her as an orgasm shook her entire being.

As though he was a child, thirsty for life giving water, he licked the essence of her from within her pussy. "You taste delightful," he said, as he got up from the bed.

She couldn't help but notice his erect cock, attesting to the fact he hadn't been completely satisfied. "Why are you leaving me?"

"I'm not leaving you, only rinsing my mouth out. As much as I enjoyed the taste of you, I doubt you would want to taste yourself when I kiss you, and I plan to kiss you over and over again."

She watched as he first rinsed his mouth and then pulled a small tin from the pocket of his pants. To her surprise, he took out a mint leaf and began to chew it. She usually chewed a piece of fresh mint in the morning after she cleansed her teeth, but she had no idea a man would think of doing such a thing.

"I keep a box of mint leaves on my dresser," she said when he returned to bed. "I didn't expect a gunslinger to enjoy the same thing."

"You forget I grew up in a household of women. Each of them kept mint in their rooms and insisted I do the same. It's a habit I never outgrew. I like the way it makes my mouth feel after I cleanse my teeth. I often chew a piece of mint during the day as well. I find the taste of it refreshing. For now, I really don't want to talk about mint."

He leaned over and kissed her tenderly. With their lips locked and their tongues doing battle, he began touching areas she wouldn't have thought of as erotic zones. To her delight, they produced the same sensation in her pussy that his caresses to her clit had given her. He was an expert, of that she was certain.

It took only moments for her to be ready to have him enter her and begin the true act of lovemaking. As he plunged his cock in and out of her, she tried to draw him in as far as possible. When at last they came together for the second time in one day, they both lay spent. Snuggling into his embrace, she fell asleep. For the first time in her life, another person shared her bed and provided her with the protection of his arms for an entire night.

Chapter Eight

Black woke and, for the first time in his life, realized a woman occupied his bed. His companions had always left after he'd satisfied himself, usually in search of another customer rather than listen to him snoring contentedly. It was the manner of the business, but what he had shared with Belle last night was far from business. It was pure pleasure on both their parts.

Many times he had heard the girls at his mother's ranch talking about the men sucking their clit until they came, and then the men licking their essence from them. They made it sound delightful, but he had never found anyone to whom he wanted to give such pleasure. Just looking at the painted whores who usually didn't bathe between customers, made the thought of doing something like that repulsive.

Belle was different. She wasn't a whore, and she wasn't an experienced lover. He liked that. There were so many things he wanted to show her, so many positions he wanted to try. He knew their nights would never get dull. The winter would be long, but it would certainly be interesting. When he left on his next assignment, it would be with enough memories to last him a lifetime.

Beside him, Belle stirred and, from downstairs, he heard the mantle clock strike five times. As much as he wanted to take her again, it was time to start the day.

After disentangling himself from her arms, he got up and poured water into the basin in order to wash up and shave. In the mirror about the washstand, he saw her stretch, as though she was a cat, waking up and stretching before welcoming the new day.

"Good morning," she said her voice still heavy with sleep. "Any idea what time it is?"

"I heard the clock strike five a while ago. I thought it was high time I got up and dressed for the day so I could give you some privacy while you cleaned up."

"What about your privacy?" she questioned.

"Men aren't the same as women. It doesn't take us long to clean up and get a start on the day. Women are completely different. They need time to primp and the privacy to cleanse those more personal parts of their bodies."

He scraped the last of his whiskers from his face before getting dressed. He was surprised to see a new pair of long johns laid out for him along with clean britches and shirt. After pulling on his clothes, he left the room, all the while wishing he could stay and watch her do her morning ritual. He knew it was a foolish wish. He'd seen enough of her magnificent body last night to satisfy any curiosity as well as make him anxious for the night to come.

On his way to the outhouse, he saw Annie in the kitchen, but bodily needs overcame his manners. It was one thing to use the piss pot in the middle of the night, but something else entirely once he was up and dressed.

By the time he returned to the kitchen, Annie was more than willing to sit down and share a cup of coffee with him.

"I suppose I have you to thank for moving my things last night," he said, once she joined him at the table.

"It was Roy's idea," she replied. "I only agreed. It's high time some man paid attention to Belle."

"Didn't you think you were pushing things a bit?"

"Not after seeing the two of you yesterday when you rode in from taking those cattle back to Clayte. I would have had to be blind not to have realized you'd awakened the woman inside her while you were gone. I expected you back by two, and, when you didn't get here until after four, I knew something happened. She's a beautiful girl and not one who should be alone for her entire life."

"If you're suggesting I should stay on here, you'd better rethink your position. Once this assignment ends, Ed will send me somewhere else. He always does."

Annie took a long sip of her coffee. "I know you'll be leaving once Clayte and the others who are responsible for the rustling are caught, but while you're here you can at least give Belle a taste of what it's like to be loved by a man."

* * * *

After the passengers from the stage finished breakfast and left, Kate gave out the assignments telling Black to ride with Janna and check to ensure there were no more breaks in the fence. Belle swallowed her jealousy of Black and Janna going to the east range together and went to the study to do some of the bookwork that always seemed to be waiting for her.

"Did it bother you that I sent Black and Janna out together?" Kate said.

Belle jumped at the intrusion into her silent thoughts. "A little, I guess. Of course, if we don't treat Black like any of the other hand, it might arouse suspicion."

"He's not just another hand, is he?"

Belle shook her head. "If he was another hand, he wouldn't still be here. He would have run off like all the others who didn't want to work for a woman. He's here to do a job, and it has nothing to do with either the Double Bar B or any of us."

"Do you think he can get enough proof against Clayte to get him arrested?"

"It's not going to be easy. You should have seen the expression on Clayte's face when we brought back those cattle yesterday. Just by that I was convinced of his guilt, but you can't arrest a man because of his expression."

"What about the men who were driving the cattle? Did any of them say anything?"

Belle searched her memory for what Black had told her. "Two of them were dead before he could get to them. Black thinks he got both of them and winged the one who got away. The one Roy shot lived for a little while, but he didn't know who hired him. He said that someone came up to him in the Purple Moon and offered him money to join with the others. Being a stranger in town, he didn't know who it was. Considering he died before he could say more, we know absolutely nothing other than our gut feelings. It's possible that it was one of the other rustlers who hired the man, but that's nothing to go on. I have a feeling getting the evidence we need isn't going to be easy."

"What about you, Belle? How will you react once this is all over? From the looks Black was giving you, coupled with the fact I saw him come out of your room this morning, I have a good idea about what's going on between the two of you. If you ask me, it's high time, but what happens when he leaves?"

"I'll continue the same way as I always have. I thought I loved Ronald, and he destroyed me. I won't fall into the same trap with Black. He's here to do a job. And, if in doing it he ends up in my bed and gives me pleasure, I'll take it as just that. I might as well act the part I've been accused of playing for so long."

"The only thing is you aren't acting. I can tell you're falling in love with him. If you weren't, you certainly would have put up more of a fit when Annie moved his things into your room. Just a word to the wise from a more experienced whore, don't let this destroy you. He will leave, and, when he does, you'd better be ready to find a replacement for the man, or you could fall apart."

Kate went out to start the morning, leaving Belle alone with her thoughts. She was falling in love with Black. Hell she'd been in love with him from the first moment she laid eyes on him.

It wasn't like when she'd first met Ronald. She was no longer a cowed eyed child who took attention from the first man to give it to her. She'd played that part and for eleven years wanted no further part of it. No, this was different. Black had swept into her life and turned her emotions to mush. She couldn't help but wonder if that had been part of Ed's plan from the very beginning.

Thoughts of Ed brought to mind the first time she'd seen him after returning from Ohio. At the time, she thought she needed a man in her life, but Ed wasn't interested. He did kiss her once, but it had been the kind of kiss a woman got from her brother, not someone who would love and cherish her for the rest of her life.

Since then he'd corresponded with her, always telling her someday the right man would come to the Double Bar B and when he did, she'd know it.

Well, Ed had sent the right man and she did know it. The problem was that just as Ed sent Black here, he would be taking him away to a new assignment and Belle would still be alone. It wasn't fair, but what could she do about it now?

* * * *

Black rode alongside Janna to the east range, all the while thinking about the turn of events since he arrived on the Double Bar B. He'd expected nights of lovemaking with the whores, but he'd never thought he'd be in the boss' bed so soon after his arrival.

"Will you be visiting my bed, Black?" Janna said, as they rode along the line of fence that separated Double Bar B and Diamond A land.

"No offense meant, Janna, but I don't think so."

"That's what I thought. I knew the first morning, after you had Kate that it wasn't any of us you wanted. Belle's a fine figure of a woman, and you could do far worse."

"This is just a job," Black replied. "Belle and I, well that's between the two of us. When the men who are behind all this rustling are caught, I'll be sent onto another assignment. It's the way I've lived my life for the past ten years."

"And before that?"

"I thought you all knew what I did. I was a hired gun. It isn't easy living with the fact I've killed over thirty men. It wasn't what I thought I'd be doing with my life, but it's the hand I was dealt. My ma had big plans for me, but when she was killed it all changed."

Janna nodded. "I know what you mean. I was going to get married and have a whole brood of kids, but Pa decided to come west. When he was killed in an Indian raid on the wagon train, I was left to fend for myself. The only thing a woman alone is good for is spreading her legs for money, at least that's what the wagon master said when he left me at the first town we reached. He took me straight to the saloon and told the owner to put me to work.

"It took a while for me to learn to enjoy what I was doing. At least I had a friend there who told me that I should find something special to do with the fucking so I could demand more money. She suggested a lot of things, but I preferred using the feather she gave me. At first it was just an old bird feather, but one day a peddler man came to town and had genuine peacock feathers. I was the first in line to buy one. That dollar was the best money I ever spent. I've made it back many times over in the extra money the men pay after I use it on them."

Black laughed at her comment. "I don't doubt you did. The whores at my ma's ranch all had their special ways of fucking, but I never knew what they were. I was too young for such things, I guess."

Talking about home brought a lump to his throat. He'd known so little about life when everything he held dear had been ripped away from him. Coming to the Double Bar B brought back memories and made him aware of what had been taken from him.

His other assignments had led him to areas where there were no ranches to work and no soft beds to enjoy. He'd spent his time on the open range as well as in rooms about the saloons in whatever town he found himself in with a paid companion.

For the first time in far too many years, he was part of a family like the family he'd had. Belle was nothing like his mother. She didn't take men to her bed. At least she hadn't until last night. He was honored to think he was the first in over ten years to enjoy the delights between her legs.

"Do you know how to use that thing?" Janna said, as they pulled the lunch Annie had packed from their saddlebags.

He looked to see what she was pointing at and realized she had focused on the bullwhip that hung on the opposite side of his saddle as his rifle. "Yup. My ma couldn't shoot a gun, but she could wield a bullwhip. It was the death of her, too."

"How so?"

"We had a neighbor who wanted our ranch, just like Clayte wants this place. What we didn't know was he'd killed my pa to get it. Ma held out for almost ten years before he came to the ranch one day when she was alone and got her whip away from her. He beat her to death with it and claimed the land as soon as the sheriff ran me and the women off."

"What did you do?"

"I took the only proof I had that the taxes had been paid on the land and Mike had no claim to it with me when I went to Mexico to bury my mother on my grandfather's ranch. A year later I returned. By that time I was as good with a gun as I was with the bullwhip. After I killed Mike Slade, I knew where my future would take me. I left the ranch that held so many memories, both good and bad, behind and never looked back."

"Do you still own it?"

"No, I was fourteen when I sold it to a man I knew would make it prosper. I went back once, but no one knew I was there. There were steers grazing and he'd made a lot of improvements to the house. It was enough to know the place was loved and well managed. Back then I had no intentions of ever being a rancher. Now I wish I had kept that place, but I was a kid, and I couldn't run it alone. After I killed Slade, I knew there would be no one who would want to work for me."

"What about your grandfather?"

"I don't know if he's dead or alive. I've been thinking about writing him a letter, but I hardly know where to start."

"How about with Dear Grandpa? After that, the words will come real easy."

"It sounds like you've done this before."

"I have. I'd been working for about three years when I wrote my grandparents about what happened to Pa and the life I was living. They told me no matter what I did for a living, they loved me and prayed for me. It was all I could ask."

Black took a bite of the sandwich and chewed on the meat along with what Janna had said. He'd been thinking about writing to his grandfather. Maybe now was the time for him to send a letter to Mexico. It wasn't like he expected an answer, but it was worth a try.

While Janna took a short nap, he pulled a pencil and paper from his saddlebag.

Dear Grandfather and Grandmother,

It's been a long time since I left your place. A lot has happened to me, and now I think it's time to tell you about my life. I went back to Ma's ranch and killed the man who murdered her. It was a fair fight. He drew first. After that I retrieved Ma's treasures from beneath the floorboards of the kitchen and sold the ranch.

I spent a lot of years as a gunslinger, but now I'm working as a U.S. Marshal. I'm not proud of the number of men I've killed, but it was never murder.

My latest assignment has me on a ranch in Montana, working for a woman named Belle Barton. If I were the kind of man who was set on getting married and settling down, it would be with someone like Belle. She's beautiful, and, like Ma, she gets what she wants out of life.

There's a man here that reminds me of Mike Slade. He wants Belle's ranch, but it's my job to arrest him for the rustling he's been doing in this area. Once that's done, I'll be off to my next assignment, but I will keep in touch.

If you feel you should reply to this letter, you can write to the U.S. Marshal's Office in care of Ed Heath in Denver, Colorado. He's my boss and will get your letter to me no matter where I am.

I know I never told you I loved you, but I really did. Whenever I get into a town that has a church, I go and say a prayer for all that you did for me when I was a kid.

"I guess I fell asleep," Janna said, just as Black was finishing the letter to his grandparents. "That was a damn foolish thing to do, but on the mornings after the stage rolls in, I'm right tired."

Black smiled. He knew all about that kind of tired. After last night with Belle, he wasn't as wide-awake as he should have been. Life on this ranch would certainly take a lot of getting used to.

Once they remounted their horses, they rode south along the line of fence that ran across the entire boundary of the ranch, with the exception of the area leading into the dooryard from the north. By the time they got back to the house it was already getting dark.

Black looked at the clouds that appeared to be full of either snow or rain. The way the temperature had dropped while they were out, he was certain there would be snow by morning. This was the time of year he disliked the most. The darkness of night came far too early for his liking, and, if what he'd heard about Montana winters were true, they would be snowbound from the first of October until the middle of April or maybe even longer.

He knew once winter set in, Clayte would slink back into his hidey-hole and not come out again until spring when tracking him would be a hell of a lot harder because the snow would be gone.

* * * *

Belle stood at the window in her office and watched for Janna and Black to return. She knew it was foolish for her to be jealous of Black riding with Janna, but she couldn't help herself. After one afternoon and one evening with Black she felt as though he was her man. If only he wouldn't be leaving once the men responsible for the rustling were behind bars she would be happy. Black was the kind of man she'd dreamed of all her life. He was well spoken, handsome, and a considerate lover. What more could a woman ask for?

At last she saw them ride into the dooryard. As he had the day before, Black allowed Janna to dismount and come into the house while he took care of their horses.

"Did you find any more breaks in the wire?" Belle said as soon as Janna entered the kitchen.

"No, everything was good. Black doesn't think they'll hit us again until spring. He thinks we'll get snow tonight. It was good to ride with Black today and get to know him better."

"Better?" Belle said, almost afraid to hear what Janna would say next.

"Not in the way you're thinking. I asked if he'd be coming to my bed, and he turned me down. That man has it bad for you, even if he doesn't want to admit it. Why don't you come up to my room while I get cleaned up for supper and I'll show you what to do with one of my feathers? I think that man would purely love it if you were to torture him so delightfully."

"You mean he didn't..." Belle couldn't bring herself to finish the last of her sentence.

"No, Belle, he didn't fuck me out in the open the way he did you yesterday. He's one of those odd men who once they find a woman they want, they don't dally with whores or anyone else who crosses their path. I did ask him about that bullwhip he carries on his saddle, and he assures me he can use it as expertly as he does his guns. Can't see where that would come in handy, but then again I don't know how to use one. I plan to ask him to teach me over the winter. We have to have something to do to pass the time. It won't take much to keep an eye on the cattle, and, if he's right and the rustling calms down, he won't be able to do any further investigation until spring. Do you think Annie's son planned it that way?"

Belle pondered Janna's question as they went up to her room. "I don't know," she said, once she entered the bedroom. "I know he didn't come himself and that could mean that he figured it would take all winter for Black to get the evidence he needs to arrest Clayte, if he is the one behind the rustling."

Belle watched as Janna stripped off her trail dusty clothes and poured water from the pitcher into the basin. From the steam that came from the pitcher, Belle knew Annie had filled it with boiling water as soon as she saw Black and Janna ride up to the house. If this pitcher were filled with hot water, the one in her room would be filled as well so that Black could clean up before supper.

Rather than watch Janna take her sponge bath, Belle concentrated on the trappings of the room. It was a house rule that the women had to keep their own rooms clean. It was too much to ask of Annie, and Belle knew there were things that were private, the women's bedrooms were one of those things. The only time Annie came to their rooms was when she brought up the laundry and filled their pitchers with hot water.

On the dresser a picture Belle decided must be of Janna's parents, sat beside two vases, each filled with beautiful feathers. They ranged from exotic peacock feathers to an eagle feather and even a goose feather. The colors of each feather made them look like a beautiful bouquet of flowers.

"Take your pick of those feathers, Belle," Janna said, without turning from her washstand.

Belle was embarrassed to be caught gawking at the array of feathers in the vases. "I … I didn't mean…"

"Of course you did. Everyone looks at them and wonders what I do with them. My suggestion would be the peacock feather. It's larger and softer than most. It's the easiest to use on a man's body, especially his cock and his balls, and it drives them crazy. I should know. I've made enough money off of them."

Belle sat down on the neatly made bed. "What do you plan to do with all your money? I mean each of you women have substantial bank accounts. I know one day you'll all leave me. Where will you go?"

"You'll laugh at me."

"No, I won't," Belle replied. "It's been a long time since I've had a girlfriend to exchange confidences with."

Janna buttoned her dress before sitting next to Belle on the bed. "Well, all of us have been talking about it, and we all want the same thing. There are a lot of kids who lose their folks. They either get killed or get sick and die. Most of them, like Cara and me get shipped off to the first whorehouse that comes along and the rest is history. Kids shouldn't be made to work like that. Now that Clayte could turn out to be the rustler, I can't help but wonder what will happen to his kids. With Nettie gone they're far too young to fend for themselves like Cara and me had to do."

Belle nodded. She too had been thinking about Clayte's kids lately. Even though she didn't want to be his wife, she did wonder what would happen to them when Black found out Clayte was the one behind the rustling. They certainly weren't old enough to take care of themselves and none of them had asked to be born, especially as Clayte's kids. In all rights, the Diamond A belonged to them, but even the oldest wasn't of an age to run it.

"I think it sounds like a good idea, and it might come about sooner than you think."

"What are you talking about?"

"When the stage came in the other night, the driver gave me a letter from the stage line. It seems the railroad will be coming through Larson's Gap next summer and means the stage will stop running, putting us out of business, at least for the stage stop. That leaves me with the addition to the house. Without the passengers, you will be out of work and the addition will be empty. It would make a perfect orphanage, if that's what you have in mind."

"Do you mean it, Belle?" Janna said, her eyes sparkling with excitement. "Lacy contacted the proper authorities and even though we had enough money to meet the requirements, we didn't have a place to open an orphanage. Without that, we couldn't get our certification or our funding. The territorial government pays for each orphan. That's how orphanages make their money to stay open. If we could use the addition to the house, it would be perfect. I've talked to people who have run away from orphanages because they were in the middle of the city and the kids couldn't get out to play. Here they could play all day, and, when they were old enough, they could learn about ranching."

"Don't get too excited yet. We'll have to see if the railroad really comes through town. Then we can start planning for this orphanage, if that's what you and the others want. At least you wouldn't be leaving me, and Annie would be thrilled to be able to play nursemaid to all those kids."

Chapter Nine

Black stood on the front porch enjoying an after supper cigarette. The wind had shifted from the west to the north and the chill of it made him shiver. The clouds he'd watched earlier in the day now obliterated the moon making him more certain that by morning there would be fresh snow on the ground. He hoped it wouldn't be too deep. There was a cave at the far end of the ranch he wanted to check out in the morning. If the snowfall were too heavy, he wouldn't be able to get to it right away.

He couldn't put his finger on why he wanted to explore it, but something in his gut told him such an exploration would be worth his time. It seemed as though it would be the perfect place to hide both men and horses. If that were the case, maybe it was where the rustler he'd winged was holed up.

"A penny for your thoughts," Belle said as she joined him on the porch, her shawl wrapped tightly around her shoulders.

"I was just thinking about some of the land I saw today when we were riding the fence line. Have you done any exploring around here?"

"A little, why?"

"I noticed some caves along the bluffs overlooking the creek. How big are they?"

"From Pa's letters, they have to be pretty good sized. He said that him and Roy prospected for gold up there one winter, but didn't ever find any. I always meant to go out and explore them, but once Pa died, there wasn't enough time to do the things I wanted and still run this place, especially since I couldn't get any men to work for me. Your best bet would be to ask Roy about them. I'm certain he knows every inch of those caves after prospecting."

Black stubbed out his cigarette and turned to face Belle. "That can wait until tomorrow. I have more important things on my mind," he said as he put his arm around her shoulder and guided her back inside the house. "It's far too cold out here for you. I can think of some things that would warm you up quickly."

When they entered the kitchen, it came as no surprise to see everyone else had already gone to bed. Even Roy and Annie had left for the night and were more than likely enjoying each other in the warmth of their bedroom. They were if Black could believe everything Roy said about the nights he spent making love to his wife.

* * * *

Belle thought of the night she had planned for Black. Earlier in the day, Kate had instructed her on the fine art of sucking a man's cock until he came in your mouth. Somehow she couldn't get past the idea of sticking a living pulsing organ into her mouth. It made her almost gag to think of having to swallow his cum. As for the pulsing part, she'd felt that inside her just the night before and it had been as exciting as the act itself.

Janna's feathers were more to her liking. They put her in control without having to put her lips around his cock and his balls. She'd taken the peacock feather Janna offered her and placed it on the stand beside her bed. Tonight, Mr. Black Conley was in for a pleasant surprise.

With his arm securely around her waist, Belle knew their night together would be an exciting one. Just the feel of his hand through the fabric of her dress excited her. She knew having him in her bed would be even more so.

As they made their way through the house, she stopped at each burning lamp and turned them out for the night, leaving a trail of darkness behind them. At the top of the stairs, the soft glow of the lamp burning in Belle's bedroom illuminated the hallway, giving credence to the fact the other women were already in bed. The only door open belonged to Belle.

Once inside the room, Black kicked the door shut and pulled her into an even tighter embrace. When he slipped his hand down the front of her dress to caress her breast, she pulled away.

"Is something wrong?" he said, as though bewildered by her action.

"Nothing is wrong, it's just last night you were the one to give me the pleasure, and tonight I plan to return the favor."

A wicked smile crossed his lips. "Just what do you have in mind, Miss Barton?"

"You'll see, but you have to give yourself over to me entirely." She reached up to undo the buttons on his coat and then to loosen his string tie and open his shirt so she could inspect his magnificent chest. With great care, she slipped the coat and shirt from his arms and proceeded to run her hands over the mat of hair on his chest before tweaking his nipples between her thumb and forefinger until they became hardened pebbles.

He didn't move but moaned softly as though she was giving him the greatest pleasure in the world. Being a novice at the game of lovemaking, she wondered if he was pretending to please her or if he was actually aroused by what she did.

When she moved her hands to the buttons on his britches, she opened them one at a time exposing his cock. The long johns were gone and there was no hint of any other undergarments to get in her way of freeing his cock from his pants.

As soon as it reached the open air, it stood at attention and begged her to take it in her hands. As she did, she remembered what Kate had told her earlier. What would it feel like to suck him dry and then beg for him to be aroused again so he could come inside her body rather than her mouth?

"Take off your clothes for me," he whispered, once her fingers curled around his cock.

She smiled at him coyly, but did as he said. The chill of the room didn't seem to bother her, as she stood before him completely naked. She liked the way he looked at her body as though he were a little boy eyeing a big piece of chocolate cake.

"I know you want tonight to be about me," he said as he pulled her into his arms, "but I need to feel you against me. Having you stand there and not being able to touch you is sheer torture."

They moved toward the bed as though they were one. Once he sat down on the edge of the bed, he pulled her down with him. She knew if she wasn't careful, her plans would easily be altered and the new techniques she had learned would not be used.

Being on top, she slid from his embrace until she was on the same level as his cock. The thought that had been so repulsive only hours earlier now drew her like a magnet. The feather forgotten, she slid her lips down his velvety foreskin as she kissed every inch of him. For the first time she had a close up view of his balls and they completely fascinated her. Taking the sack in her hands, she opened her mouth and took the length of his cock inside her.

Just as she imagined, the hard organ pulsed with a life of its own prompting her to suckle it while she played with the sac she held in her hand. Kate told her to be gentle, because a man's balls were the most vulnerable part of his body.

Without warning he came in her mouth. She wondered if she would be able to swallow it without gagging, but found it slid down her throat easily, leaving the salty taste of him in her mouth.

"Are you sure you've never done any of this before?" he said when she got out of bed to rinse her mouth and chew on the mint the way he'd done the night before.

"Positive, but I have good teachers."

"I'm afraid to ask what else they've taught you. Come back to bed and let me make love to you in the proper way. I don't think I can take any more of your lessons tonight."

When she turned back to the bed, she saw he was fingering the feather. The pleasure she had thought she would give to him had changed hands. It was entirely possible he planned something wicked with the instrument of love she'd borrowed from Janna.

When she returned to the bed, she noticed he was sitting on the edge. Before she could react, he grabbed her wrist and pulled her down across his knees. The coarse hair on his legs prickled against her stomach and breasts, arousing her far more than she ever thought possible.

Once she was in this position, he stuck his finger first into her asshole and then into her cunt. The pleasure exceeded anything she ever imagined. Then to her horror, he removed his hand from her pussy and smacked her squarely on the bottom.

"What are you doing?" she said, wincing from the pain.

"Just showing you a little of the lessons I learned from Kate. It seems pleasure and pain go together to make the sexual experience far more enjoyable."

Again his hand smacked her bottom. Rather than feel his fingers press deeply inside her, she felt the feather as he trailed it up the inside of her legs. Her body shuddered as though she was on the brink of orgasm only to have him smack her again.

This time it was her breasts that garnered his attention. Instead of dreading the spanking that came next, she anticipated it and could hardly wait for his hand to connect with her bare bottom. She couldn't help but wonder where he would pleasure her next, when he shoved his fingers deep inside her.

"Just as I thought," he declared, "you're more than ready to be fucked."

Gently he lifted her to a standing position before he lay her down on the bed. Once her legs were spread for him, he entered her with a force that was so different from the night before. He was a powerful lover, but their first encounters had been sweet in comparison to this. Out of instinct, she wrapped her legs around his waist, pushing him even deeper within her.

How long their lovemaking lasted, she'd never know. What she did know was he had taken her to heights she never thought possible.

"Thank you," she whispered, as she lay entwined in his arms.

"For what?" His voice was heavy with the sleep that would soon overtake both of them.

"For teaching me more lessons than I thought possible. I hope this won't be the last time you treat me like a disobedient child. The experience was wonderful. Where did you learn to do those things?"

He chuckled and then pulled her closer to him. "I've had my share of whores but none of them liked to be spanked. I learned that lesson from Kate. I admit I always was up for whatever the whores I bedded wanted to do and took to heart what they had to teach me."

"Only whores? Haven't you ever been with someone other than a paid companion?"

"Not until yesterday. There aren't a lot of upstanding women who are willing to bed Black Conley the gunslinger. They're afraid I'd wreck their reputations. I suppose I would."

"Then why me?"

"Because you're the first woman who made me want her for more than fulfilling a need. With the whores, it's a release. With you, it's the desire to be with you the way a man is with a woman. Even though when this assignment is over I'll be leaving, I knew I had to bring you to full womanhood before I left."

Thoughts of him leaving brought tears to her eyes, but she refused to shed them. She'd wanted him as much as he did her, and, no matter how long their relationship lasted, she planned to enjoy every minute. She knew when he was gone, there was no one who could take away her memories of the nights spent in his loving embrace. She fell asleep snuggled against him dreaming dreams she never though would enter her subconscious.

* * * *

Black lay with her in his arms long after she went to sleep. He'd felt her tense when he mentioned leaving the Double Bar B. He had to admit the thought bothered him as well.

Never before had he dreaded an assignment coming to an end. He knew there would always be another to take it's place and looked forward to the challenge. This time the thought of leaving bothered him. He wondered if this was where he was supposed to put down roots. If it were, would Belle accept him for what he was? Could she be content with a gunslinger turned lawman who had more experience in bed than she could ever imagine?

Rather than continue to worry his mind about what might be, Black closed his eyes, pulled Belle closer to him, and went to sleep. There would be time to contemplate his future by the light of day. For now, he needed his rest and wanted to enjoy the feel of Belle in his arms for the remainder of the night.

With sleep came dreams of the men he killed. Each of them stood between him and Belle, threatening to destroy any love she might have felt for him.

"What kind of a woman would want you as her husband?" Mike Slade said as he walked up to the dream-state Black. "I'm thinkin' you're no more than a snot nosed kid who doesn't know his place. You're no better than that whore mother of yours. The sheriff was right to tell you she couldn't be buried with decent folks. I only wish I'd been faster with my gun, then you'd be the one who was dead rather than me.'

One by one the other men came forward each saying much the same thing. Even though Belle knew about the ranch where he'd grown up, would she be able to say yes to being with him for the rest of her life? If he listened to the men he'd killed, he would start having doubts.

"I know you killed all these men," Belle said. "It doesn't make any difference. I love you Black Conley."

The nightmare gave way to more pleasant dreams of a life with Belle by his side. Even as his subconscious played out his dreams, his mind wondered if that was all they were, nightmares and dreams. Would

Belle ever be able to love him in the same way he was coming to love her?

Chapter Ten

The next morning, Black was surprised to see Roy sitting at the kitchen table sipping a cup of coffee. "What are you doing here?"

"When the weather is bad, I never let Mama come over here alone, especially in the morning. With last night's snow, I brought her in the wagon."

Black glanced toward the window for the first time. "How much snow did we get?"

"Only about an inch or two, but it rained before it snowed, so it's icy under the snow. It wouldn't do for Mama to fall and break something. Of course, that's not the only reason I came over here this morning."

Black looked at the old man quizzically. Could he have read Black's mind? Had he come because Black had been thinking about talking to the old man this morning?

"So what is the other reason for you to come out on such a cold morning?"

"Last night I got to thinkin' about that rustler you winged. He couldn't' have gotten far. If I don't miss my guess, he's holed up in one of those caves up by the creek."

Black laughed. "Now I know you're a mind reader. I was thinkin' the same thing last night. I'd planned to come over to your place this morning to find out just how big those caves are."

Roy joined Black's laughter. "Guess great minds do think alike. When Matt and I first came here, we were young and green as grass. We knew about ranching, but we wanted to get rich a hell of a lot quicker than by raisin' cattle. When we saw those caves, we decided we'd strike gold and be so rich we'd never have to work again."

"What did you find?"

"In the first cave, we found a bear was using it as a winter den. You can jolly well bet we didn't hang around for him to come home and find us. In the second one, there was hardly enough room for the two of us in there, but it was evident someone had used it in the past. There was a black spot on the floor where a fire had been laid, and the walls had drawings of animals all over them. It was the third cave where we finally struck pay dirt, or so we thought. It ended up to be fool's gold, but it kept us busy for an entire winter. What a disappointment we had the next spring when Matt rode down to Denver to have it assayed. That's when we decided we were better off if we stuck to something we knew, like ranching."

"So, this cave where you found the fool's gold, how big is it?"

"Big enough so a lot of men and horses could hole up there and be right comfortable. There's a stream in the back with some of the best water you'll ever taste, and it faces east so those northerly and westerly winds don't hit it. When we were working it, we stripped down to shirtsleeves since it was too warm to work with our coats on. Of course, once you stepped outside, you knew it was winter."

"What do you say you and me take a ride up there this morning? I'd like to do a little exploring, and maybe even find a rustler or two hiding out there."

"I don't like the idea of you going on a manhunt, Roy," Annie said, without ever turning away from the stove. "It could be downright dangerous, and I don't intend to lose you just yet. Isn't there someone else who could go with you, Black?"

"Not without tipping my hand. I could send a wire to Denver, but by the time someone got here, anyone holed up in that cave could be long gone. I promise I won't let anything happen to Roy. If I did, I'd have Ed to contend with, and I don't plan on tangling with him."

One by one, Belle and the women joined the discussion until at last Annie served breakfast, and Belle deemed talk of rustlers and caves wasn't proper breakfast conversation.

Kate and Janna said they were planning to check on the cattle, while Cara and Lacy took care of the horses, leaving Black free to do any exploring he wanted.

"I want to go with you," Belle declared.

"Ain't no fittin' place for a lady," Roy argued.

"Then I guess I ain't a lady," Belle replied. "It's my cattle being rustled and my responsibility to see at least one of the men responsible is brought to justice. It would give me great pleasure to see one of Clayte's men hang for what he's been doing to me."

"Don't go jumping to conclusions," Black warned. "Even though we have our suspicions, we don't have any concrete proof of who's responsible. We can't ask the other ranchers for help. They saw Clayte's steers mixed in the bunch those rustlers were running across your land, but that doesn't mean jack shit. As far as anyone other than those of us on this ranch knows, I'm just a gunslinger who's trying to get out of the business. It wouldn't do for anyone to guess I'm really a U.S. Marshal. That's information I don't want out until I'm ready to arrest the men responsible for these raids."

"Then can I go?"

"It won't be an easy ride, and there could be gunplay," Black countered.

"I'm as good with a gun as Roy is. I should be, he taught me how to shoot and told me to practice until I was comfortable with it. I can handle a six shooter as well as I can a rifle."

"We might as well let her come along," Roy finally said. "If we don't, she'll follow us. This little gal has more spunk than most, and I gave up saying no to her years ago."

Even though Black didn't like the idea of Belle coming with them, he decided it was better than having her follow them and ride alone. There was always safety in numbers, at least that's what is Ma always said. He'd been a loner for so long, he'd forgotten what it was like to have someone watching his back.

"I don't think this is any job for you," Annie continued to argue as Black pulled on his coat and went out to saddle the horses.

"Do you think Annie will convince Belle to stay behind today?" Black said, once he and Roy were outside.

"It would be easier to convince a bull not to go after a cow when she's in heat. Belle will win out, but Annie will have her say and that's enough to satisfy her."

Black nodded. He didn't known any of these people well, but he'd been around them long enough that he knew Belle usually got her way. He chuckled at the thought he'd broken her down so quickly. Her desire not to grace a man's bed had been foolish. He knew it the minute he kissed her. She wanted him as badly as he wanted her. It would have been only a matter of time before it happened. It was a good thing he was able to convince her sooner rather than later. The thought of bedding the other women had been tempting, but not practical since Belle was the one he wanted.

* * * *

"At least dress warmly," Annie finally conceded. "With daylight, that north wind could pick up. It was fairly mild when Roy and I came over this morning, but you know how the weather can turn when you least expect it."

"I know," Belle agreed. "I've got on my long johns as well as my britches and shirt. Those, along with my coat and gloves I should keep me warm enough."

When she stepped out onto the porch, she saw Black and Roy leading her horse toward the house. At least they hadn't listened to Annie's protests about her going. She'd expected the temperature to be mild considering the snow last night, but instead it was crisp and cold enough for her to see her breath. She was glad she'd dressed for the cold weather.

In a way she wished Roy wasn't going with them. If they didn't find anything, it would have been the perfect opportunity to make love to Black in one of the caves and pretend they were Indians seeking shelter from the cold.

As soon as the thought crossed her mind, she dismissed it. Lovemaking was best enjoyed in the warmth and privacy of the bedroom, although she had like it when he took her on the east pasture.

"Are you ready to ride?" Black said as she came down the steps to join them.

"I am, and I have some sandwiches Annie packed for us in case we're still out at noon."

Roy laughed heartily. "That old woman worries far too much, but I guess that's why I love her."

After packing the sandwiches in their saddlebags, they rode out in silence. As they did, Belle thought about the tracks they left in the fresh snow. It was almost a shame to disturb the pristine whiteness, but she knew soon it would be crisscrossed with the tracks of other animals seeking food or going from one den to another.

They rode for almost an hour before coming to the caves dotting the bluffs. No tracks led to any of them making Belle believe this had become a wild goose chase.

"That first cave is the one where we found the bear," Roy said, pointing to the dark opening in the earth. "The second one is just an opening, not large enough for a man to even stand upright. It's the one on our far left that offers the best possibility."

Roy pointed to the cave and Belle looked in that direction as well. To her surprise, smoke came from the opening. There had to be someone in there to have a fire going.

They left their horses a ways back from the opening and each grabbed rifles before going the rest of the way on foot. Black was the first to enter the cave, his rifle in his right hand and his six-shooter in his left. Roy followed, leaving Belle to trail behind.

"Who are you?" she heard Black ask.

She couldn't make out the words the man spoke, and stepped closer inside in order to see what was evident to her companions. Once she did, she saw a man lying on the floor of the cave in front of a dying fire.

Black knelt next to the man. "I asked who you are." he repeated.

"My name's Martin Newman," he replied, his voice weak from the loss of blood. "I'm dying, but I need to have you let my wife know what happened to me. I…" The man's words were cut off by a fit of coughing. When he regained his composure, he held out a piece of paper to Black.

"Who hired you?" Black said without looking at the paper.

"Never got his name. He was a big man with sandy brown hair and a heavy mustache. He said he'd give us fifty dollars right then and there to take cattle from one end of his boss's ranch to the other. He said when we came back and told him the job was done, he'd give us another fifty dollars. The only catch was that when we were finished he said we'd have to leave the area. That made it a hundred dollars and that's a lot of money spilt four ways." Again the man began to cough. The few words he'd spoken seemed to have exhausted him.

Roy built up the fire, while Black and Belle assessed the man's injury. The bullet had done a lot of damage and with the amount of blood the man lost, they knew he could never make it to town. As it was, it looked like he was living on borrowed time because the wound was infected. The area around the bullet's entry point was red and pussy.

Following Roy's instructions, Belle went to the back of the cave to get some water. Even though the man tried to take a sip of it, the effort seemed to be too much. For the first time in her life she watched another human being die. It was terrible. His breathing became more and more ragged as time went on until at last he stopped breathing altogether.

Belle wept at the man's passing, but Black and Roy were already preparing his body to be put on the back of the horse they'd found hobbled at the back of the cave.

"The description that man gave certainly didn't match either Clayte or Joe," Black said once the man was securely tied to the back of his horse.

"No," Roy said, "but it fits his foreman Rance Landers. At least we've got a little more to go on now than we did before."

"It's too bad he died," Belle said with regret. "He could have implicated Rance once he got to town. Now it's just our word against his."

"I doubt Joe would have believed him," Black said. "He's in this as deep as Clayte, and he would have found a way to shut Newman up before he said much. It wouldn't be the first time a prisoner mysteriously died in his cell when he was about to name the people he worked for. It's best if we keep this information to ourselves for a while. Sooner or later either Clayte or Joe will tip their hand, and we'll be able to put them away where they belong."

Belle tended to agree with Black. When the two men pulled the sandwiches from their saddlebags and began to eat, she knew she couldn't stomach food right now. She'd just watched a man die and didn't particularly like what she saw. Instead of eating, she explored the cave.

Just as Roy had said, there was enough room for several men and horses. Crude pictures of animals decorated the walls. She studied the pictures and decided they were nothing drawn recently. Hundreds of years ago other men must have found this cave and had taken shelter here. It was entirely possible they had drawn the pictures to pass the time during the cold winter months when hunting was much harder than it was during the spring, summer and fall.

* * * *

"Whatcha got there?" Joe said as he came out of his office to meet them.

"Black and me decided to visit the caves to see if we could find that rustler who got away," Roy replied, dismounting from his horse to stand face to face with Joe.

"Looks like you found him all right," Joe said, picking the dead man's head up by the hair. "Don't suppose you got a name for him. I don't like burying men without proper names like I had to do for those last three you brought into town."

"He was dead when we got there," Black said. "We found this piece of paper along side him. The way it reads, it's the name of his wife."

He held out the paper to Joe so he could read it aloud. "My name is Martin Newman and I'm dying. Please let my wife know. Her name is Patricia and she lives in Omaha."

Joe started to crumple the paper, but Black stopped him. "If you won't honor a man's dying wish, I will. I won't let that woman go on wondering what happened to her husband."

"Don't see why," Joe said, spitting a stream of tobacco juice into the street. "He wasn't anything more than a low down rustler. He came a long way to do his business."

Black held his tongue. From the things he'd found in Newman's saddlebags it was evident he hadn't come to Montana with the intention of stealing cattle. He'd come to look for gold and, when he hadn't found it, took the easy money offered him to rustle cattle.

After taking back the piece of paper, Black and Roy remounted their horses and nodded to Belle. It was time to get back to the ranch and figure out exactly what was going on and who was involved.

* * * *

Belle was glad to be back at the house. The morning and early afternoon had been trying to say the least. Not only had she watched Martin Newman die, but she had been sickened by the way Joe acted. At one time she had considered him an honorable man. After the way he'd treated her when her cattle were disappearing and how he acted today she had no respect for him whatsoever. It was a wonder his wife could stand to be anywhere near him.

In the parlor, a fire burned in the grate and the women were relaxing, wearing dresses rather than the britches they wore when they were working.

"Did you find anything?" Kate said when Belle sat down on one of the chairs closest to the fire.

She related what had happened in the cave as well as in town. As she did, tears ran down her cheeks. She couldn't understand why she was crying or why she had cried at the cave. She didn't know Martin Newman, probably would have never met him if he hadn't survived the gun battle with Black, Roy, and the other ranchers, and yet his passing saddened her.

"So, what did he say about the man who hired him?" Lacy said.

"He gave a description. It could have easily been Rance, but Black doesn't want that to be public knowledge. He figures sooner or later Clayte will try to rustle cattle again, and he doesn't want to scare him off. From the way Joe acted when we were in town, I have no doubt he's in this as deeply as Clayte."

A knock at the door interrupted what her. Reluctantly, Belle left the warmth of the parlor to see who was calling.

To her surprise, Clayte stood on the porch. "I was just in town and heard about you finding the last of the rustlers. What in the hell were you doing going to that cave? Doesn't that drifter you hired have any more sense than to drag you out on a cold day like today, to say nothing about putting you in danger?"

Before Belle could answer, Black came up behind Clayte on the porch. "I can tell you ain't never tried to reason with Miss Barton, Mr. Adamson. I've found it's a bit like trying to talk a rattler out of bitin' you when you try to talk her into being sensible. She just didn't see eye to eye with Roy and me. Seems she's got this fool idea that since it's her cattle being rustled, she should be in on trackin' down the rustlers. At least she wasn't with us the night the lead was flyin' in all directions. Come to think about it, you weren't there either. 'Course before that night you weren't the one concerned about losing cattle to those rustlers. Then again, we did find some of your steers with the ones being driven across Double Bar B land. Why do you think that is?"

Belle watched as Clayte began to fidget. "My cattle are usually guarded better than those of my neighbors. It's entirely possible the rustlers saw my men riding nighthawk and decided to leave my cattle alone. That night, my men were in town socializing so to say. I had a talk with them, and it won't be happening again."

Black nodded. "Sounds reasonable. Now, just what did you come here to say?"

"I was concerned for Belle's safety. Anything could have happened to her going up to that cave with you and Roy."

"Ah, that's right, that first day we met you told me you and Miss Barton were getting hitched. It seems right funny she couldn't remember such an agreement when I asked her about it."

"Well, ah, well…"

"Don't stammer Clayte," Belle said. "I never told you any such a thing. As I recollect, I ordered you off the Double Bar B when you first mentioned it. I have no intentions of marrying you now or ever. If you didn't hear me when I told you the first time, I'll tell you again. You aren't welcome here."

"You'll change your mind, Belle. Mark my words. You'll change your mind. One of these days you'll learn you can't run this place with a run-down old man and a passel of whores. The way I hear it, this Texican of yours is planning to move on as soon as spring comes and the real work starts. He's just as lazy as any other Mex I've ever run across. He's using you, Belle. All he wants is three meals a day, a soft bed, and a bunch of whores to warm it at night."

Before Belle could respond, another rider came into the dooryard. "I've come out here to arrest you for murder, Black." Joe said, as he mounted the steps to the porch.

"Murder!" Belle exclaimed. "Why?"

"It's about that man you three paraded into town this afternoon. You had to have shot him from behind. He's the Crystal Creek Kid. Ain't no one faster than him. There's no way you could have killed him in a fair fight."

Belle watched as Black turned on Joe. "You're as crazy as a hoot. Did you even examine the body? When we brought in the bodies of the other three men we told you we'd winged one of them. Roy and I got to thinking on it and decided he couldn't have gotten too far with his wounds. So we went up to the caves to see if he'd gone there to hold up until he was ready to ride."

"And you made certain he wouldn't talk."

"We made certain of nothing. He was dead when we got there. Wouldn't have even known his name if he hadn't had that piece of paper in his hand with the name of his wife on it. As for him being the Crystal Creek Kid, I doubt it. I heard tell he's spending time in the Colorado State Penitentiary."

"But what about him being back shot?" Joe continued.

"The boy ain't lyin', Joe," Roy said as he and Annie joined the group. "I was in that shootout. In the dark it's hard to tell if you're shooting someone from in front or behind. It could have been any of us who shot him. I ain't no doctor, but I can tell you the wound that man had was from the front and didn't go out the back. It wasn't so much the bullet as it was the infection that killed him. Ain't never seen anything so infected in my life. It was enough to make me sick to my stomach. Now, if my word ain't good enough for you, maybe we'd all better take a ride into town and see the undertaker. The body won't do no lyin'. 'Course we could talk to them other ranchers who were with us the night of the raid. I'm sure they'd all agree about what happened."

"Well, I … I just thought…"

"That's your problem, Joe, you tried to think, and you ain't got the mind for it."

"But he looked a lot like the Crystal Creek Kid. I just got his wanted poster in a couple of months ago and…"

"Black told you that the man is in prison," Belle interrupted. "I know Black was a gunslinger. I can tell you that if I were in that line of business I would know where to find any man who might be a threat to me. Now I'll tell you, like I told Clayte, you aren't welcome here, so get off my property."

Belle watched as Clayte and Joe mounted their horses and prepared to leave. Once they were out of sight, she turned to Black. "Are you certain the Crystal Creek Kid is in jail?"

"I should be," Black replied. "I was there when the marshals arrested him in Colorado Springs. By that time, I was in the process of hiring out my gun. Him and me got right chummy. I knew he was wanted for bank robbery, and, when he tried to talk me into taking one of the big banks in Denver, I arranged for one of the marshals to arrest him. At his trial, he broke down and bawled like a baby. Said he was glad he'd gotten caught and not killed. Whenever I'm in Denver, I go over to the prison and look in on him."

"Did this man resemble the Kid?" Roy said.

"I suppose if you were only going on the wanted poster you could say so. He was about the same height and weight and his hair was the same color. That's about as far as it went. I know the Kid and this man wasn't him, not by a long shot."

* * * *

Black stomped the snow from his boots before entering the warmth of the kitchen. He had to send a wire to Ed so he could get someone to contact Newman's widow, but he didn't relish going into town.

"How far is the next town?" he said when he and Roy joined the women in the parlor.

"Why do you ask?"

"I need to send a wire to Ed, but I don't want to do it in Larson's

Gap."

"You can send it from here," Cara said. "We've got a telegraph line to the house for the passengers on the stage. Didn't you see the wire?"

Black shook his head. He'd been too occupied with both the rustlers and Belle.

"You can write it out and any of us can send it for you. We wouldn't even charge you for it," Kate said.

"I'd appreciate that."

Belle went over to the desk and brought him a pencil and paper so he could word the wire correctly.

ED – NEED YOU TO HAVE SOMEONE CONTACT ELIZABETH NEWMAN IN OMAHA – HER HUSBAND SHOT AND KILLED IN LARSON'S GAP – LETTER WITH DETAILS TO FOLLOW – BLACK.

Belle scanned the wire. "If you get that letter ready it can go on the west bound stage that's due in on Monday. They pick up mail here and drop it off as well. I usually pick up mail on Sunday when I go into church and drop it off during the week. From here it will go to Missoula and then on to Denver."

Black nodded. Once Belle went to send the wire, he sat down to work on the letter he needed to send to Ed.

Ed,

Things here are worse than you expected. I'm certain Adamson is behind the rustling and the sheriff is just as bad. Your Pa and me got caught in a raid on Belle's herd, only this time they weren't taking cattle, they were bringing them onto the ranch. There were steers from every ranch in the area, including Adamson's. Luckily, the other ranchers were with us, and we killed three of the rustlers and wounded the fourth. Of course, Adamson wasn't with us. He was home in his bed dreaming of framing Belle for the rustling since he thought the others weren't coming over to check brands until morning. The look on his face when we returned his steers was priceless.

Today your Pa and me went out to the caves to see if we could find the man who got away. We did, and he implicated the foreman over at the Diamond A. Of course, we told the sheriff the man was dead when we got to him. I didn't want to tip my hand.

Don't know when this will all come to a head, but when it does, I'll need back up. I'm sure Adamson and his crew are behind this, and the sheriff is in it up to his armpits. He even came out here today to arrest me. He said that the man in the cave was the Crystal Creek Kid and that I'd shot him in the back. Now if that ain't the stupidest thing I ever heard. The Kid is safe in jail, and, besides, I'd know him if I saw him and Newman certainly wasn't the Kid.

It was a good thing I had your Pa to back me up. It's hard telling what would have happened if that lame brained sheriff had gotten me in his jail. I don't cotton to necktie parties, especially when I'm the guest of honor. I'm certain Adamson put him up to it, especially since he was here when the sheriff arrived.

I'll keep you posted on the progress of the investigation. If I need help, I'll send you another wire.

There's another thing I want you to look into. It seems Belle has a kid back east. She wasn't more than a kid herself when some guy got her in a family way. She had the baby at a convent, and the nuns said they would find it a good home. I remember the nuns at the convent down by where I grew up and they were a greedy bunch. If the baby had been a boy, you can bet they would have found a family all right, but it was a girl. If these nuns are anything like the ones I knew, they would have kept the kid to turn her into a nun. If you can find out anything, I'd appreciate knowing about it.

By the time he signed the letter, Annie called them all to dinner. Even though the women had changed their clothes, the letter had taken precedence over doing the same. For one night they would have to take him as he was, without the fancy trappings of the suit Belle insisted he wear to meals.

Chapter Eleven

Black had been at the Double Bar B for over a month. He was no closer to having enough evidence to arrest the men he held responsible for the rustling then he was when he arrived.

It had been almost a month since he'd written the letters to Ed and his grandparents and sent the wire to Ed. He was pleased he didn't have to go into town to send something by mail. With the stage stopping twice a week, he was able to put his letter in the mail sack without having to answer a lot of questions.

He had told his grandparents to contact him through Ed and knew Ed would send any mail for him to Roy and Annie to avoid suspicion. No one would question a letter from Ed coming to them, but if one came to Black it would arouse suspicion as to who the hell he really was.

He had to admit, it was one of the easiest assignments he'd had in a long time. There was no need to worry about anyone guessing he was a marshal. Living and working at the Double Bar B was far from hard to take. Annie's meals were wonderful, and Belle's bed was even better. That woman was learning things the most practiced whores didn't know. It was entirely possible the women were lending a hand in her education, but he knew he had a hand in it as well.

The snow that had fallen the first week he was at the ranch continued until the entire countryside was covered with the white stuff. It was weather like this that made him question the reason he'd left East Texas in the first place. Snow and cold were not to his liking, not one bit.

Every day he rode out to check on the herd, but found no tracks other than those of the women and himself. He also rode up to the far east end of the ranch to check on the fence. It was something he felt he had to do, even though he knew there would be no more activity by the rustlers until spring. Once the cattle were moved to the better pasture afforded by the east range, Clayte and anyone else who was involved in this scheme of his would feel more comfortable about taking Belle's cattle.

"Got a couple of letters for you," Roy announced when he arrived with Annie so she could fix supper.

Black got up from his chair in front of the fire and greeted the older man. "You must have heard from Ed."

Roy nodded. "His letters to us are usually pretty chatty, but don't say a hell of a lot. It would make Annie happy if he wrote to say he'd met a wonderful woman, and they were planning on having a passel of kids."

Black held his tongue. He knew that would never happen. Ed wasn't interested in anything other than his job, and he certainly wasn't interested in women. Black was pretty sure that was one of the reasons he'd become a marshal in the first place. It gave him an excuse for not getting married. There weren't many women who wanted to be married to a U. S. Marshal because of the risk involved in the job. For one thing, you never knew where your next assignment would take you and, for another, a bullet could end a marriage quicker than scat.

Roy took the chair on the other side of the fireplace while Black opened the letter and began to read. In no time, Roy was snoring contently, his feet propped up on one of Belle's needlepoint footstools to take the best advantage of the warmth from the fire.

Black
We located Newman's wife. She sent me a letter from her husband written just before the last raid. It gives you a lot more information concerning the people who hired him to run those cattle from the Diamond A to the Double Bar B. That's the reason it took so long for me to send you an answer. I was waiting to get the letter from Deputy Marshal Davidson.

As for that other matter you wanted me to look into for you, I found Belle's daughter was never adopted. She's living at the orphanage where Belle gave birth to her and is being raised by the nuns. I've got all the information about it, if you want to do anything further.

I'm also enclosing a letter that came to the office for you from Mexico. Got it on the same day as the one from Nebraska.

Black shuffled the papers and slipped the rest of Ed's letter to the back of the stack of papers and looked for the letter from Elizabeth Newman. The other news from Ed could wait. This letter was more important to the case than anything else Ed might have to say.

The penmanship on the paper left a lot to be desired, but Black was able to make it out, even though it was stained with the tears of a wife who wanted her husband home with her.

Dear Lizzy,

Ain't struck it rich in either gold or silver, but did get a job today. I was at the saloon in town when this big galoot came up to me and asked me if I'd like to make some easy money. Paddy and Ian, you know them boys I met up with from Ireland, were with me and so was Slim, and we all agreed it was easy money. The man who hired us told us we only had to take the cattle from one end of his boss' ranch, the Diamond A, to the other, but it had to be done by night. At this point I don't care if it had to be done in a blinding snowstorm. My share of the money is twenty-five dollars and that's enough to get me home to you before winter sets in. If this hadn't come along, I would have had to go out to the Diamond A and ask them for a job. I wasn't looking forward to that. From what I've heard, Adamson is a real bear to work for.

We're to leave to do this job tonight, so I'll finish this letter up and get it to the postmaster before I leave. I love you and can hardly wait to get back to civilization. If I ever say I want to go looking for gold again, please give me a good swift kick in the pants.

"Something interesting in that letter?" Belle said as she entered the parlor.

"There sure is. I think there's enough evidence to accelerate the investigation. The description of the man who hired Newman coupled with this letter, I think we've got more information on Clayte than we did before it arrived."

"So when do you arrest him?"

He sensed a hint of sadness in her voice. The sooner he arrested Clayte, the sooner he would be leaving the Double Bar B for good. "It won't be happening until he makes the next move. It looks like you're stuck with me until the spring thaw when we drive those cattle back to the east range."

"In that case, I'll have to go and have a talk with Cara before we eat supper. That should give you time to finish reading your letters." She winked slyly before going out to the kitchen to give Annie a hand with the preparations for supper.

Black turned back to the sheets of paper in his hand. The one he had least expected to receive drew him like a magnet.

My Dear Grandson,

Your dear grandmother and I have said so many prayers and lit so many candles for you over the past fifteen years. It is with great relief that we read of your life.

When I told Theresa about receiving your letter, she too was relieved. She said to tell you she and Manuel are happily married and they have you to thank for it. When you left, she was carrying your child, and it was Manuel who said he would be proud to be her husband and the father to your son. He is a fine boy, and your grandmother and I see him often.

Manuel and Theresa have many other children and only those of us who know the difference can tell Manual is not the father of Jose. I can see so much of you in him. I wonder what you were like at fifteen. By that time, you had killed your first man. Jose is a fine scholar and has a desire for an education. I have told his parents that any of their children that want to go on to school can do so and I will pay for it, as I would have paid for your education if you'd wanted it. Jose will be going to Mexico City next year to study at the university. It is my prayer he will become a fine doctor or perhaps a lawyer.

Never fear, for there is still more money than I will ever spend in two lifetimes. When the time comes, my lawyer has been informed to find you and make certain that this rancho becomes yours. Even if you do not come back to Mexico, Manual and Theresa will be more than fair in their management of the property and will make you a very wealthy man.

I knew you had killed Slade long before we received your letter. News travels quickly, and I did meet the man who bought your mother's ranch. He has done a good job with it, and we are in touch on a regular basis. He keeps me informed on everything he hears about you because the news from Texas is sometimes very slow in reaching this remote rancho.

Now that you have broken your silence, I pray you will keep in touch with us and tell us of the life you are leading. I know it may be too much to ask, but perhaps God has sent you to this assignment as you call it, to find a woman to love. You are no longer the young boy who left us so long ago. You are a man, and as such you deserve a settled life with a good woman by your side.

I wanted that for your mother, but her lot in life was never to be a well-loved wife and mother. Never be ashamed of what she had to do to provide a home for you. She was a proud woman and would not take money from me. As such, she led a hard life, but I feel she gave you an education far superior to any you could have gotten from most parents.

You remain in our prayers.

Roy snored loudly and jumped in the chair across from Black, causing him to put down the paper without reading his grandfather's signature. He was glad the letter was written in Spanish. It probably wouldn't do for folks around here to get wind of the fact that at any time he could go back to Mexico and live the life of a country gentleman.

"Guess I fell asleep. Damn, I hate it when I snore so loudly I wake myself up."

Black agreed, but couldn't stop thinking about the son he would never know. With the news, his worst fear had become reality. He and Belle weren't so different after all. They each had a child they would never see. He knew it tore at her just as the news now tore at him. At least Manual was a good man. The boy could have a worse man for a father.

When Black had first come to Mexico after the death of his mother, Manual had been good to him. Black wanted to work out his frustrations, and the older man gave him all the hard work he could handle. It made the days easier. It was Manual who taught Black to shoot and spent hours with him as he practiced for both a fast draw and an accurate aim.

"Supper's ready," Belle called, interrupting his thoughts yet again.

As he got up to head for the dining room, he decided it was best for his son continue to think Manual was his father and his real grandfather was nothing more than a generous patron. It was far better to be the son of a respected vaquero and ranch manager than of Black Conley the gunslinger.

* * * *

Belle immediately noticed the change in Black's disposition. She couldn't help but wonder what he learned in the letters he had received from Ed.

"What did my son have to say in his letter?" Roy said, once they were seated and had their plates loaded with roast beef, mashed potatoes, and vegetables.

"He sent me a letter he'd received from Newman's wife. It seems he wrote to her just prior to the raid. He did everything but put names to Clayte and his foreman. With this information, all Clayte has to do is make one false move and we'll have him right where we want him."

Where did they want him? Even though she knew he was the one doing the rustling, she had such mixed emotions. She and Nettie were good friends. She didn't want to raise Nettie's children and yet they deserve much better than Clayte for their father.

It had been over a month since she'd spoken with any of the women about the orphanage, but with the closing of the stage line it would be a way to keep the women on the ranch. She certainly didn't know what she would do without them.

Around her the table conversation jumped from topic to topic until at last Black went out on the porch for a smoke. Leaving the clean up of the kitchen to the women and Annie, Belle grabbed a heavy shawl and went out to join him.

"Was there bad news in the letter from Ed?" she said once she stood by his side.

Black turned to face her. For a moment, she though she saw tears in his eyes, but dismissed the idea. Black wouldn't be crying over a letter from his boss. It was the moonlight playing ticks on her.

"I have a son, Belle. He's almost fifteen, and I'll never know him."

"A son?"

"Do you remember me telling you about Theresa?"

"The girl in Mexico?"

Black nodded. "She lost her virginity on the night I took her to my bed and so did I. When I left she was carrying my child. Now, my son calls the man who taught me to use a gun father and thinks of my own grandfather as a kind patron rather than his great grandfather."

"Is the man who married Theresa a good man?" Belle said.

"Very good. Fifteen years ago he was a vaquero on my grandfather's rancho. Now he manages the entire operation. I'm pleased to think my son has such a good father, but it saddens me to think I walked away from him in search of the life of a gunslinger."

"You did what you had to do," she said, thinking of her own daughter and the nuns who ripped the girl from her arms. "We aren't so different after all. I wasn't much older than you when I had my child. There was no way I could have provided for her. At least she has a home with two loving parents, rather than a child trying to raise a child." The thought of her little girl being raised by strangers brought unbidden tears to Belle's eyes.

"You regret leaving her behind, don't you?" Black said, as he enfolded her in his arms.

Belle sniffed loudly. "More than anything in the world. I know I couldn't have cared for her properly, but just knowing there's a part of me out there that I'll never know breaks my heart."

"I feel the same way about Jose. He is my son, and yet he will never know me. In my case it's best he doesn't find out about the dark side of his father. My life is nothing a young man should be proud of. My father tells me the boy is intelligent and will be going to the university in Mexico City next year. For me, it's enough to know he has grown into the man my grandfather wanted me to be."

"You shouldn't talk like that, Black. Your son would be proud to call you father, but he has never had the chance. Give me a child, Black. Give me a part of you to have for the rest of my life."

Black pulled back from their embrace and looked deeply into her eyes. "You don't mean what you're saying. We're both grieving the loss of children we can never claim. It wouldn't be right for us to bring a child into the world. I wouldn't be here to help you raise it, and you would come to despise me for leaving you alone. It wouldn't be fair to the child."

"Don't say that. I don't expect you to stay here just because of a child. Once the railroad comes to Larson's Gap, we will no longer be a stage stop. The women are thinking of opening an orphanage and using the addition to the house where the passengers stay for housing for the children. Our child wouldn't be an only child. It would be as though he or she had several brothers and sisters to grow up with and have for playmates. I would never hold you responsible for the care or support of our child. This may be my only chance to be a mother. Please don't deprive me of that honor."

He started into her eyes for a long moment. She couldn't help but wonder about the thoughts behind his dark eyes. Were his thoughts of the child he would never acknowledge, or were they that she had completely lost her mind?

When Black pulled her closer into his embrace, she couldn't help but question her reasoning. Could she raise a child alone? The answer was a resounding yes. If the child belonged to Black, she wouldn't care. She would have a part of him to cherish long after he was gone from her life and on to the next assignment. Although she told no one, she had stopped drinking the tea to prevent pregnancy about a week earlier. Now she was glad she did. With the letter from Ed giving Black the information he needed to arrest Clayte, she might not have had the time for the effects of the tea to wear off otherwise.

"Are you sure about this?" he said as he guided her back into the warmth of the house.

"Yes, I am. Does that upset you?"

"Not really. I would like to give you a son, but my concern is for your well-being once I'm gone. Would the child know about me, or would you keep my identity a secret?"

"I would tell our child of its father with great pride. There is no reason for any of us to be ashamed of you being its father and you would be welcome to visit any time you wished. I would never hold you here against your will, but I wouldn't keep you away either."

"This will take some getting used to. I think we need to go to bed and practice making a baby before we do it for real. There is no other woman who has ever been in my life that could be a better mother to my child."

"Not even Theresa?" she teased.

"Theresa is different. I never planned to leave her with my child. At that young age, I never even considered that such a thing could happen. With you, it's different. I know what the consequences of my actions are, and I'm ready to face them."

* * * *

Black considered Belle's proposal as they made their way to bed. His cock itched to be planted deeply within her, but he worried about the child she wanted. Was she telling him she was already pregnant? He doubted it. They had talked about it, and she'd told him that she'd been drinking the tea that prevented pregnancy since before his arrival. Surely that would keep his seed from taking hold and giving her a child.

Once they were alone in their room, he looked at her intently. "You aren't in a family way now, are you?"

Her smile said volumes. "Not yet. I wanted to see your reaction. I've been thinking about it for quite some time, but didn't say anything until I saw your expression after reading your grandfather's letter. I didn't mean to make you feel trapped."

Black ran his fingers through his hair. "Trapped ain't the word I had in mind. I was thinking more of you. You know I'll be leaving when this assignment is over. What will happen when the good people of Larson's Gap brand you a whore?"

Belle laughed as though he'd said the funniest thing in the world. "My dear Black, I was branded a whore on the day I turned down Clayte's first proposal, right after Pa died and Roy got hurt. Clayte made certain no man worth his salt would work for me. That was when I brought in the women. We learned how to run this ranch together. Everyone in town knew who and what they were and so they gave me that the name as well. I was a fool not play the part before this, but there was never a man I wanted in my bed as much as I wanted you."

Black pulled her into his arms and kissed her soundly. As his tongue played with hers, his cock swelled. Unable to control himself, he worked the buttons that went down the back of her dress until the garment was loose enough to slip off her shoulders and down to the floor.

He stepped back to gaze on her breasts as they strained against the thin fabric of her undergarment. Out of instinct and desire, he rubbed his thumbs over her nipples until they hardened into taut peaks.

"Not tonight," she whispered, as she pulled away from him.

He knew his disappointment showed on his face.

"Don't look so sad. We will make love. Only tonight, I will be the one in control. I have talked to both Lacy and Cara, and they have taught me a few tricks that I think you'll enjoy."

Black looked around the room and saw the silken ties he knew Cara enjoyed as well as the whip of soft leather. He didn't think he would like either. The thought of whipping Belle or being whipped by her weren't exactly to his liking. He also didn't know about tying her up to the bedposts. He'd never taken a woman by force and now wasn't the time to start. He was falling in love with Belle and refused to degrade her in such a manner.

"I don't know if I'm up to the strange things those women do."

A strange smile crossed Belle's lips. "You won't hurt me, and I won't hurt you. Tonight, you will be my prisoner and I'll be the one in charge."

Deftly, she helped him out of his clothes, kneeling in front of him to kiss the entire length of his cock. When he thought he could stand it no longer, she slipped the silken cords around his wrists.

"I know you're the lawman, but tonight you're my lawman as well as my prisoner and my sex slave."

He smiled at her words, but wondered why she thought having him bound would be such a pleasure. Feel of her hands and lips on his body forced him to hold his tongue. Instead, he lay on the bed and allowed her to do whatever she wished with him.

To his surprise, being bound with his legs spread eagle was the most erotic feeling he'd ever encountered in his life. Even with the lamp turned low, he could see her every move and appreciate the things she was doing to him.

She started by running her fingers up his legs until she reached his cock and his balls. Once there, she proceeded to suck him in the same manner Kate had. She even ran her tongue over his balls until he shuddered over such delicious torture. When she pulled one of his balls into her mouth, while manipulating the other between her fingers, he thought he would come before he ever slipped into her velvety folds.

"You are killing me woman. Free me from these bonds so I can…"

"Not on your life, Black Conley. Tonight belongs to me, and I intend to control everything that goes on between the two of us."

Instead of continuing what she'd been doing, she got to her feet and slipped out of her undergarments. As she stood before him, she fondled her breasts in the way he longed to do before she joined him on the bed.

For a few moments, she fondled his cock until it stood tall and straight. When she was pleased with its condition, she straddled him and rode up and down, sending his cock deeply inside her. He thrashed and moaned with the pleasure as she had done so many times when she'd lain beneath him.

When they finally climaxed, she rolled from on top of him and nestled beside him. "Are you going to untie me, woman?" he said.

She reached up and kissed him, tracing her tongue around the outline of his lips. "I don't know. I rather enjoy having you as my sex slave. I wonder if I could get you aroused enough to do it again while in this position."

"It is entirely possible, but I long to hold you in my arms and feel the silkiness of your skin beneath my fingertips."

She kissed him again and then untied his wrists. Once he was free, he turned her onto her back and grabbed her wrists, pinning them behind her head.

"What are you doing?" she said.

"I'm making you my sex slave. You should have a chance to experience the pleasure of being helpless and open to whatever I want to do to you."

In one swift movement, he tied her wrists as she had done his. It pleased him that she gave no resistance. Once her hands were tied, he did likewise to her ankles, making her, indeed his prisoner.

"That's not fair," she protested. "I didn't tie your ankles. Just your wrists."

Black smiled wickedly. "I could have broken those bonds any time I pleased. To be honest, I wouldn't have protested if you had tied my ankles, but of course you didn't, giving me the pleasure of doing so to you."

Before he began, he poured some water into a bowl and cleansed her pussy to ready her for more lovemaking. "What are you doing?"

"Cleaning the remnants of our lovemaking from your body. I enjoy the clean scent of you to that of my cum clinging to your pussy."

When he finished he cleaned himself and returned to the bed, ready and willing to love her completely throughout the night. He caught a glimpse of the feather she'd used so successfully on him. Until she was tied securely, he'd forgotten about it, but now it seemed like the ideal torture for what she'd done to him. Once he picked it up, he ran it through his fingers, remembering the delights she had given him when she ran it over his body.

He enjoyed the fact her eyes widened when he picked up the feather. It would be interesting to watch her reaction to this wonderful love toy.

After joining her on the bed, he loosened the binding on one of her ankles and picked up her foot, as though he wanted to examine it. Instead, he began to message the arch and between each of her toes. When he finished, he did likewise to the other foot, until she moaned with pleasure.

With each foot again securely bound, he ran the feather over the arch of each foot and then alternated legs as he trailed it up to her pussy. Each movement of the feather was mimicked with his fingers on the opposite leg, until tears of delight ran down her cheeks.

He spread her pussy lips apart and ran the feather over her clit as well as her cunt, until her pussy wept in anticipation of the act to come.

"You are evil, Black Conley," she gasped. "Take me and end this agony."

"Not just yet my dear," he declared, as he trailed the feather up her belly and used it on her sensitive nipples. At the same time, his fingers manipulated her clit before he plunged them deep inside her.

When he thought he could wait no longer to get the release he needed, he set aside the feather and slipped his cock into her velvety folds. As he pumped against her, her muscles contracted around him making him as much her prisoner as she was his.

They came together with more force than ever before. Reluctantly, he rolled off her and untied her hands and feet. With that done, he pulled her into his arms. It wouldn't be long before they were both asleep, but he wanted this time to bask in the afterglow of what had just transpired between them.

"Did you mean what you said earlier?" he whispered, just before he was about to drift off to sleep.

"Yes, I want your child. I know with your profession I can't have you, but I can have a part of you and that's all I ask."

He pulled her closer and fell asleep, dreaming of a child that would someday think of him as his pa, even though his name would be Barton.

Chapter Twelve

"We got hit again last night," Kate declared, when she returned from her morning ride."

"Again?" Black questioned.

"That's right. I just rode out to the canyon and the fence we put across the opening was cut last night. Guess the cold weather isn't stopping anyone."

Black pushed aside his uneaten breakfast and reached for his guns and coat. "I'm riding out there for a look-see for myself."

"I'm going with you," Belle declared.

"Not on your life. This is something I'm going to be doing alone. If I catch up with them, I don't want any of you in the way in case there's gun play."

"I'll go with you," Roy declared, getting up from the breakfast table. "I ain't got my guns, but I do have a rifle in the boot of my saddle that should take care of just about anything we find."

Black nodded. He'd seen the older man shoot and was pleased to have Roy watching his back.

"Take my guns," Cara said, pressing her gun belt into Roy's hands. "It's hard telling what you two will run into. It's better to be safe than sorry."

Roy took the guns from Cara and followed Black out to the barn to get their horses.

"I didn't think Clayte would try anything while it was still so cold out," Roy said.

"I've tracked my share of rustlers in my life, and I don't put anything past any of them," Black answered.

They followed Kate's tracks in the newly fallen snow to the canyon where then fence was cut. From beyond the downed fence, the cattle could be heard, calling to one another and pawing at the ground for the grass hidden beneath the snow.

The stupidity of cows never ceased to amaze Black. Why would they paw at the ground when there was plenty of feed in the shelters built around the edge of the canyon?

The tracks of horses and cattle leaving the enclosure were fresh. Considering the snow had fallen in the early evening, it was evident the raid occurred in the early hours of the morning. Rather than follow the trail, Black rode into the canyon to assess their losses.

Once deep into the canyon, he saw a riderless horse that seemed out of place among the milling cattle. As he rode closer, he saw a body lying on the ground. It looked as though the man had been caught in a stampede of the cattle and had been trampled to death.

"Oh my God!" Roy exclaimed as he knelt in the snow next to the body. "This is Zeek Willows."

Black dismounted and went to look at the body they'd found. He was used to seeing dead bodies, but not ones of men he'd ridden with just months earlier.

As soon as he, too, knelt beside Zeek, he could see the shallow rise and fall of his chest. "He's still alive," Black declared, "and he ain't been trampled, he's been beat up pretty badly and shot. Looks like someone wanted people to think it was our cattle that did him in or worse yet that he was one of the rustlers and we shot him trying to get away with our herd. Help me get him up onto his horse and then you take him back to the house while I see how many steers we lost last night."

There was no way other than to sling Zeek over the back of his horse and secure him by tying his wrists and ankles together to get him safely back to where Belle and the women could care for him. Black regretted doing such a thing to a living man, but he had no other choice in the matter. Zeek needed care and, since he was unconscious, he wouldn't feel the pain until he awoke. Hopefully he would awaken and be able to tell them who was responsible for this.

After Roy left him in the canyon, Black took a mental count of the cattle. There seemed to be few lost, maybe ten head at the most. It wasn't the cattle these men were after. This raid was meant to frame Zeek and nothing more.

With the fence repaired, Black followed the trail left by the cattle and riders. To his surprise, it led west rather than east and ended in a rocky area where following tracks was impossible. Even so he continued on until he came to another of the many canyons that dotted Belle's property. There he found not only Belle's cattle but also ones from Zeek's herd as well as Jeb's and Pete's. It was apparent that the rustlers were trying not only to put the blame on Belle, but also on Zeek.

After scouting the area, he realized the men who brought the cattle here had left through the rocks and their trail was impossible to follow.

Rather than riding back to the house, he made his way to Jeb's ranch. The older man was at the corral when Black rode in.

"What are you doing here, Conley?" Jeb said.

"Just came to tell you that your herd got hit again last night."

"Just how would you know that, if you and Belle weren't the ones behind this?"

"Kate rode out to check on the Double Bar B herd this morning and saw the fence was cut. When Roy and I went to investigate, we saw a body among the cattle. It was Zeek Willows. He's still alive, or at least he was when we tied him to his horse so Roy could take him back to the house to be helped. Someone shot him, but before they did they beat him up. I followed the tracks and found cattle from your place, Zeek's place, and Pete's along with Double Bar B cattle in a canyon at the far end of Belle's place. I could use some of your hands to help me drive them back to where they belong."

"Do you think Zeek is behind this?"

"I doubt it. Someone wanted it to look like he was and that we'd caught him in the act, but that's not the case. With luck he'll pull through and be able to identify the real rustlers. Once we get some of your men together, we can ride over to Pete's and then stop at Zeek's place and let his wife know where he's is."

"There's no need for that. Zeek has been worried about everything that's been going on. He sent his wife and kids to visit her folks in Laramie for a while. He's been at his place alone for the past two weeks. Guess that would make him an ideal target, since no one would miss him until this morning. We'll get some of his men to help us, though."

* * * *

Belle paced the kitchen nervously. She certainly didn't like the fact Black and Roy could be riding into an ambush.

"Just what did you see out there, Kate?" she said once she turned from the window.

"Like I said, the fence was cut and there were tracks leading to the east as well as to the west. It was hard to tell which way they came from and which way they went."

Belle breathed a momentary sigh of relief. "If there were tracks leading away from the canyon, it means the rustlers are long gone. Did you check to see how many head they got away with?'

Kate shook her head. I didn't want to ride in there alone. I thought I'd come back here and get help. I never considered the fact Black wouldn't want us coming along with him."

"I know we've become used to depending on him. Of course, the fact we haven't been hit since last fall makes a difference as well. I didn't expect to have to deal with any of this until at least April or May. I can't believe they're so brazen as to come this far onto our land in the hopes of raiding our herd. I mean when it first happened in October, it was because someone was trying to frame us, but now, in the middle of a blizzard, it's just too hard to comprehend."

"Someone?" Annie said. "Don't you mean that low down snake, Clayte Adamson, and his cohort, Joe Calhoun? You know as well as I do the two of them are thick as thieves and are in this together. I don't understand why Black hasn't arrested them long before this."

"Well, I do, or at least I think I do," Lacy replied. "Until Clayte makes a wrong move, it's our word against his. I talked to Black about it one day when we were riding the fence line and he told me he has to have solid proof before he can make his move. I can understand that."

"Guess I can too," Belle agreed. "It's best if we eat our breakfast and prepare ourselves for whatever Black finds up in that canyon."

Belle played with her food, all the time concentrating on the half-eaten breakfast left on the plate at Black's place at the table. She wondered if she wanted the rustlers caught at all. If they were, Black would leave the Double Bar B and her bed for good. She didn't know if she could take the loss of the man she'd come to love and wanted to father her children.

"I don't want any tea this morning," she declared, when Annie brought a cup of the steaming liquid to the table for her.

"Land sakes, child, have you lost your mind. I know you and Black are heating up the sheets on a nightly basis. Do you have any idea what could happen if you quit drinking this tea?"

Belle nodded. "I'll get in a family way with his child. I think there's something you all should know about me and then you'll understand why I'm so desperate to have a child."

"Are you talking about that business in Ohio?" Annie said.

Belle was shocked. "I … I didn't think anyone would know."

"That aunt of yours could hardly wait to write to Matt about how his daughter had turned into the town whore. She told him you'd been sent to a convent in order to hide her shame of the bastard you were carrying. Those were her words, not mine, mind you. It was no surprise when you showed up here without the child. We all knew the sisters at that convent wouldn't allow you to keep it. There's just one question I have."

"What's that?" Belle said, still in shock that her well-guarded secret was public knowledge even out here in Montana.

"Was it a boy or a girl? I would have loved either dearly, but those old black crows wouldn't give me the chance."

Belle couldn't help but smile at the description of the nuns who had cared for her. "They certainly weren't black crows. They thought they were doing the right thing for both my daughter and me. I was so young I couldn't have taken care of a child. I didn't know how folks would take it if I showed up here with a baby and no husband."

"Did you name her?" Lacy said.

Belle again nodded. "The nuns said it would be best if I gave her a name even though she would be adopted by a family who would rename her. In that way I could pray for her safety and mention her by name. I called her Laura Leigh. I'm afraid the nuns weren't overly happy with my choice since it didn't come from the Bible, but I didn't care. I just insisted she be baptized Laura Leigh, no matter what name her new folks gave her."

"What will happen when Black leaves here for his next assignment?" Cara said.

"I'll raise our child. You said you want to turn this place into an orphanage once the railroad comes through. If we do that, my child will have plenty of playmates. I've already told Black his presence isn't necessary, and he can visit whenever he wants. I also assured him our child would know who its father is."

"You told her about the orphanage?" Lacy said.

Cara nodded. "It seemed like the proper thing to do, since the stage line won't be coming through here anymore. There's a lot of extra room in that addition, and I just know we could make the children happier here than in some convent. We wouldn't be pushing religion down their throats. We'd be teaching them useful things."

"Useful?" Annie said. "Like being whores?' The question brought laughter from everyone around the table.

"You know it wouldn't be like that, Annie," Belle said. "I've been giving this a lot of thought, and, between you and me, we could teach the girls to cook and sew and keep house. As for the boys, we could teach them about ranching and by they time they came of age, they would be prepared to face the world. I remember the kids at the convent. They spent most of their days on their knees praying for the redemption of their souls because of the actions of their mothers. As I recall, there was never enough to eat and I heard the kids crying themselves to sleep at night. The only reason I allowed them to keep Laura was because they promised me that they had a family who would take her.

"At least here the kids would get to play outside and learn some skills to take them through life."

Before anyone could answer, they heard horses in the dooryard and hurried to the door to see who was coming. The sight of Roy leading a horse with its owner slung across it's back made Belle's heart sink. Had they run into the rustlers? Had Black been injured or worse yet, killed?

She pulled herself together and took a better look at the horse. It wasn't Black's appaloosa, instead it was a chestnut gelding. The man slung across its back was Zeek Willows.

"What happened?" Annie said as she ran out onto the porch.

"We found the fence cut and Zeek lying face down among the cattle. Someone went to great lengths to make it look like he was one of the rustlers and we killed him when he was making off with our cattle. We didn't lose many, just enough to send a message. Whoever shot Zeek wasn't very good, because he's still alive. He's hurt bad and it's not just from the gunshot. Someone beat him up pretty good. We've got to get into the house so we can make him comfortable. As soon as we do, I'll go into town and bring out the doc as well as the sheriff."

"I don't want that no good son of a…"

"Slow down, Belle," Roy cautioned. "I know what you think of Joe, what we all think of Joe, but we can't leave him out of this. If we do, we'll be sending the message we're guilty, which we ain't."

"Where's Black," Belle said, her tone one of defeat. "Did they get him, too?"

"Hardly. They were gone when we got there. It looks like they drove the cattle in from the east and out to the west. Black followed the trail while I brought Zeek back here."

"Do you think that was wise?" Belle said, unable to keep the concern from her voice.

"It was the only thing we could do. We had to get Zeek back here. I'll help you women get him in the house and then I'll go to town and fetch the doc."

Belle and Kate helped Roy lift the man's body down from the back of the horse and carry him into the house. By the time they got there, Annie had the downstairs bedroom opened up and the bedcovers stripped down to the sheets.

As soon as Zeek was in bed, Roy left for town. Alone with Zeek in the bedroom, Belle unbuttoned the blood-soaked shirt from his upper body and assessed the wound. The bullet had penetrated his chest, but on the right side and not the left, missing the heart, but rendering him unconscious. When they pulled him from the horse, she'd noticed the back of his shirt had no blood on it, indicating that the bullet was still inside his body.

"Get out of my way," Annie ordered. "I need to clean up that wound and wash some of the grime from him before the doctor gets here. I don't need you in my way."

Belle stepped back and watched Annie work. It could easily be Black who had been shot. Just the thought of it brought tears to her eyes. She told herself they were because the man and his wife were close friends, but she knew it was something else entirely. Her tears were for Black and, that in his line of work, he could be shot at any time or in any place in the line of duty.

* * * *

Black herded the Double Bar B cattle into the box canyon and watched, as the hands from the other ranches became specks on the horizon. Pete and Jeb made no move to follow their hands, instead they stayed with Black until the Double Bar B steers were secured and the fence had been mended.

"Thought we'd go back to the house and check on Zeek," Pete said when he rode up next to Black.

"By the looks of the sun, it's almost noon. You boys are welcome to stay and have dinner with us. I'm certain Annie is expecting extra.

Wouldn't want to send you away hungry."

"Sounds like you're runnin' the show over here," Jeb commented. "What would Belle think of you extending her hospitality without asking her first?"

"She'd think the same thing I do, I'm bein' neighborly. Now if that don't suit you, then I guess you won't be eatin' with us, will you?"

"Black's right," Pete agreed. "Ain't never heard of Belle turning anyone away from her table. I even heard Joe Calhoun was eatin' with her that first day Black was here. Besides, I'm so hungry I could eat my horse, but one of Annie's meals sounds a hell of a lot better to me than horse meat."

The three of them rode toward the ranch in silence. Black figured it had to be because they were worried about Zeek. From what he'd seen of the wound, the man was shot bad. It was hard to tell just where the bullet went in, but one thing was for sure, it hadn't come out.

It didn't take long to arrive at the ranch house. When they did, the first thing Black noticed was the carriage that belong to the doctor as well as Joe Calhoun's horse. Annie would certainly have a full table for dinner today.

Roy greeted them as soon as they entered the house. From the look on his face, Black knew the situation wasn't good.

"So, you finally decided to show your face," Joe said as he got to his feet. "I figured you probably lit out after you tried to kill Zeek. I should arrest you."

"Arrest me?" Black said. "Roy and I are the ones who found Zeek and sent for you and the Doc. I didn't light out, as you put it. Since I knew Roy could handle things here at the house, I went to get Jeb and Pete. Together, we brought the steers from all four ranches back here and their men took them to where they belong."

"That's right, Joe," Pete said. "After Black trailed our cattle to where them rustlers stashed 'em, he came and got us. We took charge from there. It's funny, this time there wasn't one Diamond A steer in the bunch. Why do you think that is?"

"I wouldn't know, and I don't care. I just want to get the man responsible for Zeek's injuries."

"Well, you won't find him here," Jeb declared. "I suggest you ride over and talk to Clayte. Seems he's the only one of the neighbors left untouched. I'm willing to bet that he's up to his armpits in this mess and for that matter, I'm not too sure about you either."

"I … I'd never…"

"Maybe not, but you're damn quick to point fingers. If you recall, we were with Black when the rustlers hit us the last time. If he was in on it, do you think he'd willingly let us check the brands on the Double Bar B herd? For that matter, the rustling started long before Black arrived in town, so I don't think you can pin it on him so easily."

Before anyone else could speak, Dr. Franklin entered the kitchen. "I got the bullet out of him." He slumped into one of the kitchen chairs. "A couple of inches to the left and we would have been calling the undertaker. He'll be fine, but I'm afraid he'll have to stay here for several days until he can regain his strength. He took one hell of a beating. I'm certain whoever did this brought him over here after they beat the shit out of him and then shot him."

"I couldn't agree more," Black said. "There was a lot of blood in the area where we found him, but no sign of a struggle. It was as if someone had dumped him there and then shot him. It's possible he was unconscious when they brought him where they intended to kill him. It would be the perfect way to pin all of this on Belle. Unfortunately, they're a greedy lot. They must have decided to take one last batch of cattle and make it look like Zeek was one of them. 'Course they weren't too smart about it. I'm certain they thought we'd think the cattle trampled him. I've seen men caught in stampedes before, and they ain't beat up the way Zeek was."

"I need to get into town and send a wire to Zeek's wife," Joe said, pushing back his chair. "She's visiting her folks in Laramie. She should know what's going on so she can get back here to care for him."

"There's no need for you to go into town to do that," Belle said. "We have a telegraph here for the stage line. We can send the wire to Bessie right now."

Black studied Joe's face. Either he was a complete idiot, or he hadn't remembered about the telegraph line running to the Double Bar B.

"Guess you're right. We should send it right away."

"Any one of the women can do it for you," Black said. "They all know how to run the wire, but you shouldn't be so quick in bringing Mrs. Willows and the children back here. These men are desperate. They hit Zeek once and there's nothing to say they won't try to do it again. I'd feel better if there weren't women and children in the middle of it when if it happens. They're safer in Laramie than they are here at the moment."

Joe shook his head, but made no reply to Black's logic. The others looked at him in surprise. He certainly hoped he hadn't said too much and given away the fact he was a marshal sent here to investigate the rustling going on all over the place.

Chapter Thirteen

Black felt the tension that filled Belle as soon as he pulled her into his arms. The women had insisted they be the ones to take turns sitting by Zeek's bedside to tend his needs. Even so, Black knew Belle wanted to help as well. He was secretly glad the women had taken the responsibility from her to allow her to be in his bed.

"What's wrong," he said, before leaning over to nuzzle her neck.

She wrapped her arms around his neck and her tears wet his cheeks. "Make love to me. Give me your child."

"We already had this discussion, and I agreed to everything you asked. There's something else bothering you, something else that's making you cry. What is it?"

"It could have been you dragged from your bed, beaten senseless, and then left to die. I couldn't stand it if it were you. Maybe it's for the best if you didn't continue this investigation. It's too dangerous for you."

"Honey, living is too dangerous for any of us. You could ride out to check on the cattle and be thrown from your horse and die. It doesn't mean you don't continue to do your work. It's the same with me. Ever since I was fourteen years old, I've known someday there'll be a bullet with my name on it. It's the chance I took when I decided to be a gunslinger and one that continued to follow me when I became a lawman. It's the cost of living for all of us."

Belle sniffed loudly. "Then give me a part of you I can have forever. One that won't be riding away to the next assignment anytime in the near future."

Black knew exactly what she wanted. She wanted a child, but could he give her that and ride away without caring? He doubted it. Something told him if she carried his child, he'd give up the profession that had

142

been his for so long. He'd missed the entire life of his son in Mexico. He couldn't do the same thing to any child born of his blood in Montana.

He'd watched her intently at supper and noticed she took her tea from a pot separate from the women. Living with the whores on his mother's ranch, he knew the effects of the tea would linger for a while. Maybe they would linger long enough Belle wouldn't be carrying his child when he left the Double Bar B for his next assignment.

Was that what he really wanted?

He knew it wasn't. He wanted Belle to be his forever, but could he give up the life he'd lived for so long? The answer was a resounding yes, but the doubt that lingered was what would happen when he told Ed he wanted to quit being a marshal. Ed had turned Black's life around less than ten years ago. Could he turn his back on the only man he had ever called friend?

He shook his head, refusing to think of what his betrayal of Ed would do to their friendship. Instead, he lifted Belle in his arms and carried her to the bed.

Earlier they had pulled back the comforter and he knew the sheets would be cold against her bare skin. Wanting to keep her from feeling the cold, he sat down on the bed and pulled her on top of him. The chill of the sheets, prompted him to lay down without shifting her position so they could be warmed from his body before he changed places with her.

"Do you want me on top?" she said.

"Not tonight. I'm just warming the sheets for you." Her breasts dangled in front of her like a tempting play toy. When he reached up to play with them, she didn't protest. Instead, she leaned forward until her nipples were so close to his mouth, he couldn't resist pulling her down until she was laying on top of him so he could suckle her.

The mewing sounds that passed her lips were enough to arouse him completely. Unable to wait any longer, he flipped her on her back and drove his cock deeply into her body. She yelped as though surprised by his intrusion, but he knew this was what she wanted.

As he pumped against her, she wound her legs around his waist as though trying to pull him more deeply into the depths of her body.

"They say that the deeper the penetration, the more likely it is that a woman gets pregnant," she gasped.

He wanted her to shut up, but said nothing. Instead, he plunged deeper into her body than he had on any other occasion. Even the thought of leaving her with his child, couldn't dampen his pleasure at this moment. She was his and his alone. Knowing another man had been the first didn't bother him. Just the fact that he knew her heart belonged to him was enough. She had been called a ball buster and had allowed no man in her bed before he came to the Double Bar B. One kiss had changed all that, and he was glad to be the one to have awakened her sexually.

When they finally came together, the ecstasy was beyond compare. He'd been with women before — paid companions who had brought him to climax — but it had never been like this. Somehow, he knew it would never be like this with any other woman. Belle Barton had spoiled him for life. She was the only one he ever wanted in his bed.

"I stopped drinking the tea," she whispered, as they lay entwined in each other's arms.

"I noticed. There's just one thing you should keep in mind."

"What's that?"

"I don't want you disappointed if it doesn't happen right away. The effects of that tea take a while to wear off, or at least that's what my ma always said. I want you to have my child, but I don't want to leave here with you disappointed because it didn't happen. There are couples who wait years for a child that never comes."

Belle snuggled closer to him, giving him warmth in comparison to the chill of the room. "I know. Annie told me the same thing earlier. She also told me about how she and Roy tried to have more kids, but it wasn't meant to be. They lost several children after they had Ed and then she didn't even get pregnant again. I just pray that won't be the way it is between you and me."

He pulled her closer and cupped her breast in his hand as he started to doze back off to sleep.

"Belle, Black, come quick, we need you down here!"

Kate's frantic shouts woke Black. He bolted out of bed and pulled on his clothes as quickly as possible, leaving Belle to do the same as he strapped on his guns and ran barefoot for the stairs.

He was only half way down when the orange blaze coming through the window sent him back up for his boots.

"It's a fire!" he exclaimed as he pulled on his boots and again started down the stairs with Belle right behind him.

The sight of flames licking at the roof of the barn was coupled with that of the women running in and out of the burning structure to get the horses to safety.

After grabbing his coat, he joined them in their frantic efforts. "You women man the buckets," he ordered. "I'll get the rest of the stock out of there. It's not a place for any of you. It's too dangerous."

One by one he led the rest of the horses to safety and then went back in to get the saddles and other tack out of the burning building. Each time he left the barn, he felt a shower of water dripping from the burning roof. The chill of the early morning hours combined with the cold water to make him shiver, but it wasn't enough to stop him from getting out as much of the gear as possible.

"Take a rest, Black," he heard Roy say. "Between the women and me, we got the fire out. We lost the roof, but it could have been a hell of a lot worse."

Black leaned against the wall of the barn and gasped for breath. When he did, the smoke he'd inhaled brought on a fit of coughing. "Who could have done this?"

As soon as the words passed his lips, he knew the answer. It had to be the work of Clayte and whoever else was in this with him.

"Think about it, Black," Roy replied. "It had to be Clayte. This whole thing is getting out of hand. I think we should send a wire to Ed and ask for reinforcements."

"I tend to agree with you. I usually don't ask for help, but things normally don't take this long. Adamson is a threat and one I don't like. Who knows what he'll try next? We were damn lucky it wasn't the house he set on fire. There's no way we could have gotten Zeek out of there."

"Annie's put on a pot of coffee. I think we all need it. It's cold as a witch's tit out here, and, if you don't get out of those wet clothes, you'll catch pneumonia. Belle needs a lawman not another patient on her hands."

Black agreed and followed Roy to the house. The morning sky was just starting to brighten, even though sunup was a long way off. As it did, he turned back toward the barn to see it standing starkly against the horizon without its roof. In the corral, the horses milled around, still frightened by the lingering smell of the smoke that hung in the cold morning air.

* * * *

"I'll ride into town and get the lumber we need to repair the roof," Belle announced as they ate breakfast.

"I'm going with you," Black declared.

"I don't think so. If you go with me, it leaves this place unguarded. We can't risk anything more happening, especially with Zeek still unconscious in the downstairs bedroom."

"Belle's right," Roy said. "I'll ride into town with her. It's best you stay here in case Zeek comes to his senses. In the meantime, one of the women can send a wire to Ed asking for his help."

"What about the stage that's due in tonight?" Kate said. "Do we dare put the passengers in the middle of this mess?"

"Of course we can't." Belle replied. "When you send that wire to Denver, send one to the stage stop before this one and explain we have trouble here and we don't want the stage stopping tonight. It's early enough we can catch the driver before he leaves."

Belle finished her breakfast and hurried upstairs to change her clothes before going to town. Once in the bedroom, she looked at the bed where she and Black shared their many hours of pleasure. The covers were rumpled from last night's lovemaking, but she knew soon Annie would make it and erase all signs of what she and Black had shared.

She ran her hands over the sheets he had warmed with his body hours earlier and thought about the lie she'd told everyone. She had quit drinking the tea, but it hadn't been last night. She quit weeks earlier. She knew, even then she wanted Black's child.

Once she changed into clothing appropriate for a trip to town, she put her hand over her flat stomach. "Dear God," she prayed, "let me be carrying Black's child. Things are moving so quickly he could leave any day now. I want part of him so badly I know I did the right thing by not drinking the tea for these past couple of weeks."

* * * *

Black watched as Belle drove out of the dooryard, followed by Roy on his horse. The women were taking the time to rest because they'd been up all night and the light snow now falling would hamper anything to be done outside. It would take a while for Belle and Roy to return with the materials to replace the roof on the barn. That left him with nothing to do but to sit by Zeek's bedside.

"I won't leave you here with Zeek for too long," Annie promised. "I have to get upstairs and make the beds, but as soon as I finish, I'll be down here to spell you."

"It's no trouble, Annie. After last night, I need a little sittin' time. Last night was hard on all of us."

"You're a good man, Black Conley. I just hope you can put an end to all the goings on around here."

Black seated himself next to Zeek's bed and prayed Annie was right. The way things were going he wondered if he'd ever have the evidence he needed to stop the raids on Belle's ranch. He needed to put the men responsible behind bars and get on with his life.

If Belle got pregnant with his child, would he get on with his life in the way he had before? He doubted it. Things would never be the same for him. He couldn't leave another child without a father. Maybe it was time for him to settle down.

Black dozed off only to be awakened by Zeek's moans. The sound in the previously quiet room brought him to full attention.

"Zeek, can you hear me?" he said as he got to his feet and moved closer to the old man so he heard his whispered words.

"Black? What are you doin' here?"

"You're at the Double Bar B, Zeek. Someone wanted you dead. It's a wonder we found you when we did."

"Wouldn't have happened if I hadn't been ridin' nighthawk on my herd. Damn fools tried to take my cattle. When I recognized them, they started beatin' on me."

"Who were they?" Black said, getting even closer.

"You were right, they were from the Diamond A. I didn't see Clayte with them, but that foreman of his, Rance, was there. He's the one who beat me while the others held me."

Black inhaled deeply. This was the information he needed. Even if one of the women had already sent a wire to Ed, he could send another one and request back up as soon as possible. It would have been different if the hands on this ranch were men, but women didn't stand a chance against the Diamond A bunch. There was no way he wanted to put any one of them in danger. Especially not Belle, and she was the one who would insist on being smack dab in the middle of everything.

"I think that's just the information we need," Black said. "You need to rest, but until this is settled, no one will know you've come around."

"What do you mean until this is settled? Just who are you, Black? I know your reputation with a gun, but there's more to it than that. You ain't no ordinary drifter, and you certainly ain't no ranch hand."

"It don't matter none who or what I am. For now it's best you think

I'm what I've told everyone else I am, a retired gunslinger who drifted into this town looking for a job. Annie should be down from upstairs by now. I'll send her in to sit with you."

Black started to get up to leave, but Zeek's hand on his arm stopped him. "My wife, has anyone let her know what happened?"

"One of the women was going to send her a wire this morning. She should have it by now. We decided it was best if we told her not to come back home until the danger is over. They've hit you once and there's no telling when or if they'll hit you again. Your men are watching your herd and from what I can tell they're all mighty good with their guns. I don't think you'll have anymore trouble, but one never knows."

Once Black left the room, he saw Annie coming down the stairs. "You should go in a sit with Zeek," Black advised her. "He's conscious and could use some of that broth you've got simmering on the stove. I've got to send another wire to Ed."

Annie agreed and left Black standing alone in the parlor. From the room Belle used as her office, he could hear the clicking of the telegraph. As soon as he entered the room, he saw Kate taking down the message spelled out by the dots and dashes the clicks indicated.

"It's for you," Kate said, without turning around.

"From Ed?"

Kate nodded, as she handed him the neatly printed piece of paper.

Black scanned the words and understood their meaning. It hadn't come from Ed, but it was from Denver. Ed's superiors were strapped for men, but they would round up anyone they could and come out to help as soon as possible.

"I've got another wire to send," Black said, after reviewing the message.

NEED HELP IMMEDIATELY IF NOT SOONER – HAVE THE PROOF WE NEED – DON'T TRUST THE SHERIFF – BLACK

Kate read the message before looking up at him with questions in her eyes. "If you've got proof, it had to come from Zeek. What did he say?"

"It's not for public knowledge, but he told me it was Diamond A hands who raided his ranch the other night. If he hadn't been riding nighthawk, he wouldn't have known. As soon as he recognized him, they beat him senseless and tried to kill him. As far as anyone outside of this house is to know, Zeek is still unconscious."

Before Kate could reply, the kitchen door opened and Roy started calling Belle's name. Black left Kate to send the message and went out to the kitchen to find out why Roy was calling for someone who should have been with him.

"Belle's been with you," Black began, "so why are you yelling for her like a banshee?"

"Because she ain't with me. I went over to the sheriff's office to report the fire and before I could get back to where I'd left her, she took off with the lumber to repair the roof. Ned Palmer over at the store told me she took off like a bat out of hell. He said she told him to tell me she wanted to get back here so you and the women could start repairing the barn. I thought she'd be here, but the buckboard and team aren't anywhere in sight."

"That bastard Adamson has her. We just have to figure out where."

"How can you be so sure it's Clayte who is behind this?" Roy said.

"First it's my job, and, secondly, Zeek regained consciousness. He told me it was Clayte's foreman, Rance was with the rustlers. It didn't take much to figure out the rest of it based on the suspicions we've all had ever since I got here."

"Suppose not. Do you think we should wait for them to send a ransom note?"

"They won't be asking for money. Clayte wants Belle as well as the Double Bar B. We just have to figure out where they've taken her."

"I remember there was an old line shack not far from our property line. I helped Clayte's daddy build it. That was back when there were no fences separating the two ranches. We both used it when our men were out on the range keeping the herds separated."

Black listened as Roy gave him the directions he didn't need. He'd seen the shack when he'd been riding the fence line on that first day and again later when he'd gone out to check for damage after the night they'd killed the rustlers.

* * * *

Belle squirmed against the bindings that cut into her wrists as the buckboard bounced across the rangeland. They'd left the main road some time earlier, and they had crossed over onto Diamond A land at least ten minutes ago.

If only she hadn't been in such a hurry to get back to the ranch. If only she'd waited for Roy, but she'd been too independent. She cursed the silly law that prohibited the wearing of guns by women while in town. If she'd had them strapped on, she would have at least been able to defend herself. As it was, she only had her rifle and that was in the bed of the wagon, too far out of reach for her to handle the team and reach for it at the same time.

The men seemed to have come out of nowhere, and, when they caught up with her, they were quick to stop the team and jump into the wagon. One of them tied her hands while the other took over the reins.

As soon as she saw the line shack come into view, she knew exactly where they were. Would anyone else think to look so close to home? She doubted it.

The man beside her pulled the wagon to an abrupt halt leaving her to totter unsteadily. It didn't take long for the masked leader to pull her from the seat of the wagon and drag her toward the shack.

"Now what do we do with her, Rance?" one of the men said.

Belle strained to recognize the voice that sounded so familiar and yet she couldn't place.

"Shut your god-damned mouth, Charlie. Now she knows who we are."

Charlie McCasslin. She should have known. She'd fired that lazy bastard last year. This has to be his idea of revenge.

"What difference does it make? She won't be leaving here. I told you we should have set that house on fire and done away with the whole nest of 'em. Especially that fancy gunslinger she hired. But no, you said only to set fire to the barn. Now God only knows when Zeek will come around and tell them it was us."

"Zeek ain't gonna come around and you know it. He might still be alive, but he doesn't have a snowball's chance in hell of recovering. I should know. I'm the one who pumped lead into him. I might have been a bit off target, but trust me, he ain't gonna make it."

"Well, at least this is one time this bitch won't bust my balls. I plan to show Miss High and Mighty here what it's like to be fucked by a real man."

Belle gasped as Charlie started to unbutton his pants. They planned to rape her and probably kill her so Clayte could get title to the Double Bar B. She couldn't let that happen, yet how could she stop it?

The inside of the shack was overly warm from the fire that burned in the stove. Once inside, Rance untied her long enough to take off her coat, blouse and undergarment. When she was naked to the waist, he looped the rope around her wrists and shoved her down on the bed.

"What are you going to do to me?"

Rance leaned so close to her face she could smell his fetid breath. "The boss said we could have a good time with you, just as long as we didn't touch that virgin cunt of yours. Once we get those boots and britches off, there's any number of things we can do to satisfy ourselves."

Belle cringed. What would Clayte do once he realized her virginity was non-existent? Would he kill her?

"I plan to be first," Charlie said, as he pushed Rance aside. "She busted my balls when I worked for her, now I plan to show her women are good for only one thing and it ain't bossin' around men."

"What did I ever do to you?" Belle pleaded as he pulled her britches and drawers from her body to give him a good look at her.

He grabbed her wrists and brought her to her feet before attaching the rope to one slung over the rafters. "You thought you were so high and mighty then, well, you weren't. All you ever did was sashay around in front of me and tease me with something I couldn't have. Well, maybe I can't fuck you the way the boss plans to do, but I can make you regret everything you ever did to me."

Unable to defend herself, Belle could do nothing but endure Charlie's rough hands as they pinched her nipples and slipped between her legs to do the same to her clit.

When she felt like she could endure the torture no longer, Rance pushed Charlie out of the way. "You ain't no better than a stag in rut. All they do is poke at the females and fight with the males for territory. There's only one way to break a bitch and that's with a whip. I asked the boss, and he said it was time this bitch knew her place. As long as we don't fuck her the way he intends to, we can do whatever we want to her."

Belle gasped as Rance produced a cat of nine tales whip, much like the one Lacy kept in her bedroom for special customers. She watched in horror as Rance ran the strands through his hands before letting them loose on her bare breasts. The pain was horrible, but she refused to cry out.

"Now," Rance said, as though he was a schoolteacher giving a lesson, "you give her pleasure, so she equates the pain with the reward of pleasure."

He stuck his hands between her legs and played with her clit until she thought she would come at any moment. Just before she came in his hand, he pinched her clit and picked up the whip again. This time he flicked it over the tender area of her inner thighs. Then he instructed one of the men to start sucking on her injured breasts.

To keep her mind from the man who flicked his tongue over her sensitive nipple, she tried to concentrate on the conversation between Charlie and Rance.

"Where did ya learn to do that, Rance?" Charlie said.

"Spent a winter stuck in Deadwood. The only work I could get was at a whorehouse keepin' the women in line. The old gal who ran the place gave me this whip and showed me how to use it."

"Why would you have to do a thing like that?"

"Them whores were a theivin' bunch. Sadie caught them stealing more than once. One time one of the girls rolled a prospector for his poke and killed him in the process. Now Sadie didn't want the law comin' to her place, so we chucked the old man into the river. When we come back, Sadie made all the girls watch while I beat that whore to death with this whip. All the while I was doin' the pain and pleasure thing that Sadie showed me. It was almost as good as fuckin' one of them whores all night. When I finished we chucked her in the river right alongside the old man."

Belle thought she was going to be sick. The look on Rance's face when he described the terrible thing he'd done was enough to turn anyone's stomach. He was enjoying it. She didn't have to look down at his crotch to know he was hard. Since Clayte had given instructions not to take her the way a man takes a woman, sooner or later he'd have to go outside and relieve himself.

Her inner thoughts were interrupted when Rance pulled the man away from her and again raised the whip. To her horror, she could feel a wetness pooling between her legs. Rance was right. She was beginning to equate pleasure with pain.

"That's enough for now," Rance said. "We have to let the boss know we have her. Frank, you ride back to the house and tell him. I'd go, but I don't trust either of you to keep your hands to yourself while I'm gone. If the boss took her and found out you'd taken her virginity before he got her, there'd be hell to pay, and you can bet I'd be diggin' more than one grave."

The man who had sucked her breast came toward her to loosen the bindings on her hands and take her to the bed probably full of bugs. The way the cabin smelled it had housed many unwashed bodies in the past, and it was unlikely the men had gone outside to relieve themselves in the winter.

"Can I at least have my clothes back?" she said, speaking for the first time since the ordeal of pain and pleasure had begun.

"Much as I enjoy the sight of your naked body, Belle, I suppose we should give you a blanket to cover yourself. Wouldn't do for you to get sick and die on the boss before he gets a child from you. We'd all be lookin' at an early grave if that was the case."

"It ain't fair," Charlie complained. "I didn't get a chance at her."

"Take your chance now, but with all your clothes on. I don't want you getting' any wild ideas about fuckin' her right and proper."

Once Belle was on the bed, her hands were tied over her head, exposing her breasts to the prying eyes of these men. It didn't come as a surprise that once Frank left, Charlie climbed on top of her.

First he tried to kiss her, but she turned her head so his mouth came in contact with her ear rather than her lips. The only thing that got her was a slap that stung as badly as the whip had earlier.

"What the hell do you think you're doin'?" Rance demanded.

"It's my version of your game of pain and pleasure."

"You'll bruise her."

"Isn't that what you did with that whip of yours? She's got welts on her backside as well as her legs and tits. They'll pain her for a good while longer than the little love tap I just gave her."

He shifted his weight and shoved his knee between her legs so that he could reach her clit with one hand while sucking her breast. Alternately he'd bite her nipple and pinch her clit until she thought she was going to pass out from the agony.

Abruptly, Rance pulled Charlie away from her. "That's enough," Rance declared. "You don't want her all wore out before the boss gets here. He said we could watch how he takes a virgin, considering it ain't likely any of us will ever get the chance. That's one show I want to see. I hear tell they squeal like a stuck pig the first time a real cock slides in and breaks that barrier."

"I know they do," Charlie said as he rubbed the bulge in his pants. "The first gal I fucked was a virgin. She cried the whole time, but I ain't ever have a cunt that tight again. I can almost feel it constricting around my cock just thinkin' about it."

Belle tried to close out the vulgar conversation Charlie and Rance engaged in, but to do so brought on the pain of her injuries. Her breasts ached, not only from the whip, but also from the way Charlie had raked his teeth over her nipples. Her legs and backside stung from the welts left by the whip and her clit, well as the rest of her woman's parts, felt like it was on fire.

With no one knowing where she was, she would have to endure the humiliation of being raped by Clayte while his men watched. Just the thought of it brought tears to her eyes, but she refused to shed them. She vowed not to give these pigs the pleasure to see her woman's weakness. At least she hadn't cried out when they beat her so viciously.

She was hardly aware of the end to the conversation. The only thing she felt was the scratchiness of the wool blanket they threw over her naked body.

Chapter Fourteen

"I'm going after her," Black declared. "I know where that shack is. Kate, you come with me. The rest of you stay here."

"Let me come, too," Lacy pleaded.

"I can't chance it. You're not as good with a gun as Kate. There's too much of a chance you'd get hurt."

"And you and Kate won't? I may not be a crack shot, but I know my way around whips. I've been practicing with that one of yours all winter, and I can be as deadly as you are with your guns. At least let me come along to watch your back."

"The girl's got a point, Black," Roy said. "Anna and the women have their hands full here, and I think I should hang back to protect them and Zeek. It wouldn't hurt to have someone else watching your back. I've seen Lacy with that whip of yours, and she ain't half bad. I'd hate to be on the receiving end of it."

Black shook his head in defeat. "All right, Lacy can come, but no one else. This is something best handled with fewer people. Too many and we risk the chance of detection."

After saddling their horses, they headed southeast toward the line shack where they were certain they would find Belle. "They probably have the buckboard," Lacy said. "Do you think we should bring it back with us?"

"There won't be time. We need to get in and get out before they can react and stop us. The wagon would only slow us down. We'll take care of the men who are in the shack with Belle and get her out of there as quickly as possible. I don't want to take a chance of losing any of you."

He glanced at his companions and realized that neither of them were wearing guns. "I thought you'd be armed, Kate."

"I am," she replied glancing down at her rifle.

"A rifle ain't no good in a close fight. Once we get there, you take one of my guns and be ready to use it."

By the time they arrived at the line shack, they saw the buckboard and team sitting off to one side. Either they were ignorant bastards or they had set a trap for him. Either way he had to go in and get her out of there. He prayed they hadn't hurt her.

From a safe distance, they walked their horses close enough so Kate could peek into one of the windows and see what they were up against.

"They've got Belle tied to a bed. I'm pretty sure she's naked. They have her covered with a blanket."

Black closed his eyes and tried to envision the layout of the shack. It was, more than likely, identical to every other such building used by the ranch hands when they worked long stretches away from the bunkhouse. There would be a rickety table, a couple of chairs, and a bed along with a stove where cans of beans could be heated for their less than satisfying meals.

Black took a moment to think about his strategy. Having no idea how many men were in the shack made him stop to reconsider his position. It hadn't occurred to him to ask Kate if she saw how many men were guarding Belle. He must be slipping, either that or he was too damn close to this one to think straight.

"Did you see any men in there with her?" he finally said.

"Only two. One of them is Claye's foreman, Rance, the other is that no good drifter, Charlie McCasslin. He worked for us about a year ago, and, when he couldn't get Belle to spread her legs for him, he quit. She kept telling him he could have a go at any of the rest of us, but he wasn't buying, and we were just as happy not to have him in our beds. You could smell him coming a mile away."

If the situation hadn't been so serious, Black would have laughed at Kate's description of Charlie McCasslin. Unfortunately, Black knew exactly who she was describing.

Charlie McCasslin had to be the man who directed him to the Double Bar B on his first night in town. If that was the case, getting Belle out of there just got ten times more important. The man had a powerful hate for Belle and was exactly the kind of man who would follow any directions Clayte and Rance gave him without question.

After a moment, Black motioned for the women to come back to where they'd left the horses so they could talk without having to worry about anyone overhearing them.

"What we have to do is get their attention," he began his voice hardly louder than a whisper. "Kate, you take my gun and go around the back side of the cabin so when one of them comes out you can take care of him but for God's sake don't kill anyone. When the second one comes out, Lacy can take care of him with either a gun or a bullwhip. I don't care which. Once they're out in the open, I'll go in and get Belle. By that time one of you can have the horses up here."

"How are you going to get them out of there?" Lacy said.

"I'll get their attention once the two of you are in place. Take my rope. Once you have them under control, tie them up. Don't want anyone accusing us of murder, even though that's what I'm certain they planned when they shot Zeek."

Both women nodded and hurried off to take up positions on either side of the front door to the shack. Once they were in place, Black snuck up to the shack and threw a stone against the wall.

As he'd anticipated, the door opened and Charlie McCasslin came out only to be cracked on the back of the head by Kate using Black's gun. As quickly as possible she dragged him away from the entrance before Rance came out to investigate what was happening.

When the door opened, Black watched as Lacy wrapped the whip around Rance's upper body while Kate cracked him on the head as well with Black's gun.

While the women tied up both men, Black rushed in and untied Belle. The bruises on her face along with the welts on her breasts and arms made him sick to his stomach. He knew he had to get her home and to hell with the wagon loaded with lumber to repair the barn.

"Black," she said when he scooped her into his arms. "How did you find me?"

"That's not important. What we have to do is get you out of here and back to the Double Bar B."

"My clothes," she pleaded.

"Leave them," he replied as he helped her to put on his coat and then pulled the vermin-infested blanket closer around her before hurrying out of the shack.

Kate and Lacy waited for him with the horses. Once he hoisted Belle onto the back of his horse, the three of them headed toward the Double Bar B and the safety their own place afforded them. When they got there, they would barricade themselves into the house in preparation for the retaliation certain to come from the Diamond A.

Black didn't realize they were being followed until he heard the report of gunfire from behind him. Ahead of him, the women were riding toward the ranch house. Rather than look back, he spurred his horse praying Belle had a good grip on the saddle horn.

The pain of a bullet slamming into his back made him realize just how close their pursuers actually were. Rather than slowing because of his wound, he dug his heels deeper into the sides of his horse.

His strength was fading as the ranch house came in view. If he could make it a few more yards, Belle would be safe. If the bullet took his life, it would make no difference. Roy would see to Belle's safety and the women would be able to defend the ranch once they barricaded themselves behind the locked doors.

Through his blurred vision, Black could saw several horses in the dooryard. How had Clayte and his men gotten here ahead of him? How could he hope to protect Belle and the women, when the blackness of unconsciousness threatened to overcome him? How...

* * * *

Belle clung to the saddle horn. The sound of shots from behind them frightened her more than anything. What if Clayte and his men caught up with them? What if they were caught? Would they kill Black so Clayte could rape her and force her into a marriage she neither wanted nor would approve? Would they make Black watch what Clayte did to her before they killed him?

Hot tears stung her eyes and blurred her vision as the roofless barn and the house she so loved came into view. They had made it. They were safe. Roy would know what to do.

As they neared the house, Black slumped against her. Had he been hit during the wild ride? Had he died getting her to safety?

She grabbed the reins of the horse and pulled him to a halt. Once she did, she saw Roy and Annie along with the women and several armed men on the porch. Were they safe? Were these men friends or foes?

Someone pulled the reins from her hands and reached up to help Black down from the back of the horse. Once he did, someone else helped her. She didn't recognize the man at first, and then realized it was Roy who now held her protectively while the other men carried Black into the house.

"I have to go to him!" she shouted, as she tried to untangle herself from Roy's arms.

"Let them get him in the house. We'll follow. Didn't you see the stain on the back of his shirt? Someone shot him. He's unconscious."

Belle nodded. "I felt him go limp as we got closer to the house. I heard the shots. I didn't think he'd been hit."

With the tension of their wild ride behind her, Belle began to shake. She wondered if it was from the severity of her wounds, the cold, or the relief of being in her own home and at last safe.

"Let's get you in and get you warmed up. Ed can take care of Black while I see to you."

"Ed? Ed's here? When?"

"You'll get answers to all your questions, but for now, we need to get you into the house. You're chilled to the bone."

Roy held Belle close as he carried her into the house. With safety just a few steps away, she tried to relax in his arms.

The house was a beehive of activity. Men, both familiar and unknown crowded into the large kitchen, making it look small and cramped. She immediately recognized Jeb and Pete. With them were three other men all wearing badges and of course, the women from the ranch.

"Who?" she said, before Annie insisted on taking her upstairs to rest.

"As soon as the doc finishes with Black, I'll send him over to check on you," Roy said, after Annie helped Belle into a nightdress and put her to bed.

"I don't see why," Belle protested, even though she winced at the pain prompted by the flannel nightdress against the welts that covered her breasts, legs and back.

"Because you're injured," Annie replied, once Roy closed the bedroom door.

The fact that Roy said the doctor was with Black finally registered in her mind. "Where's Black? How badly is he hurt?" she said, needing to know more than what anyone was willing to tell her to put her mind at ease.

"He's across the hall. It was a good thing the doctor was here checking on Zeek. Ed's certain the bullet is still in Black's back."

"It's all because of me. What if he dies? How can I live with that?"

"Ssh," Annie said, as she rubbed Belle's hand.

Annie's gesture was soothing and Belle closed her eyes to think the positive thoughts Annie wanted her to think. If Black hadn't come to her rescue, Clayte would have surely raped her. Once he was finished and realized she wasn't a virgin, it was likely he would have given her to the other four for them to enjoy her body as well.

From outside the house, shots rang out. She heard glass shattering and prayed no one inside the house was hurt. Almost immediately, the gunfire was answered with shots from within.

"What's happening?" she pleaded.

Belle watched as Annie carefully peeked out the window. "It looks like Clayte and several others are firing on the house. I'm certain they expected it to be just us here. They have to know Black was hit. I'm sure they expected to find us women alone. I'll bet they never expected to run into the sheriff from the next county as well as two U. S. Marshals ready to return fire. Ed would be in on it too if he weren't with Black."

Annie no more than spoke the words, than Belle heard someone rush down the stairs. It had to be Ed getting in on his share of the action. She knew there had always been a powerful hatred between Ed and Clayte. From her father's letters, they had crossed paths more than once and never did get along.

It seemed as though the fighting went on for hours until at last all was quiet. Belle finally relaxed. She had wanted to get in on the fight to save what was hers, but Annie hadn't allowed her to stir from her bed.

"It's over," Ed announced when he entered Belle's room.

"Did anyone get killed?" Belle said, not really wanting to hear the answer to her question.

"One of Clayte's hands is dead, but that's it. Clayte and some of his men are wounded and in the custody of the marshals who came with me. They're guarding the lot of them in the old bunkhouse you no longer use."

"How did you get here so quickly? Black just sent the wire last night."

"Black's been checking in with me regularly through the mail. I had an assignment in Sheridan. When it was finished, the men who were with me agreed we should come up here and see what was going on with Black. We were at the stage stop when the wire came through this morning that there was trouble here, and the stage shouldn't stop today.

We'd tied our horses to the back of the stage so we were able to get here quickly. Along the way we recruited the help of the sheriff from the next county. I was shocked when we got here and found not only the barn roof gone but learned you were missing. I had no doubt Black would bring you back here, but I never expected to have him shot in the back."

"Is he going to be alright?"

"He'll hurt like hell for a few days, but that's about all. The bullet was in his shoulder. The only reason he passed out was because of the loss of blood. Of course he won't be any good with his left hand for a couple of months."

"Can I see him?"

"He's still out of it. He won't even know you're there, but I don't see no harm in it after the doc checks you over."

* * * *

Consciousness returned to Black slowly. With it came memories of rescuing Belle and the breakneck ride to get her to safety. Had he made it? He hoped so. As the memories returned so did the pain caused by the bullet that hit his back. He tried to move his left arm and found it was in a sling. Someone had patched him up, but who? It certainly wouldn't have been Clayte and his bunch. If he'd been captured by them, he wouldn't be waking up. They'd make sure he was dead and left for the buzzards.

Slowly he opened his eyes. As things came into focus, he realized it was night and he was in the room he occupied the first few nights he was on the Double Bar B. After getting his bearings, he turned his head. A lamp on the dresser gave the room a soft glow. In it's light, he saw Belle sitting in one of the chairs and Ed in the other.

"Welcome back to the land of the living," Ed greeted him, his voice hardly more than a whisper.

A closer look at Belle told Black why his friend wasn't speaking loud. She had fallen asleep.

"How bad?"

"Not bad enough to keep you down for too long. I think you've earned the rest."

"How did you know to get here?"

"I read between the lines of your letters. It wasn't hard to figure out things were coming to a head. I had Rogers and Morris with me in Sheridan, so I decided we should head north rather than go back to Denver right away. It's a good thing we did."

"Did you get Clayte and his bunch?"

"They're locked in Belle's bunkhouse until a judge can get out here from Billings. I stopped in the next county and recruited the sheriff. He's guarded the bunkhouse while Rogers and Morris went into town to arrest Joe. Tomorrow morning we'll take the others into town to join him in his own jail."

Before Black could respond to what Ed told him, he saw Belle get to her feet.

"I was so worried about you," she said.

He half expected her to burst into tears. Instead, she sat dry eyed beside him on the bed.

"Takes more than a bullet to stop me for long. Give me a couple of days and I'll be ready to take on the world, or at least take on you in that bed across the hall. That is of course if you're up to it."

"Trust me, Black Conley, I'm in much better shape than you are. The doctor gave me some ointment for the welts, and it took the pain away. The worst pain was sitting here waiting for you to wake up."

Chapter Fifteen

March had turned to April before the trial of Clayte and the others got underway. Belle sat with Black and Ed in the chairs set up in the saloon, which now served as a courtroom.

Clayte and his men looked less menacing as they were paraded into the makeshift courtroom, their hands and feet shackled. Seeing them in such shape made her almost feel sorry for them.

Black squeezed her hand reassuringly, as though he could read her thoughts. "Whatever happens will be for the best," he whispered, just as Clayte's children were ushered into the saloon.

Around them, people whispered about how terrible it was that if the trial went wrong, these poor innocent lambs would be orphans. The very thought made Belle's heart melt. She knew the children had been sent to various households in town and that just wasn't right. They should be together.

One by one people testified against Clayte. Belle listened as Jeb and Pete told of losing cattle and Zeek related the story of how he was beaten and shot in an attempt to make it look like the rustling had been Belle's fault.

At last, it was Belle's turn to testify. With confidence, she faced the people who were assembled as well as the jury of her friends and neighbors. With as much composure as she could muster, she began to relate the details of her kidnapping and torture at the hands of Rance and Charlie. To implicate Clayte, she told of how they talked about their boss taking her virginity. Not even the cross examination from Clayte's lawyer could shake her calm or get her to change her story one bit.

When she finished, Black took the stand and told of everything that had happened since his arrival in September. The most damaging evidence was the letter he produced from the widow of the man he had found dying in the cave on Belle's property.

By noon, the testimony was finished and the people who had packed the saloon brought in food they had prepared. Clayte and the others were taken back to the jail.

"Thank you," Belle heard someone say. She turned to see Nora Calhoun standing behind her.

"Oh, Nora, why are you thanking me? This has turned your life into a living hell."

"Nothing could be compared to being Joe's wife and living in this town knowing everyone suspected him of wrong doing. Since his arrest, I've been able to take care of my children without having to worry about his beatings, or being sold to Clayte whenever he doesn't want to be with the girls at the Purple Moon." Belle slid closer to Black leaving room for Nora to sit beside her.

"What will you do now, Mrs. Calhoun?" Black said.

"My house is very large. I've always wanted to open a boarding house, and the banker thinks it's a good idea. He's lending me the money to start my operation, and I already have a boarder who will pay me well. There's also money in the bank. Joe was too cheap to spend anything he didn't have to. I think he had the idea I would be the first to die and leave him with all that money. I have no doubt he will be going to jail for a long time. It will give me something to live on when he's gone. I'll be fine, the ones I worry about are Clayte and Nettie's children. They're the innocent ones in all of this."

"Indeed they are," Belle agreed. "I've had word the railroad will be coming through town and will be here by June. Since that's the case, I won't have the passengers from the stage line to supplement my income. The women who work for me want to open an orphanage. I'm certain we'd have room for all of Clatye's children until they are old enough to take over the running of the Diamond A. In the meantime, I'll hire men to work that spread so the children have at least something from their father. I'd hate to see them deprived of what their grandfather worked so hard to build."

Nora nodded and then got to her feet to return to the table where her children were sitting.

"Do you know what you just did?" Black said.

"I put voice to the plans my crew and I have been making over the winter. I can't stand to see those children growing up without one another. I know what it's like to be taken away from your family. They deserve to be together just as they deserve to have the ranch that would have belonged to them if their father hadn't been such a greedy man."

* * * *

Black finished eating and excused himself, allowing the ladies time to talk. Once outside, he joined Ed in a smoke.

"How do you think it's going?" Ed said.

Black shrugged his shoulders. "It's hard to tell. If it were up to me, I'd find every one of them guilty. It's a shame we couldn't have this trial in Denver. At least there'd be no question about what would happen. I hate to think about how many of those men on the jury are drinking buddies with at least one of the ones on trial."

"I know what you mean. It's hard to find twelve men in this town who don't genuinely like Clayte. Up until all this started happening, I think Belle was the only rancher with a problem with the man."

Black nodded his head in agreement. "I remember when I first got here, Jeb and the others were dead set on blaming her instead of the man who was responsible for the rustling. It didn't take long for us to set them straight, but for a while there, Belle was mighty upset."

"Her being upset bothered you, right?" Ed paused, waiting for Black's affirmative nod. "So since it did, what about you and Belle?"

"What about us?"

"Don't act innocent with me, Black Conley, I've known you for too long. Do you really think you can ride on to the next assignment and leave her here? You have feelings for her. I can see it not only in your eyes, but also in your actions."

"My feelings have nothing to do with it. I have a job to do. I can't put Belle and the others in danger because of who I am."

"That job might not be waiting for you. I saw the damage that bullet did. I want you to see a specialist in Denver. If I'm right, I doubt you'll ever get back the full use of your left arm. If that's the case, your career with the marshals is over."

Black made no comment. He'd been thinking the same thing. As much as he'd come to love Belle, he couldn't stay. There were too many things he had to do before he could even think about asking Belle to share his life. When the time was right, they could begin a family, one in which he could play an active part. At least he knew she wasn't carrying his child. She had only just stopped taking the tea the night before the kidnapping. Things like that didn't happen over night and since the shooting, he hadn't been up to the nightly activity he'd participated in ever since he arrived at the Double Bar B.

"Did you hear me?" Ed said.

"I heard you. I was just thinking."

"What's there to think about? Either you want Belle in your life or you don't. Which is it? So help me if you've only been telling her what she wants to hear…"

"I've told her nothing other than I'm not the man for her. She has told me she understands and doesn't want a commitment from me. Why can't you understand there are things that must be done before I can do anything like that?"

Ed stared at him as though he was a stranger rather than a trusted friend.

"The jury's back," Roy said as he joined them.

Black was glad for the reprieve. He certainly didn't want to continue the conversation about commitment and Belle that he'd somehow found himself in the middle of.

"What do you think, Pa?" Ed said. "Will they find them guilty?"

Roy scratched his head as though searching for the answer to his son's questions. "I don't know. Clayte and the others are acting like this is just one big party. I heard Clayte say that the drinks were on him as soon as they were found innocent."

"How in the hell can anyone find them innocent?" Black demanded. "They were caught by the marshals when they were firing on Belle's house. The jury has heard Zeek's testimony about who it was that beat and shot him. Then there's that letter from the widow of the man we killed last fall."

"You're forgetting one thing," Roy commented. "That jury is made up of a lot of Clayte's friends. It's possible they could be looking past the law and relying on friendship alone for their decision. We just have to wait and see how this all comes out."

* * * *

Belle watched the batwing doors of the saloon, all the while wishing Black would return. The jury had been brought back in and she, like everyone else, was anxious to hear their decision. She just didn't want to hear it alone.

Relief flooded her being when she saw Black, Ed, and Roy return to the room. Once Black seated himself next to her she was more confident. The jury had to find Clayte guilty. If they didn't, the man would make her life a living hell. Without Black by her side, she didn't know if she could survive.

"Gentlemen of the jury have you reached a decision?" the circuit judge said, just as Black took his seat.

"We have," Red Kline replied. "The whole passel of them are guilty as sin. Makes us ashamed to say we even know them. I've heard…"

"What you've heard has no place here," the judge warned. "Then your verdict is guilty. That being the case, I sentence all of you to twenty years at hard labor in the state prison up at Helena. All that is except for you, Mr. Adamson. It appears you were the one behind all of this. Your greed will cost you your life. Tomorrow morning, you hang by the neck until you are dead."

"But … but you can't," Clayte sputtered. "I have a ranch to run and seven children to raise. You can't leave my kids without a father."

"You can and you will. Your children will become a ward of the state and your ranch will be sold to support them until they are of an age when they can become independent."

"May I be heard, your honor?" Belle said as she got to her feet. All around her people began to whisper. She paid them no mind as she cleared her throat in preparation for permission to have her say.

"What could you have to say that would be of interest to this court, Miss Barton?"

"I have a solution for what will become of Clayte's kids."

"And just what would that be?"

"Everyone here knows I run my ranch with the whores who weren't welcome in this town. They've never entertained any of the men from this area while they've been in my employ. They've reserved that honor for the men on the stage. Now the railroad is coming to this area and the stage won't be stopping anymore.

"I added a large addition to my home to accommodate the passengers. The women have been talking it over and they'd like to turn it into an orphanage. That way the children could have good meals, fresh air, and learn how to do something other than sit and feel sorry for themselves. As for Clayte's children, the Diamond A is their inheritance. I'd be willing to take over running it for them until they were of an age to run it themselves. Clayte's oldest boy is eight now. In a couple of years he will be ready to start riding with the men and learning how to make that spread prosper."

"What do whores know about children?" Clayte demanded.

"More than you do. I've heard the way you've talked about them since Nettie died. They deserve better than that. Would you rather have them sent off to some orphanage and split up? Our plan would give them the opportunity to learn how to run not only a ranch but also a home. They'd be given love and respect, and they wouldn't have to be separated."

"You have a point, Miss Barton," the judge said. "The only problem is that an orphanage has to be approved by the state. I'm afraid you're going into this blindly. What if the state doesn't approve of this venture?"

Before Belle could speak, Cara was on her feet. "We've already got the approval of the state. Since the Diamond A would more than pay for the raising of these children, it wouldn't cost the taxpayers a red cent. We want to do this, your honor. We were talking about it long before any of this ever happened. As a matter of fact, we've had the blessing of the state for the past six months. Of course, at that time, we were expecting the state to have to pay us for taking the children into the house. Now that isn't necessary. We all have a lot of love to give. None of us grew up wanting to become whores. We were all forced into it in one way or another. Why can't anyone believe we could ever become respectable members of this community?"

One by one the women in the room got to their feet and applauded not only the words Belle had spoken but Cara's as well.

"We'll all help you get the place ready," Grace Harrington offered. "Since we have children, we know exactly what you'll need. Until it's ready, the children can stay in the homes where they are now."

Everyone started talking at once until the judge banged his gavel for quiet. "Your offer is a generous one, Miss Barton, but what about the profession your women have worked at for so long? How can you expect to give these children a normal life if…"

"That's right judge," Clayte said, getting to his feet. "I don't want my girls learning to be whores."

"Would you rather they learned to be rustlers, murderers, and kidnappers?" Belle retorted.

Again the gavel banged against the wood of the bar. "Mr. Adamson,

Miss Barton, this isn't the time for arguments. I will agree to this only if I will be allowed to inspect your home on a regular basis. If I hear of any nonsense going on out there, the children will be sent to another orphanage and the Diamond A sold."

"The eastbound tracks are within three miles of town and the westbound are within five that means the trains should start running through here in June," Belle said. "That will give us two months to get the house ready. Since the women in town are willing to help, you can come out anytime after that and see how we care for the children."

"Then so be it," the judge declared. "The defendant, Clayton Adamson will be hung by the neck until dead at noon tomorrow."

Clayte and the others were ashen as they were led from the courtroom. Adding to the finality of the judge's ruling, Clayte's own children each turned away from their father, as though disgusted by what they had seen and heard.

"Don't you want to say goodbye to your father?" Belle said when she caught up with Clayte's oldest son, Matthew.

"Why? It weren't just you he hurt. Now he can't beat us any more."

As the boy turned and hurried off to be with his sister, Belle looked up at the woman who had taken the two oldest children into her home.

"It's true," Martha Worthing said. "When those children came to me, they were bruised in places a child should never be bruised. When I showed my husband the bruises, he said that the undertaker said Netter was bruised in much the same way and it wasn't from her fall down those stairs. It's a good thing you didn't fall for his sweet talk."

Martha's words came as a shock to Belle. "How did you know about that?"

"Clayte told everyone who would listen you were going to be his wife just as soon as you came to your senses and accepted his proposal. I've known about it for almost six months now. When my William came home with that story after playing poker with Clayte over at the Purple Moon, I told him I knew you had much better sense than to fall for any such a thing. William agreed but he also said Clayte could be mighty persuasive when he wanted to be. I guess we all know how he planned to get you to marry him."

Belle was still shaken when Martha hurried to join the children. She knew Clayte had bragged to Black about how the two of them were going to be married, but she never thought he would have told the entire town. It was no wonder people looked at her strangely when she walked into church on Sunday morning.

"Are you all right?' Black said as he put his arm protectively around her shoulder.

"I will be once we get home. Make love to me tonight, Black. Please make love to me. I want to erase all the terrible things I've seen and heard today."

"You know I can't say no to you. Let's get something to eat over at the hotel and then head for the ranch. With everyone in town, I know Annie won't be doing any cooking tonight. For what I have planned, we'll both need all our strength to survive the night."

Belle smiled at Black's comment. There would be no need for her to try and get pregnant tonight, since it had already happened. She'd missed her last cycle over a week ago, even though she'd banned Black from her bed as though it had come. Once the hanging was over tomorrow, Black as well as Ed would be leaving for their next assignments. She didn't want to make Black feel as though he had to stay just because she carried his child. It would be better this way. Once the child was born, she would contact Ed and have him tell Black he was a father. His son or daughter would be raised to know the name of their father and respect the man behind the façade.

* * * *

Black planned the night with Belle carefully. In the morning, he would pack his gear, and, after watching Clayte hang, he would leave Larson's Gap.

He had a powerful amount of thinking to do along the way. Being around Belle, he knew he couldn't think straight about the future.

Future, what an odd thing for him to think about? He never thought there would come a day when he wouldn't be a marshal and now he wasn't so certain. If the doctor confirms the suspicions Ed and I have, I'm going to have to find something else to do with my life.

"Anything else I can do for you?" Ed said, as he and Roy poured buckets of steaming water into the tub that sat in Belle's bedroom.

"Can't think of anything," Black replied, pleased to get a reprieve from the inner thought consuming him. "The way I see it, the only thing left to do is get the two of you out of here. I have a very special evening planned with the lovely Miss Belle, and it doesn't include either of you watching what we do."

"Are you sure you want to leave her after the hanging, son?" Roy said. "I ain't seen Belle happier than you've made her these past few months. You could have a good life here. Besides there'll be more than enough work keeping both the Double Bar B and the Diamond A going."

"I have my own job to do," Black protested. Even though the job could be gone without warning, he used it as a ploy to give him an excuse to do the things he needed to do before making Belle his own.

Roy looked at him skeptically. "From what my boy here says, you won't be able to go back to marshaling."

Black glared at Ed. "Your boy ought to keep his mouth shut."

Roy and Ed left the room without making comment, although their laughter trailed back to Black's ears as they went down the stairs.

"What was so funny?" Belle said, as she joined him in the bedroom.

"Just my so called friends' warped sense of humor. For tonight, let's not think about anyone but us. Tomorrow…"

Belle put her arms around his neck and silenced him with a kiss. "I don't want to think about tomorrow. For tonight, tomorrow doesn't exist. I know you're leaving. I won't try to stop you, but for tonight we're together and nothing else matters."

Black pulled her closer and again kissed her long and hard. When they separated, he unbuttoned her dress to gaze upon the white mounds of her breasts as they strained against her undergarment. With her nipples already puckered, he teased each of them until they were completely hard.

He wondered if it was his imagination or had Belle winced as though the way he paid homage to her breasts had hurt. "Did I hurt you?" he said, knowing he certainly didn't want her last memory of him as one of pain.

She turned her face up until their eyes met. Those beautiful blue eyes were enough to drive him crazy.

"You aren't hurting me," she said, leaving him to wonder if she was telling him the truth or just what he wanted to hear. "For tonight I don't want the teasing that leads to lovemaking between us. Tonight I want you inside me for as long as the two of us can be connected. Do you think I'm crazy?"

"If this is crazy, I don't ever want to see you sane."

She laughed softly and began to unbutton his shirt as well as his pants. With the promise of spring, he hadn't put on fresh long johns this morning before going to the trial. As soon as she opened his trousers, his cock sprang to life and practically fell into her hand.

The feel of her fingers curling around the entire length of him was almost more than he could stand. Like her, he wanted to plant his cock firmly within the velvety folds of her and make love to her until the first rays of dawning crested the eastern horizon.

As soon as they finished undressing, he lifted her into his arms and put her in the tub of water that had now cooled sufficiently so that neither of them were uncomfortable. Once she was seated in the water, he climbed in behind her and began to make a lather with the soap she kept exclusively for herself. The scent of lavender filled the room and reminded him of her. Never again would he smell lavender without thinking of the precious gift he'd been allowed to love for an entire winter.

* * * *

Belle relaxed until her back was against Black's chest and his cock was bumping against her backside. She'd known he wanted the two of them to bathe together before they made love. It was the reason she had set out a fresh cake of the soap she ordered especially for herself from the east.

She was glad the only reminder of what she'd endured at the hands of Clayte's men were the scars that probably wouldn't ever go away. At least the pain she'd endured because of them was gone and Black had seen them. In their stead, her breasts were tender because of her pregnancy. She didn't dare let on to him how much it hurt to have him even touch them. He'd come dangerously close to the truth when he had played with them earlier. She knew she winced, but had thought quickly enough to assure him there had been no pain.

As though he sensed her agony at having him wash her breasts, he lingered only a moment before moving the soft cloth down her belly to the juncture of her thighs. At least that was one area the pregnancy hadn't made tender.

He slipped his soap slick fingers into her crevice and massaged her clit until she thought she would be wet with cum even before his cock entered her body.

Did other pregnant women desire their men as much as she desired Black? It certainly wasn't this way with Ronald. Once she was this far along she had wanted nothing to do with him.

Unbidden the memory of being so sick the thought of being with Ronald was enough to make her sick all over again. As though it was yesterday, she remembered him telling her the child she carried could not belong to him. She had to have been with another man, and she could go to him with her story and see how far it got her.

She wondered if Black would react in the same way if he knew she carried his child. She doubted it. Rather than dwell on his reaction to something he would never know, she returned to the pleasure his touch gave her. Would she ever be content with the dildo after being with Black? She doubted it. This night would have to become a memory to sustain her through her entire life. Never again would she love anyone with the passion she had for him.

With their bath finished, Black lifted her from the tub and dried her with one of the towels she had laid out earlier. Every swipe of the towel made her want him more than ever. When at last he carried her to the bed, she was more than willing for a night of delightful lovemaking. She prayed it would do no harm to the child, but she also knew the babe was hidden deep in her body and was in no danger from Black's cock, no matter how large it was.

Rather than their usual foreplay, Black slid his cock into her willing body and began to pump back and forth. They both knew tonight was not the night for anything other than serious loving, anything but him inside of her for as long as either of them could make love without falling into the exhaustion of sleep.

Tomorrow he would be gone and she would continue on as the owner of the Double Bar B as well as the overseer of the Diamond A. In two months, the stage would no longer be coming, and she would have the addition to the house turned into an orphanage for children like those Clayte would leave fatherless because of his selfish actions.

Tonight was far too important to her to dwell on the future. Tonight would be the last time she would lie in Black's arms and feel him pulsing inside her. The child would always know about its father, but she swore Black would never again know the agony of the child he had left behind. Ever since he had received the letter from his grandfather, she'd seen the difference in him. He regretted never knowing his son. She vowed he would never know regret just because she wanted his child so badly.

* * * *

Black felt as though he could continue making love to Belle all through the night. It was only fitting they were together like this for one last time before he left. He couldn't help wondering if tonight he would leave her carrying his child.

The inner walls of her cunt gripped him firmly and prolonged the climax when they both came at the same time. Even so, he never broke the connection between them and found it took only a few minutes for him to want her again. Over and over again, he peaked and ebbed until the first rays of dawning came through the windows, alerting him to the fact they hadn't slept at all during the long night of love making.

"I can't believe it's morning," he said after kissing her long and hard for probably the hundredth time since they went to bed.

"It's morning all right," she replied. "In a matter of hours, Clayte will be dead. I wonder if that's what I really want."

"No one wants such a thing, but it's the law. Rustlin', kidnappin', attempted murder, and murder, if you count them men he sent here to plant the cattle on your range. Those are all big offenses. I think the judge was fair. Even if he had sent Clayte to jail, his children would have suffered. I know what it's like to be young and have no parents in your life. It's hard living with strangers. Clayte's kids are lucky to have you and the others caring for them. You all have a lot to teach. I ought to know. The whores at my mother's ranch taught me more than I can ever repay."

"Like what?"

"They taught me manners, made me study and do my best in school, taught me to speak and read Spanish, and insisted I learn the Bible. That last part probably didn't take considering the profession I chose for myself."

"There aren't many people who could boast such accomplishments. I know I learned about the Bible and God when I was young, but those nuns managed to kill that for me. It wasn't until I came back home and started going to church with Pa that I changed my mind and started believing again."

Black thought about his own faith. He hadn't been in a church in years, even though the one thing of this mother's that he carried in his saddlebag was her Bible. He knew he wasn't a good enough man to go to church, but that didn't mean he didn't believe. Maybe once he did what he planned to do after he left the Double Bar B he could come back, make Belle his own and lead the life of a respectable citizen of Larson's Gap.

Chapter Sixteen

A warm breeze blew down the main street of Larson Gap. To the west, storm clouds gathered just over the mountains. It they were lucky, the rain would hold off until after the hanging.

Even though Black insisted Belle shouldn't go into town, she hitched up her buggy and along with Kate, Janna, and Lacy drove in just as they were leading Clayte from the jail to the scaffold with the hangman's noose at the top. Behind them came Roy and Annie with Cara.

"Damn fool women," Black commented to Ed, once he saw Belle arrive. "This certainly ain't no place for the likes of Belle and the others."

"It may not be the place, but she's here, and I doubt there's not a man here who would deny her the right to see justice done. Considering everything Clayte did to her, it's no wonder she wants to be here."

"But a hanging ain't a pretty sight. It will give her nightmares for weeks."

"Is that what a hanging does to you?"

Black nodded. "I can't help but think that if it wasn't for meeting you, I might be the one on the end of that rope. I killed my share of men in my life. In any of those towns, I could have been arrested for murder. I was just damn lucky it didn't happen."

Ed slapped him on the back. "You certainly were. I knew the minute I laid eyes on you that you weren't the cold-blooded killer I'd heard about. I decided right then and there I wanted you on the side of the law. If that isn't possible, what will you do?"

"Someday in the future, I'll come back here and ask Belle to marry me."

"Someday? Why not now? Why leave Larson's Gap?"

"I don't expect you to understand, but I have a lot of bridges to mend. I have grandparents in Mexico. I haven't seen them in over fifteen years. I need to see them before it's too late. I also have a son in Mexico. I can't ever let him know that I'm his father, but I want to see what kind of a man he's become and thank the man he calls father for giving him a good life."

"Is that all you have to do?"

"No, I've got a hankerin' to go east. Before I settle down, I want to see the places I've only heard and read about in books and newspapers."

"You wouldn't be heading toward Ohio, would you?"

"There's a little girl in an orphanage who needs a ma and a pa. I think I know the perfect people to become her parents."

Ed said nothing, but Black knew Ed understood his need to bring Belle's daughter home. It was one thing he could do for the woman he loved that he couldn't do for himself. His son would never know him, but he would always keep the boy in a special place in his heart.

* * * *

Belle was shocked at the number of people assembled on the main street of Larson's Gap. Even though the breeze was warm, snow still clung to the areas between the buildings where the warming rays of the sun couldn't reach.

She pulled her shawl tighter around her shoulders as she watched Clayte walk toward the gallows. "I know the punishment is fitting, but it's hard to believe they're planning to hang Clayte," she said to Roy.

"That's why Black and I didn't want you to come into town today. A hangin' ain't a pretty sight. Maybe you should go on back to the ranch until this is over."

"No, I have to be here. This is the last chance I'll have to see Black before he leaves."

"Why don't you tell him about the baby?" Kate said.

"Because he'd think he had to stay because of it and that's not what I want. If he comes back to me, so be it. If he doesn't, I'll know he never loved me. I wouldn't ever saddle him with a responsibility he wants no part of."

"Suit yourself, but I think you're doing the wrong thing."

Before Belle could comment on what Kate just said, Clayte turned in her direction. "I ain't the only one who should be swinging from this rope today," he shouted. "Belle Barton should be up here with me. If she'd accepted my proposal of marriage ten years ago to say nothing of last summer, none of this would have happened. It's all her fault, and she should be made to pay along with me."

With his declaration, all eyes turned to Belle making her blood run cold. The urge to answer Clayte's accusations and give credence to what he said was a hard one to suppress.

"You all know what goes on over at the Double Bar B. I tried to make an honest woman out of her and she refused. I had no other options. I needed her as my wife and mother to my kids, and she wouldn't have me. Any one of you would have done the same thing in my place."

The stares of those gathered turned from ones of shock to one of pity. It was obvious Clayte had lost his mind and blamed Belle to get sympathy for himself.

"That's enough," one of the marshals who had come with Ed ordered as he pushed Clayte toward the waiting gallows. "You were found guilty by a jury of twelve men. This is your punishment. No one other than you is responsible for your actions."

"But she…" Clayte began as he lunged toward Belle.

She saw Black and Ed tighten their grip on their rifles and take a step closer to Clayte before the marshal tightened his hold on Clayte's arm.

"It's time Clayte," Ed said. "Do this like a man. Don't let your kids grow up knowing you made a fool out of yourself during your last few minutes of life. This is hard enough on them as it is. Don't make it any harder."

Clayte turned from the crowd and mounted the first step. He stopped. With each step he lagged more. One by one Belle counted off the steps that seemed more like a hundred than mandatory thirteen leading to the gallows.

At the tenth step, he allowed his body to go limp, forcing the marshal and Ed to carry him up the last three steps. Once at the top, Clayte began to sob like a child as the black hood was placed over his head and the rope noose around his neck.

"I'll see you in hell, Belle Barton. Mark my words, I'll see you in hell," he shouted just before someone pulled the lever to release the trap door and he swung freely.

The hideous sound of his neck snapping was one Belle knew would haunt her for the rest of her life.

It took several minutes for the men to take him down and the doctor pronounce him dead. During those minutes, Belle thought of the last words to come from Clayte's mouth. They weren't pleas for forgiveness. They were ones of condemnation of her for not bending to his will and agreeing to become his wife.

"Why did you come here today?" Black said, his tone one of concern. "This is the last place I wanted to see you."

"I had to come and see justice done," she replied, all the while wanting him to take her in his arms and tell her he loved her. "His anger was directed at me in life as it was in death. I couldn't sit at home and not see what he'd come to be."

"Well, you saw it. Did it make any of this easier to live with? Does it bring back the cattle you lost? Does it take away the nightmare of being kidnapped or the beating Zeek took any less real?"

She hung her head, shamed by his words. "No."

"Vengeance is mine, sayeth the Lord." His quote from the Bible came as a surprise. "We are only the means to an end. Right now Clayte is meeting his maker and having to explain his actions. He won't be talking to the people who were once his friends. He will be addressing the Lord and telling him his reasons for what he did. I doubt the Lord will believe one word of what he has to say."

"I didn't know you were a believer, I mean…"

He put his finger under her chin and tilted her head up so he could capture her lips with his and cut off the words she was about to say. "Just because I don't go to church on Sunday and act like I'm better than my neighbor, doesn't mean I don't believe. My ma and the women who worked for her, taught me to read the Bible and to pray on a nightly basis. In my line of work, I had no other option because I needed forgiveness on a daily basis."

"Did you need forgiveness for what we did together?"

"I don't think so, because what we did was special and it was mutual. It was all the meaningless relationships I had over the years that need forgiving."

"Then stay with me. We can run the Double Bar B, and you could even become the sheriff here. I've heard the position is open."

He looked down at his boots and even before speaking, she knew what his answer would be. "I have to leave, Belle. There are things I need to do, and I have to do them alone. When the time is right, I'll be back. I'm not leaving because I want to go, but because I must. Please try to understand."

With one last kiss, he turned and walked away from her. The only thing she could do was to stand and watch as he mounted his horse and rode out of town with Ed.

Someone put their arm around her shoulder, and she turned to see Roy at her side. "That wasn't right, it just wasn't right," he said.

"It doesn't matter," she replied, trying hard to keep the tears dammed behind her eyes. "He never promised he would stay. His job is important to him. I would never deprive him of that."

"He would have stayed if you'd told him about the child."

"I don't want him on those terms. If he couldn't stay because of me, I don't want him because of the child. I planned to have this child alone, I just didn't think that watching him ride away would be so damned difficult."

* * * *

"Are you certain this is what you want to do?" Ed said once they were several miles outside of town.

"You know it's not what I want. It's what I have to do. There are things I must do before I can ever go back to her."

"If that ain't the worst logic I've ever heard. You could give me your resignation right here and now and be back in her bed by nightfall."

"I could, but that ain't the only thing I need to do. Like you said, I need to see that specialist in Denver and then I have a few personal fences to mend."

Ed pulled on the reins and brought his horse to a halt, prompting Black to do the same. "What kind of personal fences? Until this morning I ain't never heard you talk about anything in your past. What's so urgent you're prepared to leave Belle to do it?"

"I never talked about family, because it hurt too much. That letter you forwarded to me from Mexico was from my grandfather. When my ma was killed, I stayed with them for almost a year. When I left, I vowed I'd never return. I knew the life I led was nothing of which they would be proud. Being here with Belle, made me realize I needed my family so I broke my silence. I learned I have a son in Mexico. Not only do I need to see my grandparents, but I want to see the boy as well. I won't be telling him that I'm his pa, but I will be thanking the man who stepped in and took my place."

Ed looked at him, a puzzled expression on his face. "Why not tell the boy you're his pa?"

"Because he has a pa. Manuel is a good man, one he can be proud to call Papa. My grandfather has been helping them to give all their children a good life. Next year the boy will be going to the university in Mexico City. He, like his brothers and sisters, think my grandfather is a kind patron. I won't do anything to change their opinions. Let's just say I want to see what I could have been if I hadn't been so consumed by hate and the need for revenge."

"Do I have to ask if there are any other places you plan to visit?"

"I have money in a bank in Texas that I plan to get and then I'm heading east. I think there might be a little girl in a convent in Ohio who could use the love of her ma."

"Belle's daughter?"

Black nodded.

"Just how will you know her?"

"With luck those nuns won't have changed her name. I doubt there will be a lot of little girls in that place called Laura Leigh. I'm also hoping she takes after Belle. Can't think of a better present to give her than to bring back the daughter who was taken away from her so long ago."

Chapter Seventeen

The train made its way east. Under the click-clack of the wheels on the tracks, Black thought of the past five months since he'd ridden out of Larson's Gap.

He'd left his horse, along with his badge in Denver. Ed promised that when he was ready to have the horse back, he would bring him to the Double Bar B.

After withdrawing the money he had in the bank in Denver, Black boarded a train for Texas. His first stop had been the ranch where his mother had lost her life. The man who had bought it had made many improvements and the payments he'd promised to make had been deposited in the bank. After assuring himself that his money was safe, he told the banker sometime in the future he would be sending a wire to have the money sent north.

From there, he went on to Mexico and the rancho of his grandfather. Instead of his black shirt and pants, he invested in clothes that said he was a prosperous man. He wanted his grandparents to see him, not as a gunslinger, but as a man of whom they would be proud.

As he expected, his grandmother cried and his grandfather glowed with pride as he told them of his exploits over the years. When he mentioned Belle and the Double Bar B, they insisted he give them enough warning so that they could attend the wedding.

He'd told them he didn't know if she'd have him after leaving her the way he did, but they assured him she must love him if she'd begged him for a child, even knowing he wouldn't be there to help raise it. He prayed they were correct.

After that reunion, he had gone to see Theresa and Manual. As his father had written, Jose was a fine young man. Black could tell Manual and Theresa were concerned about what he would tell the boy, but he assured them he was no more the boy's father than anyone other than Manual.

Now he was nearing the last stop on his journey to complete the assignments he'd given himself. He prayed this one would be as rewarding as the others he'd made.

The train pulled into Cincinnati, and Black found himself standing on the platform, waiting for the carriage that would take him to the best hotel in the city. Here he wouldn't be the gunslinger, Black Conley. Here he would be Phillip Conley, a rancher from Montana who had come to adopt a child. The hotel was more than willing to rent him their best suite and directed him to the stable where he could rent a fine carriage.

After a good night's sleep, he asked directions to the convent where he knew he would find Belle's daughter. It was still early when he drove out into the country to the remote convent. Just seeing it in the distance made his blood run cold. How could Belle's aunt have sent her to a place like this when she'd been so young?

He was met at the door by a sour looking older woman. "What is your business here?" she demanded.

"My wife and I are looking to adopt a child. She was brought up in a convent much like this one and told me to check into a convent while I was in Ohio on business. I asked around and was told that you have children who are orphans here. I was hoping you could help us make our family complete."

"Come with me and we will speak with Mother Superior about this. It is very irregular for anyone to come here looking to adopt one of these poor unfortunates."

He could tell she was looking at his expensive suit and the silver ring his grandfather had insisted on giving him before he left Mexico. A similar ring was with his belongings at the hotel for Belle. It would grace her delicate finger once she agreed to become his wife.

It took an hour of intense questioning by Mother Superior for her to agree to allow him to see the children. "Adoption is something that comes at a high price," she finally said. "If you are willing to pay for the privilege of having a child, I'm certain there are several boys who would be happy to go west with you. You will not be disappointed in any of them because they all know how to work as well as to obey. You will be raising them in a good Catholic home, won't you?"

"I was raised Catholic, Ma'am, but there aren't a lot of priests in

Montana. The child will be going to church on a regular basis and taught from the Bible. As for playmates, my wife runs an orphanage from our home and there are many children there to keep her company."

"Her? I thought you would want a son."

"My wife had a hankerin' for a daughter, and I wouldn't want to disappoint her. Now can I see the children?"

Laura Leigh wasn't hard to spot. She looked exactly like what he thought Belle looked like at her age. Even dressed identically to the other girls and her hair in desperate need of washing, her beauty shone through.

"This is the child I want to be my daughter," Black said, as he put his hand on her shoulder.

"You can't be serious," Mother Superior retorted. "Her mother was a common whore. There are other children here who would be much better suited for the life you're able to give them."

Black tried to hide his horror at the woman's words. "A whore or a girl who found herself in trouble? I tend to think the latter. As I said this is the child I want. Will you draw up the papers, or will I have to go to Cincinnati and hire a lawyer in order to take her home with me? If that is the case, then I will not be paying the convent one red cent for the privilege of calling this delightful child my daughter."

Greed eventually overcame the woman's indignation as she informed Laura Leigh to go to her room and prepare to leave with the man who would become her father.

"You don't need to pack anything," Black told her. "Once we get to Cincinnati, we will do some shopping, that is after you have a good hot bath and wash your hair. I don't know much about little girls, but I do know they like to be clean and beautiful. I doubt if you're used to this, but you will see what it's like, and I have not doubt you'll like it."

Laura Leigh gave him a smile that reminded him so much of Belle, he wanted to leave here and return to Montana as soon as he possible could. The smell of this place and the sight of the sisters who cared for these children was turning his stomach.

After an hour of waiting for Mother Superior to draw up the papers, Black left the convent with Laura Leigh in tow and one hundred and fifty dollars of his hard-earned money in the woman's hands.

"Are we really going to a ranch in Montana, or are you taking me to a whore house like Sister Caroline says?" Laura Leigh said. "She told me my mother was a whore and that's all I'm good for if I don't take my vows and become a nun."

Black reined the horse drawing his rented carriage to a halt. "Do you want to become a nun?"

"No sir, but I don't want to be a whore either. It's sinful."

"You won't be a whore and neither was your mother. I'm taking you back to her, and if we're lucky, she'll agree to marry me."

"But you said you were married."

"I told a small lie. I needed to be able to return you to the woman who loves you more than you'll ever know. She tries to hide it, but I could see through her. She was a young girl, not much older than you when she got into trouble and was sent to the nuns. When you were born, they took you from her. At the time, they promised you would have a good home with loving parents. I made some inquiries and found you were still with the nuns. I knew I couldn't ask her to be my wife if I didn't do everything in my power to bring you back to her."

"Even though you paid a lot of money? Sister Caroline says that you would have to pay a lot to Mother Superior in order to adopt me."

"Money isn't as important as you are. Now, before we get to the hotel, we will go shopping and pick out one complete outfit for you to change into after you have your bath. When that is done, we'll go back to the hotel and have one of the maids help you wash the grime of your past life from your body. Our train leaves the day after tomorrow and that will give us enough time to get you a whole new wardrobe so your mother will see what a beautiful girl you are."

"Am I beautiful? Sister Caroline says that whores are ugly and since—"

"We'll have no more talk of that. You're a beautiful young lady, just as your mother is a beautiful woman." As he spoke the words, he began to wonder if the child had any conception of what a whore really was. "Do you know what a whore is?"

She looked up at him with the innocence of youth. "Sister Caroline says they are vile people who are damned to hell for existing. I don't want to be damned to hell."

Black pulled her into a fatherly embrace. "Oh, my dear Laura, you couldn't be further from the truth. Whores are women who have no option but to be with men for money. Many of them are alone in the world with no other way to support themselves. Outside, they do what must be done to survive, but inside they are beautiful people. You have led a sheltered life, and I can understand why you would believe what you've been told, but things will change and so will your opinion of the people of this world."

"Will I still be able to go to church?"

The fact she had changed the subject told him she had no understanding of what he had said. Why should she? She'd been raised with the same beliefs since birth. A few words from him wouldn't change her perceptions of the world overnight.

"Yes, you will go to church. I'll even buy you your own Bible before we leave here. You can read, can't you?"

She lowered her eyes. "We weren't taught to read. That was for the boys. We were taught to pray, to keep the convent clean, and to cook."

"Well, then you're in for a great . On the trip to Montana, we will start your lessons in reading."

"May I still have the Bible?"

"You may have anything your heart desires."

Once they arrived back in the city, Black stopped at the first store he found. There he purchased a complete outfit for Laura, along with paper, pencils, and a book the storekeeper assured him was one of the first books teachers in the school used to teach the children reading.

He could tell that everything in the city was amazing and yet frightening to Laura. It was evident she had never been outside the walls of the convent before.

At the hotel, he arranged for a tub with hot water to be delivered to his suite, along with a maid to bathe Laura.

"I don't need help to bathe," Laura protested.

"Perhaps not, but it's always fun to be pampered now and again."

While the maid and Laura went into the second bedroom of the suite, Black relaxed in one of the overstuffed chairs in the sitting room and lit a cigarette. It had been trying dealing with the nuns and disappointing to learn they hadn't even taught Laura to read or write. He knew he wasn't the best teacher, but he would try.

"Mr. Conley," the maid said as she entered the room wringing her hands. "I think you should come in here and see this."

"See what, woman? I don't want to embarrass my daughter."

"I doubt you'll think the same once you've seen what I have to show you."

Black got up and followed the woman into the room. The tub was large and made Laura look like a very small and fragile child in comparison.

"Show your father your back, child," the woman requested.

Laura sat forward and for the first time Black saw what had so disturbed the maid. Laura's back was crisscrossed with white scars and ugly red welts.

"Who did such a thing to you?" he demanded, all the while knowing the answer.

"The sisters said that they had to beat the sins of our mothers from us. Three times a week when we knelt in prayer we were beaten. It is our penance for being born to whores."

"You said we. Were there more than one of you who were beaten?"

"There were three girls who were not adopted when they were babies. We are good friends. Deborah was so happy for me when you came to get me."

"You said three, what about the other girl, wasn't she happy for you?"

"Mary died last month. Her back became infected and God's angels came to take her to heaven. Mother Superior said it was because God was afraid Mary would become a whore and he wanted her at his side to protect her from that."

Black rolled his eyes. "I saw some boys there. Were they beaten as well?"

"Michael and Jonathan are brothers. They came when their parents were killed in a flood. They were only beaten when they didn't get their work done. They both say that as soon as they are old enough, they'll run away, but I doubt that will ever happen. The nuns guard them closely."

Black's anger surged. No child should have to live in such conditions when there were people in the world who would love them.

"Did I say something wrong, sir?" Laura questioned.

"No darling, you didn't, but please don't call me sir. If you can't bring yourself to call me Pa, then Black will do. No one calls me sir or mister for that matter. Now you enjoy your bath. I have some business I have to finish. When you're done, why don't you take a nap and when you wake up, I'll be back with a pleasant surprise for you."

Laura nodded and rubbed the scented soap the hotel provided onto the soft cloth so that she could begin washing her body. As she did, Black motioned for the maid to follow him into the sitting room.

"I'm going out there after those other three children. Can you stay with my daughter while I'm gone? I'll pay you extra. When I get back, I'll need three more tubs of water brought up here."

"Yes, sir, but I don't know what you can do. I doubt those old crows will let those children all go. The boys were sons of people who were passing through town and got caught in a flash flood. They were settlers heading west. The nuns took them in and—"

"And what?"

"I've heard they are grooming them to take care of their sexual needs when they are old enough. My husband was brought up out there and when he was old enough, he was made to service the nuns, if you know what I mean. He ran away as soon as he was able to and came to town."

"What's your husband's name? Maybe he can help me."

"It's Collier Trent."

Black wondered why the name sounded so familiar and then it hit him. "Is he a U. S. Marshal?"

"Why yes he is. How did you know?"

"I don't have time to explain, but please keep a close eye on my daughter and see if you can get some salve for those welts. I'll be back as soon as I can."

When the woman returned to the room where Laura was bathing, Black went into the bedroom where he'd spent the previous night and got his guns. Once armed, he headed for the U. S. Marshal's office to talk to Collier Trent.

"Are you Collier Trent?" he said as soon as he entered the office.

"Yes, sir. What can I do to help you?"

"You can tell me why you haven't cleaned out that nest of black crows at the convent."

The look on the man's face was a mixture of hatred, shame, and shock. "What do you mean?"

"I just adopted a child from there and found out exactly what the nuns do. Your wife says you were brought up there and forced to service those women."

"She had no right to say that. I've told no one but her about that time in my life."

"She had every right. If I'm not mistaken, you were the one who found out Laura Leigh was still there. Now, I need your help to get the other three children who are being mistreated out of there."

"Are you Black Conley?" Collier said, eyeing Black's guns.

"It doesn't matter who I am, but yes, I'm Black Conley. Now are you going to help me?"

"Of course I'll help you, but I doubt anyone else in this town will. They all think those nuns can do no wrong. That's why I've never told people about what really goes on out there. I doubt anyone would believe me. Just what do you plan to do with those children once they're out of there?"

"I'm going to adopt them and take them to Montana. I know a ranch where there's an orphanage that's run with a lot of love. The work is hard, but so is the country. They'll grow up to become productive men and women rather than studs to nuns in heat."

Collier strapped on his guns and then called to two other deputies to join them. While the others rode their horses out toward the convent, Black drove the carriage. As much as he wanted to be mounted as well, he knew he would need the carriage to bring the children into town with him.

Once there, he knocked on the same door he'd knocked on earlier. It was the same old woman who answered the summons. "Mr. Conley, what are you doing here? Has Laura displeased you? If so, we will gladly take her back and see she's punished for her sins." She tried to look around the bulk of his body to see if Laura was in the carriage.

"Laura has been punished enough. At this moment, her wounds are being cared for. I've come for Deborah, Michael, and Jonathan."

"But ... but you can't. They belong here. Mother Superior—"

"Mother Superior can go to hell. I've come for those children and when I'm leave, it will be with adoption papers for all of them in my pocket."

The old woman crossed herself at his use of profanity, but stepped aside to allow him entrance to the convent. As he stepped across the threshold, he heard the men behind him enter as well.

"Just what is the meaning of this, Mr. Conley?" Mother Superior said, as she came out of the office where he'd signed the papers to make Laura his.

"I've come for Deborah, Michael, and Jonathan. I will not allow the mistreatment they've received to continue."

"I cannot allow that."

"You can and you will," Collier said. "I've kept my mouth shut about what went on out here, but Black made it perfectly clear shame was no reason to allow it to continue. I'm here to arrest all of you and find homes for these children. Black has agreed to take the older ones, and my wife and I will gladly take the little ones. Any home would be better than what you give them."

"Black?" Mother Superior questioned. "I thought your name was Phillip. As for you Collier Trent, I know who you are and what you've done. Do you think the people of Cincinnati will accept you once they know of your life here?"

Black drew his gun and stepped up until he was toe to toe with the irate woman. "I've heard enough about what goes on out here today to be so outraged I'd press charges against you. Instead. I'm taking away the children. It's the best thing for everyone concerned. As for my name, the one I was born with was Philippe, for my Grandfather. I was called Black from birth because of my coloring. I'm assuming the name means something to you."

"Who hasn't heard of the gunslinger, Black Conley? Your reputation is well documented in the newspapers."

"So, you do know how to read. If that's the case, why haven't you taught the girls in your care to do the same?"

"It wasn't necessary. My parents taught me to read, but my calling was the church, just as these girls are called to serve God. There is no need for them to be able to read. That is not mandatory to become a nun."

"Look, lady, I'm letting you off easy. I'd prefer to see you behind bars for what you've done to these children. I'll settle for papers giving custody of them to Collier and myself. How many children are we talking about?"

He didn't know if he had intimidated her by his tone or by the gun pointed at her heart. In either case she told him that besides the three older children there were two toddlers and one infant.

Within the hour, the children were all piled into his carriage and were being escorted back to Cincinnati by the marshals. He couldn't help but wonder how Belle would react when he arrived in Larson's Gap with not only her daughter but also three other children in tow. He prayed he had done the right thing.

Chapter Eighteen

"Push, Belle, push!" Kate's words cut through the pain of labor.

"Damn you, Black Conley, you should be here for this," Belle heard Annie say.

With all her might, Belle pushed one more time and then heard the lusty cries of a newborn baby. Too exhausted to care about anything, she lay back against the pillows and allowed the women and Annie to care for her.

"You have a fine son," Annie announced as she lay the screaming infant in Belle's arms. "He's got a beautiful head of black hair and a pair of lungs that will raise the rafters of this old house. It's been a long time since there's been a little one around here."

"A long time, hell, what about those seven children of Clayte's?" Kate responded.

"For the most part, they're old enough to take care of themselves. This little guy is completely dependant on all of us."

Belle cradled her son in arms and marveled at the perfect being she'd just brought into the world. Each little finger and toe was accounted for and his darker skin made him look less like the pink helpless child she'd given birth to in the convent. This little boy was meant for greatness.

"What are you going to call him?" Lacy said.

"Matthew, for my father. He'd like that."

Within a few days, Belle was back into the routine of running the ranches as well as the orphanage. Clayte's children had proven to be a joy in her life. At first they were timid, but as time went on they had become outgoing and more than willing to do their share of the work around the ranches. Even though they weren't old enough to work independently, the boys gladly helped clean the barns and care for the animals. From Clayte's stock, she'd made certain each of them had their own horse and saddle and gave their schooling in ranch matters over to Roy. The old man had glowed at the prospect of teaching youngsters everything he knew.

As for the girls, the older ones helped with the younger ones and were adept in the kitchen. The addition of the house was kept spotless without Annie ever having to remind them of the chores that needed doing.

Since the older children were enrolled in school, Cara took over taking them to their classes and picking them up every day in the buckboard. She also oversaw their homework and monitored their progress through meetings with the teacher, Mr. O'Donnell.

The train had brought not only the end of the stage line, but also prosperity to Larson's Gap. No longer did people look down on her and the women who helped her run the ranch. She had been able to employ several new hands and reopened the bunkhouse.

Zeek had recovered and helped her to find someone to manage the Diamond A and to live in the house until Clayte's boys were of an age to run the place themselves.

The only thing missing from her life was Black. She hadn't heard a word from him since he left the day of the hanging. Even though Belle knew it was for the best, she longed to know again the security of his arms and the sweetness of his lovemaking.

Matthew was two weeks old, when Clayte's oldest son, Joshua, came running into the house. "There's a wagon coming and it's loaded down with a bunch of kids."

Belle inwardly cringed. She wasn't certain just how many more children she could accommodate at the orphanage. They'd already had to build on another addition to the house to accommodate Clayte's seven children and the four others who had showed up on her doorstep.

She laid Matthew in his cradle next to the stove in the kitchen and went out onto the porch to see who could possibly be bringing children to her now. To her surprise, it was Black driving the wagon.

"Sorry it took me so long to get here, darlin'," Black said as he jumped down from the driver's seat of the wagon. "I had a special delivery I had to pick up for you in Ohio."

As much as she wanted to run to his arms, his words stopped her short. She looked past him to the four children in the wagon. There was no denying that one of the girls was her daughter, but who were the rest of them?

"How did you find her?"

"It wasn't hard," he replied. "She never left the convent. After I found her, she told me about the other children, and I just couldn't leave them behind. Would you accept me as your husband and these four children that I adopted?"

"Five," she said. "That is if you want to claim your son. He's sleeping in the kitchen."

Black's eyes sparkled, and he smiled broadly. "You had my son? You had to have known before I left. Why didn't you tell me?"

"Because I wanted you to return for me, not because you felt compelled to do the right thing. Judging by this special delivery you have for me, I can see you were doing what you considered the right thing."

"Are you really my mother?" Laura said.

Belle hurried to the side of the wagon and watched as Black helped each of the children to get down. "Yes, darling, I am your mother, and it looks like you came with a ready-made family. I'm so excited to get to know you and to be mother to all of you."

"Do we really have a new brother in the house?" one of the boys said.

"Yes, you do."

The other little girl tugged at Belle's skirt. "Will there be enough love for all five of us, like Pa says there will?"

"That's Deborah," Black said giving a name to the child whose red hair stood in direct contrast to Laura's silver blond locks.

"Yes, Deborah, more than enough. Besides Matthew, there are eleven other children who live here, because their parents have died and left them alone."

"I'm Michael," the older of the two boys declared. "I want to know if Pa was right when he said no one would beat us here."

"Beat you?" Belle said. "No, Michael, no one will beat you. There will be a lot of hard work and even more good meals. You'll be expected to do your share and also your school work, but no child here is ever mistreated."

"Good, than Jonathan and me will stay."

"Jonathan and I," Belle corrected before hugging each of the children in turn.

"Can you stretch dinner to accommodate five more hungry people?" she said when Annie came out onto the porch to investigate what was happening.

"Of course we can," Annie replied. "Four more children, land sakes I never did see the likes of it. After we eat, Black, I suggest you go into town and get some bedding for these angels. I'm certain Roy will want to help you build new beds."

Black gave Annie a hug. "There's no need for that. I stopped in town and bought everything we need. It will all be delivered after dinner. I just hope you have room for the new beds."

"There's always room for more children, Black Conley, and there's certainly room for you."

Belle watched as the children followed Annie into the kitchen leaving her and Black alone.

"I've waited forever to do this," Black said as he took her in his arms and kissed her tenderly. "If I'd known about the baby I'd have come back sooner, but—"

"But you're here now and that's all that matters. After dinner, we'll get the children settled."

"I never thought about where they would sleep until we were getting off the train this morning. Will you have room? I mean the girls could use the room that I had and the boys could be in the bunk house."

"The bunk house is occupied by a full crew. There's plenty of room in the addition for the children. I just have one question, how did you manage to adopt four children?"

"It's a long story, and one best told over dinner. Of course, you never answered my question. Will you marry me and give these children a mother?"

"You name the day, Black Conley, and I'll be there. I've waited almost a year for you to come back. Don't think, for even one minute, that I'll let you get away from me again."

"That's good, because I sent a wire to my grandparents before I left Ohio and told them we were going to be married two weeks from Saturday. They wrote back and said that they were coming and will bring Jose with them. I've already made reservations for them at the hotel."

"You saw your son?"

"Yes, and, even though I didn't plan on it, we told him I was his natural father. I assured him Manuel was the man who deserved the title, and while I was with my grandparents, we became friends. If you don't mind, I'd like to have him and Ed stand up with me at the wedding."

"I don't mind, but I think you'll need more men at your side than that, since I want all the girls to be my bridesmaids and I plan to have Roy give me away."

"I think that could be arranged," Black said, as he swept her into his arms and carried her into the house.

* * * *

The morning of the wedding dawned bright and clear. The blue of the October sky promised no snow would be falling on this special day.

Black waited at the front of the church with Ed, Jose, Jeb, and Pete, and someone played softly on the piano. The first pews were filled with the fifteen children from the ranch as well as Annie holding baby Matthew.

The tone of the music changed as one by one Belle's girls came down the aisle. Even though they stood in direct contrast to one another, they all looked beautiful in the gowns they had been working on for the past two weeks.

At last Belle and Roy appeared at the end of the aisle. Black couldn't believe how lovely she looked. She wore a dress of ivory satin. He'd heard about the row of buttons down the back from Laura and Deborah, who had a terrible time keeping a secret. He knew he'd have just as hard a time getting all those little buttons undone in order to make love to his wife.

He had purposely occupied the room across the hall from Belle ever since his arrival. Having just had the baby, he knew she wouldn't be ready for sex until after the wedding. As for the children, they had insisted on staying in the addition with all the others. They told him it wouldn't be right for them to stay in the main house and make themselves appear different.

At last, Belle stood by his side and allowed him to hold her hand. Just her touch made him harden, but he tried to control his desires until it was time for the two of them to retire for the night.

"Do you, Philippe Conley, take Isabelle Barton to be your lawful wife? Will you love, honor and cherish her, forsaking all others for as long as you both shall live?"

"I do."

"Do you, Isabelle Barton, take Philippe Conley to be your lawful husband? Will you love, honor and obey him, forsaking all others for as long as you both shall live?"

Belle hesitated for a moment. Black knew why. He doubted she would obey him anymore than he would expect her to obey him. After an awkward pause, her 'I do' echoed loud and clear throughout the church.

When Black finally took her in his arms and kissed her, the children cheered. Without even looking, he knew his grandmother was crying and his grandfather was beaming with pride. Today he had become the man they had prayed he would become.

It was well after midnight when the last of the wedding guests left. With Matthew fed and in his cradle, Black prepared for a night of lovemaking with his new wife.

Once alone, he undid the buttons that ran down the length of her spine until he was finally able to slip the dress from her shoulders. It seemed like an eternity since he'd seen her naked body. Like a child turned loose in a candy store, he helped her out of the dress and undergarments before he began to kiss ever inch of her body.

As much as he wanted to take her enlarged nipples into his mouth, he refrained. They were now meant to give nourishment to his son, not pleasure to him.

When they finally lay naked together on the bed, he ran his hand down the length of her body until his fingers became entangled in the hair at the juncture of her thighs. He easily slipped them into the moistness of her and teased her clit before putting them into her cunt. He marveled at how a child had passed through this opening just weeks earlier and yet it had shrunk to the perfect size to accommodate his cock again.

Carefully, he positioned himself over her and allowed her muscles to grip his cock. Even though he'd been afraid of hurting her, once inside, it didn't matter. This was his woman, his wife, and making love to her was as natural as breathing. He pumped against her bringing them both to the brink many times and pulling back to prolong the delightful agony. When at last they came, it was with a force unlike any other either of them had ever felt.

She wasn't a paid companion. She wasn't his boss who had generously let him into her bed. She was his wife and the most cherished of all his possessions. Theirs would be a marriage of mutual love and trust mingled with delightful lovemaking and many more children.

About the Author

Mild Mannered wife, mother and grandmother by day, Shari Dare spends her nights writing and writing and writing. Having been inspired by an English assignment in her sophomore year of high school, she had never quite finished the assignment. New stories pop into her head every day with never enough time to write them all.

A Wisconsin native, she grew up a country girl, but enjoys her "city" home. She and her husband of over 40 years, Bob, live in a mid-sized town close to the Illinois border. Deeming Bob "A Saint" for putting up with her she has never regretted marrying her high school sweetheart just two days after graduation in 1964.

http://www.derr-wille.com

Other Books by the author with Melange

Man in the Forest

www.ingramcontent.com/pod-product-compliance
Lightning Source LLC
Chambersburg PA
CBHW020434180626
46812CB00003B/1227